I0573512

WITH MURDER IN COMMON
FRIENDSHIP IS INEVITABLE.

In the town of Hollow Creek, South Carolina two separate murders, fifteen years apart, unite fifteen-year-old Pleasant Day and sixty-year-old Clarissa Blackwell. As Pleasant Day struggles with her mother's distance, her father's infidelity and the death of her best friend, she draws closer to Clarissa, an older woman with the secrets to heal her. But Clarissa has struggles of her own as she faces betrayal and seeks to come to terms with old wounds. With her unpredictable psychic ability to 'read people' Clarissa uncovers the answers to a deadly crime and to Pleasant's true identity. In the end, both Pleasant and Clarissa's worlds are transformed by the truths they're forced to accept, and both find solace and strength in the histories that have shaped them.

Absolutely unputdownable, a real page turner. Be pre-pared to clear your schedule for the day. You're going to read this one straight through! This is Vera Jane Cook's best one yet!—Wall to Wall Books .

"A beautiful blend of past and present with loveable, memorable characters and a page turning pace, I was sorry I couldn't read it in one sitting."—Jenn Doyle, Books & Life.

PLEASANT DAY
Vera Jane Cook

This book is a work of fiction. Names, characters, places and incidents are products of the author's imagination or are used fictitiously. Any resemblance to actual events, locales or persons, living or dead, is entirely coincidental.

ISBN: 978-1-64456-318-2
MOBI: 978-1-64456-319-9
EPUB: 978-1-64456-320-5

Library of Congress Control Number: 2021938577

Copyright © 2015 by Vera Jane Cook
Published July 2021
by Indies United Publishing House, LLC

SECOND EDITION

All rights reserved. No part of this book may be reproduced in whole or in part without written permission from the publisher except by reviewers who may quote brief excerpts in connection with a review in a newspaper, magazine or electronic publication; nor may any part of this book be reproduced, stored in a retrieval system or transmitted in any form or by any means electronic, mechanical, photocopying, recording or any other means, without written permission from the publisher.

INDIES UNITED PUBLISHING HOUSE, LLC
P.O. BOX 3071
QUINCY, IL 62305-3071
indiesunited.net

Dedication
For my Aunt Leda, in loving memory.

Also by Vera Jane Cook

Dancing Backward in Paradise

The Story of Sassy Sweetwater

Where the Wildflowers Grow

Lies a River Deep

Marybeth, Hollister & Jane

The Fourniers: Book One, When Hannah Played Ragtime

By Olivia Hardy Ray

(pen name of Vera Jane Cook)

Annabel Horton, Lost Witch of Salem

Annabel Horton and the Black Witch of Pau

Pharaoh's Star

PLEASANT DAY

INDIES UNITED PUBLISHING HOUSE, LLC

PART I

Chaos is Come Again

Chapter One
Pleasant Day

I wanted to let loose with a good right hook to his grin. Son of a bitch was always treating me like I had nothing in my head but air, no way to reason or form thoughts. I had no purpose on this earth but to appease his need to be believed. Little bastard would never get as tall as the tales he told.

"Ain't that something," he said.

He stood there breathing hard, getting fat on bad news. Of course it wasn't true, meant to scare me away from giving John Peter two minutes of my time. I raised my eyes to the sky and put my hands in the pockets of my jeans.

"You shocked?" he asked.

Now listen here, bull shit is not my middle name. I shoot straight from the hip, tell it like it is. But you throw bull shit my way it's going back atcha, that you can be sure. I don't' take any crap from anyone and I don't give it. So don't go trying to sell me the frigging Gervais Street Bridge 'cause you can't put a price on something that can't be bought.

"You owe me five shiny quarters for that little bit of news."

"Kiss my white, southern little ass, Angus."

He stared at me like I was a detour he'd come up against, his free ride to money took a sharp left, right off the road. The little bastard was stumped, like a jeopardy question that froze him up. "Duh, what is a summer's day? Can't get much easier than that."

He squinched up his nose, his leprechaun impression, I guess. He looked Irish as a shamrock, eyes the color of a glossy post card pea green sea and his jaw line was just begging to be grown into, waiting for him to get handsome, which one day he would be, I guess. But for now, he was irregular looking, like his poor features didn't know where to go to get caught up with.

"I never understand what the hell you're talking about," he said.

He wasn't too smart. "Shall I compare thee to....."

"What? I swear, Pleasant, you're out of your mind."

"What is a summer's day, asshole. It's a Jeopardy question. It's Shakespeare."

He made some whishing sound in his throat and kicked the dirt, like he wished I was getting the benefit of the end of his shoe. I always made him angry, angry as my daddy gets when he looks at his paycheck and wonders where the zeros went.

"You hear what I'm saying, Pleasant? You're nuts."

"Good thing to be, I hear."

He made a whishing sound again. "Can you believe what I just told you? I wasn't lying. Hell, I wish I was. What the hell reason would I have to be lying about a thing like that?"

"You want to play Jeopardy or not?"

"No. You listening to me?"

"I hear words falling like bricks from your mouth. They have no meaning but they are awfully heavy, hard to bare."

"Why do I bother telling you anything?"

"You don't tell me shit, you are one big piece of crap and your mouth is filled with things that don't mean nothing. Your mind is the same."

"You don't believe me?"

"You want me to believe that Mrs. Clottey found a dead body in her son's box-spring? You really want me to believe that?"

"It's the truth."

"No truth on this goddamn planet ever made its way out of your mouth. If truth was hanging out of your nose you'd blow that goddamn truth bugger into a snot rag and toss it into a fire pit."

"Fuck you, Pleasant." And off he walked.

Damn Angus Ray would have me believe that Pluto is the planet with rings and Mars got nothing to do with the God of War. Oh no, the God of War is a freaking pansy and he took his name from those little hard candies look like hearts. According to Angus we got Cupid to thank for slaughtering the assassins of Caesar.

He must think I got nothing better to do on a July afternoon but swallow any line of bull he wants to feed me.

Truth is though, I don't have much better to do on a July afternoon but join all the other aimless souls got nothing in their heads but some kind of fuzz. Damn if I understand what we're doing on this earth. I mean, I can't justify getting born. I didn't ask for it, nobody did. Then all of a sudden you're here, screaming at the top of your little lungs 'cause you know what you're in for. Hard times is what you're in for. I can't even begin to tell you what bad news is lying on my path through life but I best be ready for it. I best be putting on my armor and I'd best be prepared to fend off all the bullshit coming my way head on.

People make up things to do before they go insane doing nothing. Now, ain't that the truth? Most people I know don't take the pleasure in reading that I do. That's what keeps me from terminal aimlessness. I got my own July classroom up on Piper Hill with my copy of To Kill a Mockingbird in my knapsack and five dime store paperbacks stuffed under my arm. Beats being stuck in some dusty classroom breathing in chalk in December. I been staring at Mrs. Llewellyn's layers of flesh too many semesters of my life, sneezing at her cheap perfume and pretending I am with purpose. Knowledge is purpose, and I give that to myself. All the knowledge I need I can find in Shakespeare and other great writers. So I get lots of knowledge in July. What kind of knowledge do I get in December? It don't matter none that I can name the presidents of the United States or figure out the area of a goddamn polygon. It matters that I can feel a kinship in the presence of masters and sublimely superior in the presence of fools. Fools being Angus Ray for one, masters being Shakespeare, Charlotte Bronte and D.H. Lawrence, to name but a few.

Sawyer told me I shouldn't put Charlotte Bronte in the same category as Shakespeare but Sawyer is a fruitcake. He's never read anything; he's too busy making sure the part in his hair is straight, which is the only thing about him that is. Sawyer knows nothing, doesn't like to read. Great writing is great writing; don't matter if it's dialog or prose. I tell him he's an idiot all the time and he just slaps me upside my head and says I have no right to my opinions because my brain is yet to be fully formed. Shit, Sawyer wouldn't know Shakespeare from Humpty Dumpty. I don't know what the hell I'm doing on this earth with these people. I wonder if they believe the shit they spew.

It's other people boggle the mind with nonsense.

That's why I long to be alone most times, completely alone under a blue sky in Hollow Creek. That's in South Carolina, not too many people heard of it. Shakespeare would have thought the same 'bout Hollow Creek, that it brings the poet out in people, well, at least in me. Shakespeare was a nature lover and he had his own Hollow Creek over there in England, must have had. He fully understood the perfection of a summer day. Why, if a man compared me to a summer day I'd be honored to pass over my virginity with no strings attached. Fortunately or unfortunately, no man in Hollow Creek sees any kind of poetry in a yellow sun or a green field with dancing weeds as high as my forehead. Only thing they see is a bottle of beer on ice and an excuse to stink behind the sweat marks that are so visibly untoward under the arms of their t-shirts.

Looking over yonder I can see my mama putting clothes on a line. There's a bunch of purple flowers between me and her. The clothes are all white except for one blue towel. It looks so proud to be different. Mama's hair is dandelion yellow, golden against the daylight. She's a compliment to the natural environment around her, like an Oak tree is to a back yard and like a lone cactus would be to a wide desert. I never been to a desert but I can see the beauty of that prickly, dangerous cactus in my mind. Everything has its compliments I imagine, even me.

Mama looked up. You'd think she'd wave. I always want her to wave when she sees me but she never does, she looks off, as if my presence has disturbed her or is about to disturb her. But I bring nothing of any consequence to my mama. She need not fear that my overbearing presence will devour her. I am well practiced in avoidance and indifference though the hollowness in my soul resents her absence; I wear the mask I must.

I was surprised to see Sawyer just hanging out by the clothes line, looking like a big, fancy poodle, prancing around and beguiling her. His dark good looks unnerved me. I'm so bewitched by beauty that I always succumb to my fascination with it, my awe of it. I am unnerved by those who have no noticeable flaws. I could pray to look like Sawyer, even though he's my older brother. I could pray to own the same kind of space that his bewitching beauty encumbers, but I don't pray for that. I only pray to grow up and find that I can deal with it all. Maybe I'll be better at that then Sawyer, who knows?

"Hi, Mama."

She doesn't respond, of course. She smirks. I guess she thinks of a smirk as a greeting.

"You hear the news?" Sawyer asked.

"What news?" They both looked kind of consumed. They looked over stimulated by something that had distracted them from their usual boredom and lazy egocentric paragraphs about nothing at all that ever held any interest for me.

"Mrs. Clottey found a dead girl in John Peter's box-spring," Sawyer said. "How gross is that?"

I almost fell over myself. "Holy shit," I managed to get out. "You bullshitting me I'll break your ass, Sawyer Day."

"Don't let it upset you, Pleasant, it's no one you knew. And watch that language." Mama hooked up a shirt on the clothesline. It was white. That blue towel still held its own. I was going to find it later and use it for my bath.

"I know everyone in this town," I said.

"She wasn't from Hollow Creek. She was from Summerford." Mama looked at me like maybe I had known her and she'd have to deal with my shock and my sorrow by hugging me.

"Did you know that girl from Summerford? She only had one arm," Sawyer asked me. "Poor girl couldn't defend herself. Maybe she could have whipped his ass if she were whole. John Peter doesn't weigh much more than you."

"What?" Shock waves went through my body.

"You all right, Pleasant?" Mama asked.

Well, I sure did know that girl from Summerford and I wasn't all right at all. I slid to the ground as if the weight of my shock had compelled the weakness in my knees. I could smell it, the earth. Grass must have been mowed earlier that day, I could smell that too. Everything felt clean and right, felt good. The dichotomy made me dizzy. There ain't nothing clean and right and good about dead girls, nothing pretty about it at all. I couldn't understand how anyone could get themselves done in when the grass had just been mowed and the sun was out. That's why people make up stories about harps, and heaven and all that shit, makes death look like the better place.

"Get up off the ground, Pleasant," Mama said.

"I knew her," I whispered. "I knew her well."

They both looked at me like I was the crazy bastard stuffed her inside a box-spring.

"Tough luck," Mama said and reached out to touch my arm. Her limp attempt at solace falling short of the hug I needed. She helped me to my feet, begrudgingly, I suspect.

"You sure she's dead?" I asked, like maybe they were messing with me, they were all messing with me, Angus too.

Mama laughed, not exactly a lilt, more like she'd got something caught in her throat. "Dead as a doornail, Pleasant."

"John Peter do it?" My expression was one of deep sadness, I was sure. But I often looked at Mama that way, with sadness. Sawyer too, so I cannot blame them for not being sensitive to my loss.

I heard Sawyer laugh. "Wasn't the tooth fairy, Pleasant."

I ran to my room and sat in the window. Poor John Peter didn't kill anyone. He wet himself that day Angus and I captured a frog and tore him up. We were just curious but John Peter was screaming and crying that we were going to hell. He said he named the goddamn thing 'Preston' and the fact that we'd killed something that had a name made us low life devils. Shit, I had to tell John Peter that I prayed in church every Sunday, prayed to be forgiven for that little frog's death and would God please take that little frog to the pearly gates and treat him like a king. I told John Peter I'd spend every day of my life guilt ridden over what I'd done to that frog.

I don't think John Peter ever forgave me and I know he never forgave Angus. Now I ask you, how could he kill a girl if he couldn't even kill a frog? I figured I'd go to the Sherriff and tell him what I knew, sort of like a character witness. Millie Grady was the one armed girl that got herself killed. How could so many bad things happen to one poor girl in the span of fifteen years? Millie lost her arm when some old car her father drove smashed into a truck. They had to take off her arm to get her out of the car. I guess she should be glad she survived at all, her mama didn't. Her daddy didn't take to no other woman after that so she was raised without a mama. Her daddy wasn't as rich as mine but they lived on a rich man's property in a cottage, didn't pay any rent on it either 'cause her daddy was the grounds keeper. We lived in Summerford years ago but I don't remember it very well, I was just a baby when daddy bought us the house we're in. It's bigger and better but Mama says it reminds her of a goddamn school 'cause it's red brick and has a fence around it.

Millie's bad luck didn't stop there. She had bucked teeth and she was skinny as the cane old Mr. Wiley uses to get down the street. Old Mr. Wiley is our neighbor and he's mean as a Komodo dragon. I avoided Mr. Wiley whenever I could, which isn't easy 'cause he sits on the side of the road all day selling the jellies Mrs. Wiley spends all year making. Sometimes he throws rocks at me 'cause he says my presence on the road is a pleasure to behold, now does that make any sense?

I took pity on Millie 'cause none of the other kids would go near her. They thought she was diseased 'cause she only had one arm. They made fun of her, of course. Half of them were as ugly as water rats and the other half were goons, goons with no souls. The kind of kids that grow up and make no difference to the world except for the puke they left in your wake from their drunken binges, which happened one too many times. Those were the morons who teased poor Millie ruthlessly. She was good about it though. She'd shrug her shoulders and tell me they were just being dumb and didn't mean nothing by it. Poor Millie didn't know rot when she smelled it.

Daddy came and got me after dinner. Mama must have told him I knew that dead girl 'cause he was eyeing me all through Mama's pot roast like maybe I was going to get suicidal and hang myself from the ceiling light in my bedroom after the two helpings of dessert I took.

"Hello, Sweet Pea," he said as he stood there lingering in the open door. His trepidation was charming. That's what I loved about my daddy, he never assumed anything. He didn't take for granted that I'd want to speak with him at all, which I didn't.

"You can come in," I said. "But I don't want to talk about Millie Grady, you hear?"

"Mr. Fitzwilliam Darcy." He pointed his finger at me and sat at the edge of the bed. He wasn't as good at playing Jeopardy as Nana but I humored him most times.

"Jane Austen, Pride and Prejudice," I said. "How can I make a question out of that?"

"I don't know, maybe who created him?"

I made a face. "You don't get it."

"Does everything have to be a question, Pleasant?"

"Yes, if you're playing Jeopardy it does."

"Does every subject have to be literature?"

"It does if you want to have fun at it."

He got a crease over his nose, a sign of distress. "I'm sorry about your friend." He reached out and squeezed my leg. There was nothing limp about his touch. Matter of fact, it was so filled with emotion that it started stinging and was sure to leave a red mark on my skin.

"The rule was we wouldn't discuss it."

He latched onto my foot with his big hand and squeezed that too. I felt my toes go into a cramp.

"I don't care much for rules but I do care for a ride in my convertible when the night wind is warm."

I grinned. "It's awfully warm."

"Grab a light jacket," he said.

~

No one understood the relationship between me and my daddy, not even me, not fully anyway. I should have seen his weaknesses and only given him a section of myself but I loved him to my core, no matter who he was. There were no hidden places in my heart that would not welcome him or any sacred ground inside my being that he could not walk upon.

I watched him as the night wind lifted up his hair and he kept reaching up to push it off his forehead. Sawyer did not resemble him but neither did I. He was uniquely himself. If I live to be a hundred I'll never meet anyone that looks like him in the slightest way. He was handsome, yes, that he was, but he was uncharacteristically appealing, the way a bump on one's nose erases perfection and leaves the face vulnerably beautiful. It's all in the smile, I think. That's really where it all begins- attractiveness, seduction, charm and Daddy's smile was the first thing you noticed about him. His smile was a whole conversation just inviting you to enter in. His straight brown hair was too long at the back of his neck and his sideburns stopped a bit beyond his ears and even if you didn't like that look in a man you'd like it on him. He was approachable but he was too complex to know really well, too gifted at exaggeration to believe fully.

That's what love is all about though, being able to spot the imperfections in someone and getting beyond it, seeing beyond that which other people may call dastardly and offensive. What I saw in my daddy was the port in a storm, should I ever need it. He was the life vest tossed me when I could not swim and was out there treading water. Daddy was all the words of comfort given when I was bruised and battered by the insensitivity of others.

We were going to Buck's of course. Buck's is where we always went. Daddy didn't like Mama telling him he had a two glass alcohol limit at home, so he always found an excuse to take his Vintage convertible out for a spin, to Buck's and back, seven miles one way and seven miles the other. It's a wonder that Mama never asked why it took him so long to cover fourteen miles. Guess Mama had her own secrets.

"So, you think he did it?" Daddy asked.

"John Peter? Hell, no," I said.

"Who else could have done it?"

"Thought we weren't going to talk about this?"

"I just want you to know that nothing is going to happen to you. I want you to feel safe."

"It's not a safe world, Daddy."

He looked at me with that lopsided grin of his, the one in which I could always interpret my own incorrigibleness. He'd always grinned lopsided when he called me incorrigible, now he didn't have to say it anymore. I heard it in the grin.

"They might all be talking about it at Buck's."

"Talk without poetry is backwoods dumb. You think I got nothing better to do than put any stock in backwoods dumb?"

There was that grin again. I watched as he pulled into the parking lot, his confidence was bubbling over and it was all due to the convertible. It was a 1969 Chevy Camaro, the color of lime candy. It was pure vintage and Daddy treated it like it was the Shroud of Turin. When Daddy drove his 69' Camaro around town he was sixteen again, and he could conquer anything. I remember when he first bought it at the vintage auto show, it gave him the courage to take a second mortgage on the house and file his three years of back taxes.

Buck's was attached to an apartment house. It looked like a motel but the people that lived there had leases and kitchens and even little backyards. It was called Lilac Gardens but I never saw a lilac there in my life.

Of course everybody was talking about the murder around the bar, making fun of John Peter, saying how they never thought he had it in him, like murdering someone was a hero's act and John Peter had never shown courage before. Now it seemed like they were going to give him the medal of honor for killing Millie.

We slid into a booth with ripped red leather seats and scratches on the table so deep we could have stood our dimes up in 'em. Kidd Rock was blaring off the radio singing "Redneck Paradise" and someone's voice screams out, "little bastard probably raped her first."

"Sometimes too hot the eye of heaven shines...." Daddy was looking right in my eyes.

"For sweetest things turn sourest by their deeds; lilies that fester smell far worse than weeds."

"Different sonnet," he said.

"Same author. Same wisdom."

"Well," he said, looking around, "we could use some poetry to soften the stench of the backwoods dumb chatter."

I agreed, of course. He took a book out of the bag he'd brought in the bar with him and slid it over to me. I could read the title upside down. The Time Travelers Wife. I was used to this. Daddy always gave me a book to keep me preoccupied while he slipped over to apartment Six to get whatever Karlene McFaddy was going to give him. Whatever it was, it was fast and satisfying, that I can tell you. Daddy always came back to the table with his cheeks flushed and I could smell the mouthwash he'd swished around his mouth so Mama wouldn't smell anyone's vagina on him.

"I'll just be a minute, baby face."

I sucked in my lips and raised my eyes and avoided the anger in my gut. If he could have done it in a minute I guess he would have.

"Like the book?" He'd been gone forty minutes so when he slid back into the booth I wasn't smiling.

"I already got a book. I'm reading A Confederacy of Dunces."

"Good book, but when you're finished, read the one I gave you. It's better."

"Not one book of literature is better than another. Nana says that. It's always about what book you're reading in the moment. It's subjective. You can't compare The Brother's Karamazov to Wuthering Heights but they are both great books that I enjoyed reading."

"That so, smarty pants?"

Well, his book was good, I'd started it while he was visiting with Karlene McFaddy and getting himself laid, or whatever.

"I started it, while you were gone." I glared at him, emphasized the word 'gone' but it only made him grin wider.

"And?" he raised his eyebrows and leaned in, then he made his eyebrows move up and down, which made me laugh.

"Pretty when you're laughing," he said.

"And when I'm not?" I asked, giving him my worst mug of a scowl.

"You're downright scary."

~

When we got home Mama was watching television. She didn't even look up when we came in. It was like we were co-conspirators and we'd both been out together getting drunk on good times and country music. It was like we should have gotten a tap on the head and a slap on the ass for our wicked adolescent behavior. Of course all I did at Buck's was read a book and maybe Mama thought Daddy wouldn't cheat on her if he was with me, but I think something in the back of her mind told her that he got away with doing whatever he wanted no matter whom he was with. Maybe that's why she always looked at me like I was bad luck. She knew I was his and all of his secrets were safe with me.

Chapter Two
Pleasant Day

I wanted to see John Peter real bad, get the story straight from the horse's mouth about poor Millie Grady's dead body showing up in his box-spring. He'd never paid any attention to her. He wasn't one of those goons that made fun of her either. John Peter wasn't a joiner; he was an individual, a sensitive artistic type. Some of the goons called him queer but the only thing queer about John Peter were his ears. They were too big for his head. I imagine he was going to grow into them one day and be kind of cute, the kind of cute that lets a man get away with almost anything, like my daddy.

There were lots of cars at his house and I didn't think I'd be too welcomed if I marched in there and gave the sheriff my character reference on John Peter, about him crying over a dead frog so how could he possibly murder anyone? I wasn't going to get to him that day though, he was probably being finger printed down at the county jail so I took myself to Piper Hill.

The oddest thing is how much humor Millie would have found in her body being stuffed inside John Peter's box-spring. Out of all the boys in the world John Peter gets blamed for doing her in and she and I both know he's the last person we'd suspect of killing her. She hardly even knew him. I wished she could tell me who did this to her. I wonder why the dead can't talk, look at all the crimes we'd solve if the damn dead would just Ouija board us our answers, or tell all those weird psychic people who killed 'em.

I lied back in the grass, I couldn't even read. I wanted to commune with Millie. I just didn't understand what had happened to her and why it happened. She never did anything to anyone. I started thinking 'bout our time together and her telling me that she missed not having a mama. I told her she was probably better off but she didn't believe me. "Thanks for trying to make me feel better," she'd said. Hell, it was the truth as I knew it.

She didn't have any siblings either so her poor father was going to be terribly alone. I felt badly for him and helpless about Millie. Feeling helpless is an awful feeling, it's like you're useless to prevent something awful from happening. I knew I'd bear this burden for a long time. But what could I have done to prevent her murder? Probably nothing, but maybe I could bring some justice by trying to find out who did it. Maybe I could bring some peace.

I had my eyes closed for about ten minutes and kept seeing Millie's face behind the lids of my eyes. I made her a silent promise that I'd seek justice and that she would not be forgotten. I swore I'd visit her grave every week and tell her everything that was going on without her. When I opened my eyes I thought I was hallucinating, but over the hill who do I see coming toward me but John Peter, he didn't look none too happy either but at least, he hadn't been locked up.

Instead of saying anything, he just flopped down on the grass and looked off. The two of us never hungered for words between us but now we were both at a loss.

Finally, I took a handful of dirt and threw it at him. All he did was brush it off his pant leg and stare at me. In normal times he would have chased me all the way over to Lake Murray and dunked me in.

"It wasn't my fault this happened," he said.

I couldn't tell if he was angry or bewildered or both 'cause he started to laugh. I just sat there in silence wondering where in the hell he was finding the humor in this but it was probably a really nervous laugh.

"Ain't this a fucked up world?" He started shaking his head up and down like he didn't give a good goddamn who agreed with him, he sure as hell thought it was a fucked up world.

"The police let you go?"

"What the hell they going to hold me on? I had no cause to kill her. I couldn't even lift Millie much less stuff her inside a box-spring."

"Why was she found there in your box-spring, John Peter?"

He shrugged his shoulders and looked up at the sky. The clouds were racing by, chasing each other like they might have been running from a storm.

"They didn't find any scratches on my skin. They're hoping to get DNA from under Millie's fingernails because they said she probably scratched her killer. It's clear it wasn't me. I don't have a scratch on me."

"Maybe there was someone on your property who was hiding out there?"

Again, he shrugged his shoulders and continued to watch those fleeing clouds. "There weren't any drag marks on the grass either so they figured she was carried up to my bedroom by someone bigger and stronger than me."

"Drag marks?"

"Yeah, they think whoever killed her did it in my

back yard and then carried her into the house. I think they found a scarf of hers out there or something. That was the murder weapon, that scarf."

"So they let you go?"

"Until they figure out how I could have done it, they let me go, I guess."

"Jesus Christ, John Peter, you didn't even know Millie. I'll tell the police that."

He didn't say anything and his silence was so weighty I saw the wind around him take a dip. I thought I knew Millie better than anyone in the world and she had always looked off when I mentioned John Peter's name as if the mere mention of it bored her. I couldn't figure out what the hell she was doing at his house though. And now John Peter was looking off same way she used to.

"You didn't know her, did you?"

"We went to the same high school, Pleasant, how could I not know her?"

"Well, yeah, but you didn't hang out with her. She and I are a grade below you."

"I don't hang out with anyone but you."

"Yeah, and Millie was my friend and I never spent time with you two together. You never once took up the space that Millie and I took. I never heard one word that came out of your mouth that that girl ever heard. You didn't know her. Your breath never passed her face, your presence was never held in her eyes while I was there to claim witness to it. So what the hell was she doing at your house?"

He lay back on the grass and closed his eyes. I watched his expressions change all my life and they pretty much went from hysterical to somber with nothing in between. John Peter was high strung and when he wasn't giddy about something he was brooding about something else. According to John Peter the world pretty much sucked and the weight of it was taking him under. But then he'd get it in his mind that he was in Disney Land and he'd skip away laughing so much he'd fall down. I guess some text book would call him bipolar.

I looked at him now and his expression was soft, like he was moonstruck. "I knew her," he said.

Millie had never ever mentioned his name except once when I called him unpredictable and she said that's what made a person interesting, being unpredictable. She'd said that if you couldn't ever predict what a person was going to do maybe they'd surprise you and do something you never would have expected, like form a rock band and become famous. I remember telling Millie that John Peter couldn't carry a tune so she better hope he'd unpredictably become famous some other way, like maybe he'd win the potato sack race at the Hollow Creek fair one year.

"I was the one told her not to tell you, not to tell anyone." He looked at me and I knew he felt guilty.

I looked at him like he was expecting me to eat the dirt he kept rubbing in his hands.

"You know how all the kids made fun of her? I didn't want them to think that I couldn't do better, couldn't get a girl like Sarah Hartsdale."

"You couldn't."

"Hell I couldn't."

"You were always a dreamer, John Peter. Sarah Hartsdale wouldn't stop to drop a dime in your cup if you were begging on a city street. Not that you're not good-looking or anything but you're not popular. Most people don't even know you exist. She'd see you die right there at her feet, and then when they told her that you were the one had a crush on her back in the days she'd shake those golden locks of hers and wonder who the hell you were."

"You're harsh, Pleasant. I can't help it if I don't like sports. That's why no one likes me."

"I'm a realist."

"Millie liked me."

"She liked me too. What the hell does that mean?"

She was coming to my house when Mama was at work and we'd… fool around."

"What?" I stood up and started pacing and he kept trying to follow me with his gaze but he finally gave up and stared at the ground.

"You and Millie?"

"Yeah."

I had to take a moment of silence. I hadn't a clue. "You didn't kill her, did you?"

"No!" He stood up on his feet so fast he tripped. "Shit, no."

"Then how the hell did she get dead inside your box-spring?"

"How would I know?"

"What were you doing?"

"We were up in my room, half undressed and someone knocked on the door."

I fell back to the ground again. "Undressed? You were sleeping with her?"

"Almost. Not altogether."

"But you're both underage."

He looked at me like my brains had spilled out at my feet.

"Who the hell came to the door, John Peter?"

"We didn't answer the door. I made Millie jump out the window and beat it on home. I guess we panicked, thought we were going to get caught with our clothes off."

"When was this?"

"Day before yesterday."

"She never made it home then?"

"I guess not but I never saw her again. I stayed until the man at the door left, then I left. I rode my bike over to Forrester High and played a game of chess with Jimmy Downey."

"You tell the police this?"

"Of course."

"Her father report her missing?"

"I don't know. I guess so."

I started feeling creepy. There couldn't be anyone out there that could have had a personal vendetta against Millie. That meant there had to be some creep out there randomly killing young girls.

"You went to sleep that night with…."

"Shut up, Pleasant. I didn't know it. Mama found her next morning when she was up there cleaning my room.

She saw a leg sticking out of the bottom of the bed while she was making it. She must have screamed so loud the dead took cover. Shit, didn't mean to say that."

"Shit, John Peter. Holy shit."

Chapter Three
Clarissa Blackwell

Everything had to be put in its perfect place. Everything had a perfect place, forks to the left of the spoons, brooms to the right of the vacuum cleaner and toothpaste always hidden away in the medicine chest, not bludgeoned to death with all of its exposed white blood. Clarissa thought that was the problem with toothpaste, it always wound up looking like it had a drunken binge the night before and was spitting up all over itself. Whenever possible, she purchased toothpaste powder. Life had to have order. Wayward toothpaste and shapeless tubes did not belong in a perfect world. In a perfect world, days had purpose and toothpaste tubes had spines. Clarissa Blackwell was the creator of purpose. Life had a driver's seat and she was in it. Turmoil was unbearable and caused her too many visions she couldn't explain.

Her house was her pride and joy. Nice expression, pride and joy. It didn't matter who entered her lovely Victorian home, it only mattered that she could read on their faces how they envied her. How perfectly comfortable everything looked. That's the thing about fine things, they couldn't alienate, they had to invite, as hers did. Her garage sale finds had to whisper their desire to be picked up. Her paintings had to demand pleasing stares and the cushions on her chairs had to long for a derrière to deflate their puff. Nothing could utter pretension or scream 'Go Away.'

Clarissa Blackwell was very much like her house. She demanded notice, as well. Though she was soft spoken and never did anything out of the ordinary, people stared at her. They assumed she must be somebody, like a movie star or surely someone they'd seen on television, like a famous female sports figure. Maybe something or other to the president? A newscaster? They were always a bit distressed to learn that she was no one, no one famous that is.

Clarissa had the look of a woman who grew up well, the look of confidence, poise, flair, even though the way she felt inside was often a contradiction to her external presence. She was grateful that her intelligent face made her appear worldly and wise. She would have preferred being beautiful to looking as if she were perpetually sucking on sour drops. She would have welcomed a very straight aquiline nose to the one she had, it naturally turned up, nothing she could do about it. But it gave her a condescending demeanor as if she were constantly sniffing something foul. But when Clarissa smiled, she became approachable, like her house and all things in it. Carissa made a point to smile often.

She was approaching sixty-six, a little secret she kept from others. Well, why shouldn't she? She believed that the body was a temple one should treat with respect. She looked much younger, she was sure, because her temple of a body had not been abused for years. She ate foods that did not oink or go moo, and she power walked the distance between Summerford and Edgefield two or three times a week, a good mile and a half. Well, she power walked in between stopping at garage sales, visiting a friend or two, and lunching at her favorite coffee shop in Edgefield.

Clarissa rarely ever went into Hollow Creek. It was another half mile or more out of the way but she'd read about a new health food store opening over there called The Fine Fettle. She assumed she could get almond milk and fish oil and other absolutely fabulous things like pure goat soap and organic face creams. As wonderful as the Edgefield Café was, it was just a café and it was more prone to BLTs and burgers than soy milk shakes and protein bars.

The Fine Fettle did not disappoint. Clarissa was quite content sitting there in a nice, large comfortable booth with the sun streaming in the window. She'd treated herself to the whole wheat spiced pumpkin pancakes and organic coffee all the way from Maine. She was thinking, as she stared out the window at the picturesque town, that it was worth walking the extra half mile to get into Hollow Creek more often. She'd definitely want to return to The Fine Fettle. As she took a napkin to her mouth to wipe off the remaining homemade maple syrup, she happened to look out the window. A scream immediately caught in her throat and she held her breath—to her absolute horror, there was a girl on a bicycle riding straight toward the little café looking like a demon on fire. She was maybe fifteen or sixteen years old, old enough to know better, Clarissa thought. The girl made a sharp left at the curb and Clarissa breathed a sigh of relief. If she hadn't made that sudden turn she might have gone through the plate glass window and landed right in her lap.

It was only for a second that Clarissa had gotten a glimpse of the girl's face. In the glare of the sun the girl had looked just like Chloe Rappaport. It had to be an apparition because Chloe Rappaport had been dead for years, but Clarissa could have sworn she'd just seen her on a blue bicycle racing down the main street of Hollow Creek like a wild savage. Of course, Chloe had died at twenty-three, not at fifteen. But Clarissa had known Chloe at the age of fifteen and this girl could have been her double.

Clarissa's body shook, as if cold, as if she'd been frightened by something. The girl on the bike had startled her so much. It was like seeing Chloe again. It wasn't the familiarity in the girl's face altogether but something about the attitude of that girl, nothing cautious about her, no sensitivity to the speed at which she was going. She appeared so cocky, just like Chloe had been at that age. How close had she been to the girl, at least twenty feet away? It must have been the glare from the sun. It had made some remote resemblance appear familiar, chillingly familiar.

As Clarissa paid her check and walked out of The Fine Fettle she crossed the street toward the route that would take her back to Summerford. She was a bit distracted, so perhaps that was why she didn't see it coming, but without warning, she was knocked to the ground, as if caught in the fury of a fierce tornado. She felt the collision in her entire body, the cuts on her hand and the sting of her flesh as she slid into the cement. She was on her ass in the middle of the street and there was that same Chloe double staring down at her with a horrified expression.

"Good God," Clarissa screamed. "Ow."

The sun still glared and Clarissa put her hand up to shield her eyes. The girl's features came into view so clearly. Clarissa realized that the familiarity was not caused by the glare from the sun. The resemblance was uncanny. She immediately got 'that feeling,' the one that rattled her to the core. She called 'that feeling' a tapping, it made her heart race. She knew this bizarre run-in with the girl had been fated.

Well, perhaps she shouldn't put too much stock in this. Perhaps she exaggerated her own experiences. She didn't really know that this painful collision with the girl on the blue bicycle was meant to happen, but the tapping in her heart told her otherwise. Clarissa did what she usually did in these instances; she tried to talk herself out of what she knew to be true. After all, not everything necessarily had meaning; meaning in a glance, meaning in an accident, meaning in this or that, all too vulnerable to a subjective interpretation. But meaning in her taps always held significant pause, whether she always understood them or not.

She was disturbed; confused by the girl's resemblance to Chloe, but other than that her mind was still. There were no messages in her head of any kind. Contact had been made between she and this stranger and the only interpretation for it was that it had to be important in some way. Take heed. Listen, she told herself. But skepticism was normal. Had she really seen the resemblance or had the tapping just been the result of confusion, the pandemonium of shock as she landed on her backside?

After she'd been thrown to the ground by the girl, she knew she would not be able to walk the distance home. Her ass hurt more than her hands and she might have sprained her ankle.

"Excuse me," the girl said. "Oh, I'm so sorry." But all Clarissa could do, while she was being tapped by God only knows what, was to gasp. The significance of her encounter with this girl was overwhelming her. The taps were like a knocking on her heart but that's all it was, there was nothing else, no interpretations.

"Are you all right, lady? Can I call someone for you? Help you somewhere?"

"No, no, I'm fine."

The girl stood up straight. "You sure?"

"Chloe?" Clarissa whispered.

The girl was off, like lightning. But she left behind the unsettling recognition in Clarissa's mind of someone long dead.

Clarissa fished her cell phone out of her bag and called Dennis to come get her. She hated calling him but he was always around, doing nothing, practically at her beck and call. He'd been retired for the longest time. She never understood how he was able to do that. He'd been free to discover what to do with the rest of his life long before he was fifty. Clarissa assumed he'd probably die before he figured it out. Well, maybe it was the result of his divorce from Savannah. Maybe Savannah had to buy him off to get rid of him.

Dennis drove out to pick her up, which he always did. Whenever she called him he made himself available. He was probably still guilt ridden over making her life a living hell twenty-five years earlier and ruining her friendship with Savannah. Well, it was water under the dam, life had to go on.

≈

"Getting old, Clarissa?" Dennis swung open the door of his Lexus SUV and she jumped in.

"Fuck you, Dennis." She put her head back in the seat and recalled the young girl's face.

"I hate profanity."

"You live so well. How do you do it? Did you take up gambling after our divorce? Oh, that's right, I forgot, you married into money."

He reached out and pinched her cheek. "Still beautiful."

"Told you not to do that."

"Winded?"

"A bit."

"You know, you're not making it to Edgefield the way you used to."

"I didn't go to Edgefield, I went to Hollow Creek. You're picking me up in Hollow Creek, Dennis."

"Oh, right. What were you doing here?"

"I went to The Fine Fettle."

"A dress shop?"

Clarissa laughed. She remembered how they ate when they were married, the young cannibals devouring their way toward high blood pressure and or cancer, a perfectly normal skinny couple barbequing their way into jowly cheeks and fat thighs.

"It's an organic café."

Dennis made a face. "Ay, right, where's the fun in that?"

She decided not to get into with him. They'd had too many arguments years ago on what not to put into one's body. When she stopped flipping steaks and pouring one too many scotches at happy hour their marriage broke up. Well, actually, their marriage broke up when he took up with Savannah, but no need to carry that around like a steel necklace. Clarissa looked ten years younger and he looked, well, Clarissa forced herself to be kind, he looked his age. Despite his money, he'd spent it on toys instead of his health. Karma had its advantages and he had brought it all on himself.

"I've been thinking about Chloe," she said out of nowhere. At least it was out of nowhere for Dennis. She'd thought of nothing else since she'd been knocked to the ground in Hollow Creek.

His whole body seemed to stiffen. "Chloe? How come?"

"You remember her murder?"

Clarissa watched his face, noticed how it tensed up. He had never been close with Savannah's daughter. Chloe hated him, used to go around saying that her mother couldn't sink any lower than Dennis Haworth unless she fell in a well.

"I don't like to think about her murder," he said softly.

"Well, I don't either but I saw a girl today in Hollow Creek, looked just like her, brought a lot up for me."

He turned to her. "Really?"

"She was so much like Chloe."

"You helped solve Chloe's murder. Never got over that, still beguiles me. You're something."

"I didn't solve it at all."

"Didn't? You led them to a body. You saw it all in your mind or something. You saw the killer's face in your head, your description turned out to be a perfect rendering. They caught the son of a bitch because of you."

"I didn't see anything about Chloe in my mind at all."

"Well, whatever you saw led to the capture of a serial killer."

"Ain't I something?"

Dennis starting twirling his finger around his head, "you are one spooky woman, Clarissa Blackwell."

Chapter Four
Pleasant Day

John Peter told me that Mr. Grady was at the police station same time he was and he was crying and screaming, saying that that couldn't be his daughter's body they found because Millie was home sleeping. Sergeant Brown drove Mr. Grady to Doctor Rand's office so he could get a sedative. John Peter said he started crying himself 'cause Mr. Grady was so distraught.

"I think he's going to go a little crazy," John Peter said to me. "I never saw a man's face look like that in my life. He looked like he was taking fire into his body, burning to death. He had this horrible grimace. I swear, I couldn't look at him."

I didn't know what to say. I wanted to pay my respects to Mr. Grady but on the other hand, I never wanted to see him again in my life. I couldn't bear his distress. I even wanted to get away from John Peter and go hide under a blanket.

"I gotta go," I said. "Mama wanted me to pick up pork chops at Madison's."

I started down the block and I heard him yelling behind me to meet him up on the hill next day. I didn't know if I wanted to see John Peter again so soon. I couldn't help myself but I kept wondering if he could have saved Millie's life. If they'd only waited it out together, waited for the strange man to leave the doorstep. If he'd only not made her jump out the window then maybe the man at the door would have left and John Peter would have gone back up to the bedroom and taken Millie's virginity the whole way. Then she could have told me all about it and I'd be begging for all the clandestine details instead of flying into town, wishing I was dead too.

I was real distracted after buying the pork chops and I guess I wasn't thinking. I hopped on my bike and took the corner at top speed. Before I knew it some damn woman was on the ground under my front bike tire. I nearly flipped my lid. She looked like she was dead, the way she was staring at me, like I held a harp and had wings. I sure was relieved when she got to her feet and wiped herself off. She didn't reprimand me or anything, like someone else might have done. She had kind of a nice face.

I said I was sorry a thousand times but she just kept staring at me. I think she mistook me for someone else but I couldn't be sure.

I put the pork chops on the kitchen counter and ran back outside. I didn't want Mama to put a paring knife in my hand and a sack of potatoes in my lap. That was Sawyer's job anyway, peeling carrots and being in there to savor Mama's gastronomic wonders and telling her how absolutely French her cooking was and how she should be on television showing people how to find flavor. That boy had so much sugar in his shoes I couldn't hardly keep a straight face. He had this little dance he did over the pot when Mama asked him to salt something. I could hear the two of them laughing like hyenas from upstairs; then I'd show up in the kitchen just as hungry for attention. Mama would turn silent and Sawyer would start rattling off things that didn't make no sense, silly songs like I got a chicken in the barn, what barn, whose barn. I got a chicken in the barn.

That was like their private code, she's here, let's get stupid now. That's when I'd tell him that his head was so empty, filled with nothing but pennies, like a pig bank, and his pig head rattled so loud it kept me up nights. I'd tell him he was supposed to have brains in there like everybody else but he got out of line when they were passing them out. Mama would sigh long and hard and tell me he had her genes, that's why he liked to cook. What was that supposed to do, make me feel good? I'd say "Ha, and I have Daddy's." I didn't use that argument none too often though 'cause Mama would always say "You didn't get the better of us. You hear that, Pleasant? You didn't get the better of us."

Maybe that was Mama's way of telling me I was unique. I could read all sorts of things into that but I wasn't going to waste my time. I stayed clear of the kitchen as much as I could. Anyway, Sawyer had pissed in there and left his mark, metaphorically speaking. Fine, I metaphorically pissed all over my bedroom like a male dog too, also out the backyard and in the den, where my fruitcake brother liked to watch cooking shows.

The fence around our house wasn't too high. I sat cross-legged on the ground and stared across the road at Mr. Wiley. If he threw rocks he couldn't hit me, long as I stayed low. He was just sitting there with his sign, Homemade Jellies, $6 a jar. On the little table in front of him he had all Mrs. Wiley's jellies. I think there were five or six different kinds. I didn't like the plum but the cherry was real good and made my lips pucker. The strawberry was Sawyer's favorite. I sometimes swiped one for him. It all depended on how he'd treated me that day. The apricot jelly gave me the runs and the marmalade was made with rum so I couldn't have that.

Mr. Wiley went to the bathroom about four times a day and he left for lunch at noon. Both the bathroom and the kitchen didn't have a view of the road so I could time it just right. I'd get over there and swipe a cherry jelly right off the table, maybe a strawberry one for Sawyer. Mama always said it was so kind of Mr. Wiley not to charge us for the jelly but Daddy used to grin and tell her the only thing he wouldn't charge us for was the shit our dog, Fredo, left on his front lawn. That always got me to laughing. Mama would make her sour face and Daddy would get up and stretch. He always got up and stretched when he knew Mama was about to give him hell for using words like shit in front of us kids. That way he could turn his back real fast and avoid a confrontation.

"She'd say "Where'd the jelly come from then?"

He'd look at me while I sat there trying to make my bubble gum blow me a bubble. "Why, the wind blew it over here, Martha," he'd say and my face would be covered in gum because I'd laugh so much that pink shit would burst all over my face.

"Hell of a wind," Mama would say and she'd kick my foot as she walked by, just to let me know she knew Daddy was my ally. "Feet off the table, Pleasant."

Funny how Sawyer got to scuff up the whole house with his sneakers and all she'd do would be to run around after him with lemon oil.

Nothing worse than grey light coming in your window on a Sunday morning. Personally, I don't like the color grey. It reminds me of the absence of color. I know, I know, people say grey is a color but it isn't. It's grey. Grey like smoke, like clouds, like ash. Grey like dirt and shale. Grey is Mr. Wiley's hair and a cat bit me once was grey. Grey is a deadly color. Grey gets between me and the sun and threatens rain. It's a downer, grey is. Don't ever wear grey, people are likely to avoid you.

Daddy told Sawyer he wanted him to shadow me. He didn't want me on my own, not till they cleared up Millie's murder. Daddy said there may be a maniac walking around out there. I wanted to ask Daddy what the hell he thought Sawyer would do if he came face to face with a murderer, weep most likely, after he offered me up on a silver platter to save himself. I didn't want to rub it in though. If Daddy wanted to think of his son as some kind of protector, well he's got a right. Far be it from me to burst his bubble. Sawyer does that on his own, every time he sings and dances along to his Ricky Martin CDs and Daddy looks at him funny.

I got rid of Sawyer soon as Angus showed up to torture me with the truth. "Sawyer," I said, "I swear I won't tell Daddy if you stay out of my face for the rest of the day." Sawyer liked that idea. "And besides," I added, "Angus likes to show his fists and hike up his pants. He is definitely an adequate detour to any maniac's plans to do me in. Angus even spits on the ground to make himself evil. He likes to be taken seriously."

I gave Angus a grin and noticed he was scowling. I guess he wanted to show Sawyer he was fierce as fire.

"Guess you're in good hands," Sawyer said as he skipped away and shook his backside like a showgirl.

Angus spit right before he asked me what I thought of the body pulled out of John Peter's box-spring.

"We all got a little bit of luck, Angus."

"You believe me now, Pleasant?"

"John Peter didn't do it." I stared at him, threatening him to disagree.

He shook his head. He had grass stains all over his pants, on his backside and on his knees so it didn't matter that he sat on the damp ground. He started tossing rocks like Mr. Wiley 'cept he was aiming at a tree and not at me. "Who did it then?"

He was gangly, longer legs than any of us. He stretched out but kept tossing rocks.

"Sucks," I said.

"Yeah, you knew her, didn't you?"

"Me and her hung out. You didn't want anything to do with her. Damned if I know why."

"She only had one arm, Pleasant."

"So what?" I screamed. "She wasn't human because of that?"

He made some breathy sound, and I knew he felt bad, but I wanted him to admit to being an asshole. I wanted him to tell me he didn't even deserve my friendship because his soul was a shallow puddle.

"My mama says she was killed in John Peter's back yard. It was in the paper. So not only was she found in his box-spring, she was killed in his back yard." He looked at me pathetically and I saw his confusion.

"John Peter said someone came to the door while she was in his house and it was him must have caught her and killed her in the backyard after she jumped out the window."

"What was she doing in John Peter's house?"

I blushed and turned away but he got it all too soon.

"You insinuating they were getting it on?"

"Insinuation is not truth, just conjecture."

"Shit, everybody is doing it but us, Pleasant."

I blushed again. "You don't know whether or not I'm getting anything on except my clothes when I get out of bed in the morning."

"Ha." He turned away.

Sex was not on my agenda and when it was on my agenda, Angus Ray was not on my list of potential suitors. I had my ideal and his pants did not have grass stains and his head was filled with brown curls, not that straight yellow hair Angus had that fell into his eyes and looked weird because his mama shaved most of his scalp so his hair was only long in the front. Angus had small green eyes, sort of like olive pits. My ideal was so handsome he made your pulse race. He would be a writer, of course. Nothing harsh would ever come out of his mouth, just words that floated across the breath like petals in a pond, like he was Shakespeare or one of those English poets from the nineteenth century that wore wide lace collars and swung both ways, according to Sawyer.

"Fucking A," Angus said. "I never was so close to murder in my life. Not real murder, just all those fake TV shows. This here is real, Pleasant. We have to arm ourselves against this foul presence."

"And just how are we supposed to do that, Angus?"

"I don't know. Let's pair up. Never leave each other's side, except to go home and eat and sleep."

"You think I want to make myself crazy keeping you in my sight? You are a burden to bear, filling my head with your asininity."

"I don't know why I like you, all you do is insult me."

"Maybe it's my sweet smile, Angus."

"Yeah, right."

Chapter Five
Pleasant Day

Next day, Angus and I walked across Piper Hill toward Sumter Creek so we could put our toes in the water. The sun had burst through all those grey clouds from the day before like an angry bull, showing its deep glistening colors to the earth, prideful and glowing. Apollo Helios had usurped the grey and was showing off his plumage of yellow-gold. It made me think of that short story about the bet between the sun and the wind. Wind bets that he could get a hat off a man's head so he blows himself to death, but to no avail. The man just holds on to his hat more tightly. But the sun reigns my sky. After burning brightly down on that man he donned his hat 'cause his poor scalp was sweating heavy. The wind took cover, and would have hanged his head if he had one to hang, for there is no glory in losing. I worship the sun, it grants me a shield against the world, forces my darkest thoughts where they can't be seen or heard. When my day is brightened I am indomitable.

Angus and I were quiet. My thoughts were going where I didn't intend for them to go. Maybe it was the shade that found me. Damn Angus plopped us right under a Willow Tree, its long limbs hid the sun with frail, multitudinous branches. I felt at any moment I might be swooped up and eaten by the profound sad tales of a Weeping Willow.

Maybe it was appropriate to be under that tree for I was thinking about Mama. I had brought Millie home a thousand times and my mama didn't remember meeting her? I guess she didn't recall we'd been friends, either that or her amnesia protected her against my grief. No need to hold me in her arms if my soul was unscarred by the news of Millie's murder. Mama was a blind woman, blind to Karlene McFaddy and blind to my sorrows. After so many years, I was numb to it. I yearned for her but I learned that detachment is a weapon we both could employ.

Angus had his feet in the water. His jeans were rolled up and the blonde fuzzy hair on his legs looked soft as doll's hair. He was stern and serious as John Peter on his down days, when the bipolar swing of his personality was waist high in quick sand.

"So you really don't think John Peter did it?" he asked me, the first words he'd uttered in over an hour.

"She must have outweighed him by several pounds. She was taller too, much bigger boned. I doubt if he could have gotten her back inside the house and inside his box-spring. I knew Millie. She would have taken a punch at him."

"I guess you don't think he did it, huh?"

"No."

"I agree. She would have overpowered him, one arm or not."

"And another thing, who was the man came to the door?"

"A man came to the door?"

"Yeah."

"Could have been anybody."

"I guess. But it could have been the murderer too."

"Did John Peter see the man?"

"Maybe we can ask him. I think I see him coming up over the hill."

I squinted up my eyes and focused them on a little speck against the sky. Soon enough I could make out John Peter. I noticed he wasn't idly strolling on such a hot day, he was running. By the time he got to us the sweat was pouring off him like he'd just come in out of the rain.

He slid to his knees before me and nearly knocked me over. "Shit, Pleasant, Ike and Bodean had Sawyer in a neck hold and they were turning the hose on him, looked to me like they were going to drown him." John Peter was breathing fast and his whole body was red as a pale person's sunburn.

I stood to my feet. Damn Sawyer was always being teased. Maybe it served him right for being so neat Mama had to press his designer jeans so they never showed a wrinkle. Still, Sawyer was my brother and I wasn't going to let those two bullies end his life.

"C'mon," I yelled, "let's go help him."

John Peter grabbed my arm and held me back. "It's okay, Ike's father came out of the house and broke it up, shooed Sawyer home."

"I wonder what the hell he was doing there. Nobody in his right mind would show up on Ike's farm." I looked from Angus to John Peter, just daring them to say one nasty word against my brother, like maybe he was expecting to be the recipient of a sexual favor.

John Peter, being a bit kinder than Angus said, "Hell, Pleasant, they might have lured him there, pretended like they were befriending him or something."

"Yeah, Pleasant," Angus said, "you know how much Sawyer tries to fit it."

"He's not ever going to fit in," I said and sat back down.

The three of us looked off. We all hated Ike and Bodean. Most of the kids in school hated them but they were too afraid they'd get blown away if they stood up to them. They were boys in Sawyer's grade but they looked older, especially when they were shoving some smaller kid into a wall or threatening some black kid with a can of white paint. Both of them looked like pigs, fat, snarly, should be butchered for dinner pigs. Ike had pimples the size of snowballs and Bodean had a hump on his back made him look like a monster, but I guess they thought they were handsome. I thought their deformities must have been karma and the Lord had punished them for their past life sins by making them ugly in this incarnation.

Daddy once told me that beauty is attitude and Bodean and Ike were rich in attitude so maybe some people would consider them handsome. Every time Bodean saw me he whistled and told me he had something for me. First time he said that I was so dumb I asked him what it was and he grabbed his crotch and started hopping toward me like some deranged rabbit. I ran screaming down the road. He told me later that I should be thanking my lucky stars he found me attractive.

"I hate those guys," I said.

The three of us sat there staring at the water in the creek. The creek was clear as crystal glass and tasted like nothing you could buy in a bottle or turn on from a sink. It was as if no one had ever pissed in it and no duck had ever shit in it. It made me think of the times I'd sat there with Millie and she had filled canteen after canteen of that creek water to bring home. She said that when she grew up she was going to bottle it and call it Hollow

Creek Crystal Clear Water. She said she was going to get rich from it. Millie was pretty smart, always thinking ahead. Ike had once grabbed his crotch and started hopping at her like Bodean had hopped at me and she took a pair of scissors out of her book bag and took off after him, screaming she was going to cut his wang off. Ike hated her after that, called her a three legged cow and went around saying the only job she'd get out of school would be working for the carnival.

Angus broke through my thoughts. "Who was that man you saw that came to your door the day Millie was murdered?" he asked John Peter.

"I never saw him before in my life."

"You don't know what he looked like?" I asked.

John Peter stared at me for a moment like he was expected to know what the guy looked like. "Well, I peeked through the glass at him. He was tall, maybe six feet or so."

"How old was he?" Angus asked.

"My mama's age, maybe older." He looked over at Angus. "I didn't do it. You know I couldn't do anything like that."

"Don't worry, John Peter, me and Angus are going to solve this crime," I said. "I need to solve it, for Millie's sake." I reached out and touched his arm.

"You can't solve it," he said.

I looked at Angus, he looked a little surprised that I'd given him this daunting task but he nodded his head. "I owe you, John Peter. You're my friend and we'll solve it."

"Thank you," John Peter said. "But I don't want you going to any trouble."

"No trouble," we said in unison.

Daddy was out on the porch reading the paper when I came up the drive on the Schwinn cruiser I'd gotten for Christmas that year. Sometimes Daddy got home early as 4 p.m. He made pills at some plant. I don't know how he stood it. He worked on an assembly line stuffing medicine like paracetomal, whatever the hell that is, into soft gelatin capsules all day. Daddy liked to go around pronouncing all the names of the pills. I don't know why. Maybe he just liked the way the names ran over his tongue like some foreign language. Problem is they'd get stuck in my brain and I wouldn't be able to get rid of them. He said his job was more scientific than just pouring pills into gelatin capsules but it never sounded like anything other than boring to me. He also did odd jobs like building picket fences for people and installing gas heaters. I think that's what kept him sane after his assembly line day, that and Karlene McFaddy in apartment Six over at Lilac Gardens. I wondered if I was doomed to marry a man like my daddy, a man with so much charisma I'd forgive him almost anything. But I didn't even know if Mama forgave him for cheating on her. She scowled at him the same way she scowled at me and my only lies were those of omission.

Daddy looked up when I sat beside him. He gave me his grin, his lips lifting up into slits like the Howdy Doody dummy Mama got from a flea market and set in an old rocking chair out on our back porch. She called the puppet Handsome Howdy and said it was going to be worth something some day, that it was an antique. I thought it was the spookiest thing I'd ever seen in my whole life the way it sat there staring at me. Mama sometimes picked Howdy up and made his mouth move. Then she'd close her lips and pretend it was Handsome Howdy talking. She'd laugh like that was the funniest thing and I'd be thinking she was just as freaky as the damn dummy. Our dog, Fredo, tore Howdy up a bit and Mama got the broom to him but every time you took the broom to Fredo he'd think you were playing with him. Fredo was pretty relentless though and Handsome Howdy lost part of his little hand 'cause I'm sure Fredo thought he was the devil sitting there, same as I did. Fredo tore into him every chance he could. Mama eventually moved Handsome Howdy into her bedroom to protect him from Fredo. I guess maybe that explains Daddy's relationship with Karlene McFaddy. How the hell could he be romantic with Mama with that freakish little wooden dummy sitting there looking spooky at him?

"Here," Daddy said and gave me the only section of the newspaper I ever read, the entertainment section.

"I want the front page," I said.

He gave me one of his looks, the one he used when he knew that something unexpected was about to come out of my mouth. "Is my little girl becoming more political these days?"

"Your little girl wants to know if they caught the bastard that killed my friend, Millie Grady."

He looked at me a long time, like maybe he was debating whether or not to open his mouth. He made the wrong choice.

"She was inside John Peter's box-spring, honey."

I looked at him like he'd grown another head. "You don't really think John Peter did it?" I almost screamed.

He stared at me. "Humbert Humbert," he said and pointed his finger straight out.

I took a deep breath. "I'm not playing that game today."

"All right, all right. Calm down now honey and answer the question."

"You didn't ask one," I said through my teeth.

"Humbert Humbert was a character created by what author?"

"Who was Nabokov? The book was Lolita and you're still an idiot. You're supposed to give me an answer. I give the question."

He reached over and kissed my cheek. "I'm sorry, Sweet Pea, but face facts. The body was found in John Peter's box-spring, up in his bedroom. I think he was scared after he did it and stuffed her in there."

My tiny little eyes must have gotten round 'cause my forehead hurt. "He didn't do it.

"Prove it."

"You didn't think he did it the other night."

"I did, I just didn't say it."

"A man came to the door, how do you know he didn't do it?"

"I don't know that he did do it either."

"A man is innocent until proven guilty." I turned away and looked for agreement elsewhere, from the trees and the flowers that Mama had set out on the porch, 'cause that's the only place I was going to get it.

"John Peter is not a man yet." Daddy held out his hands and drew me to him. "But kids are capable of murder, you know." He looked at me like he felt sorry for me because I was going to try and solve something that was over my head. "I know he's your friend and you need to stand by him, but the odds are not in his favor."

"I'm going to prove his innocence, Daddy."

"How?"

"By finding that man came to the door."

Daddy nodded his head. "Okay, okay, good start Sweet Pea. Do you know anything about him?"

"He was tall."

Daddy smiled. "He was tall? Okay, okay, like I said,

good start, honey."

Sawyer got home about that time looking like someone had thrown his Jimmy Choo Portman sneakers in mud.

I stared at him and wondered if he'd tell me what had happened earlier with Ike and Bodean but he looked right through me as he ran ahead.

"Have a wet day today, Sawyer?" I called after him.

"Piss on you, Pleasant," he yelled back as he took to the stairs. I guess he knew John Peter had spread the news about his head being held in a death grip by Ike and Bodean and the hose being turned on him.

"I thought he was supposed to be shadowing you today," Daddy said, looking as disappointed as he usually looks when there's no beer in the fridge.

"He did, for a while," I said. "But then Angus came, and then John Peter so I told him he could go."

"What's he so angry about?"

"Ike and Bodean turned the hose on him. They had him by the neck. They've been known to do that."

"He's almost six feet two, he couldn't take care of himself?"

"He's slight of frame, Daddy. Ike and Bodean are deformed, big like Schwarzenegger."

He nodded his head and got quiet. I didn't think Daddy wanted to admit that Sawyer would rather darn their socks than take a punch at them.

"Listen honey, I don't want you hanging out anymore with John Peter. We can't be really sure of John Peter now, sweetheart."

"You got the wrong man, Daddy. I mean, you're smart and all but you're no judge of character. I can see that."

I heard him laugh. "You want to give me a more solid reason to believe in his innocence then something you feel?"

"Solid reasons like proof? You mean facts? I'll get them. You never trusted anything that was in your gut alone, without solid facts to back it up?"

"You can't trust what you feel, only what you can prove." Daddy winked at me like he had all the answers and I had none. "Your feelings won't keep that kid out of jail. But he's a minor, might not even go to jail. Anyway, you get some facts, little girl, then we'll talk."

He was right, of course. Believing in John Peter's innocence could only get me so far; I needed to prove who had done this to Millie. That night when I went to bed I willed Millie to come to me in a dream and tell me who had committed this crime against her. I willed Millie with all my might but the only thing I could recall when I awoke was that I had dreamed of a storm but not a normal storm, it wasn't rain that was nearly drowning me, it was blood, and I was covered in it. I guess it seemed like an appropriate dream, all things considering.

Chapter Six
Clarissa Blackwell

It was Monday morning, cleaning day, a day for dusting flea market figurines, Victorian flower bowls, Tiffany lily vases and vacuuming her antique Persian rugs upstairs and down. Clarissa enjoyed cleaning her house and took great care, the way one would when bathing an infant. Each object in her house had a place in her heart and was never discarded. That's why Clarissa bought everything she owned carefully, giving thought to its final location. Vases on the fireplace mantel, figurines on end tables shinned and polished with the best paste wax. Some priceless dishes and bowls were kept behind glass in an old vintage walnut cupboard in her pantry and displayed only at holiday parties.

At the end of the day Clarissa would sit with a glass of the finest French red wine and admire the comfort and simple beauty of her home. She enjoyed the quiet of sunset, a time when nothing had to be done or even thought about. It was so peaceful to let her eyes rest on the mixed rose hedge that neighbors continually admired, running lazily beyond her parlor windows all the way to the road. Sunset was a time to think about what was ahead of her instead of what was behind her, if she was going to think at all. But life wasn't always that uncomplicated, some days peaceful repose was impossible and she certainly wasn't calm enough for peaceful repose after her run in with the girl on the bike in Hollow Creek. She was so jittery she almost broke her majolica fruit bowl as it fell to the floor earlier that day, saved only by the thickness of the rug. She had been distracted by that girl, and the dream she hadn't had in years, the one that always woke her up in a sweat.

Clarissa hadn't been able to get the girl out of her mind. It had to mean something to run into her like that. It had to mean something that the girl resembled Chloe down to her nose and her eyes and the color of her hair. But Clarissa wasn't having any visions, or at least not any new visions. She'd only had the dream, the one in which the baby was covered in her mother's blood and Chloe was screaming for help. She couldn't trust that dream. It had started right after Chloe was murdered. Clarissa had always assumed that Chloe's baby might have been covered in her mother's blood, of course, but according to the police, it was most likely her own. Horrid thought. It was too painful to think about. She shut it out, slammed a door on her mind so fiercely that the images shattered and fell back.

But the girl's resemblance to Chloe was a shock to her spirit, memories she couldn't bear to think about were resurfacing. That's why she'd had the dream again, she imagined. Hopefully it would vanish and she wouldn't have to obsess about what had happened to Chloe or to Chloe's baby.

Tuesdays were the days Clarissa walked to Edgefield.

Each day had order and purpose and she rarely varied her schedule. She was afraid of becoming purposeless. She would only sit idly at sunset, it was a gift, sunset was, something she deserved after fulfilling so many ambitious goals during daylight hours. Purpose and fulfillment made her happy. Wednesdays were for her flowers and rose hedges and sometimes a run over to Home Depot. Thursdays she was back walking to Edgefield and stopping along the way to browse at flea markets. She knew people who would invite her for coffee and she would return the favor on Saturdays, a social day for Clarissa, a day for having friends in for lunch so they could admire her home. Fridays Clarissa had her yoga class in Edgefield and spent the rest of the day reading newspapers and novels. On Sundays she volunteered at the church to teach people English. When life took pause she filled it with more walks, more books, more yoga and more clips to her hedges.

Life was full. She'd never had children, which she only regretted at holidays, and she was only married once, to Dennis, who had spent a good deal of time over the years trying to convince her to take him back, that Savannah was a she devil that could charm Satan into a Bible class and he shouldn't be held accountable for her seduction, her attraction to him, and besides, it was so many years ago, like that excused it.

There were times when Clarissa hated Dennis to the core, times when she doubted she'd ever forgive him. He had taken Savannah away. The closeness between she and Savannah had dissolved like images on a beach when the ocean runs in and nonchalantly takes down a perfect sand sculpture. Her childhood friend had decided that a man was the only thing that could come between them.

Clarissa laced up her sneakers and made sure to

wear her sunhat for it was a hot day, but a friendly one. The humidity had gone into hiding and a gentle breeze swayed through the trees. She walked the mile and a half, the same route she took twice a week but she took a left at the fork instead of a right. She was going back to Hollow Creek. It wasn't likely that she would run into the girl but maybe she would. Her body was still sore from her fall but Clarissa would bare it. If she saw the girl again, chances are it would be worth it, if only to get a much better look at her unusual resemblance to Chloe.

The Main street in Hollow Creek was a block long, not much on it but The Fine Fettle and a few stores that sold newspapers and donuts. However, both sides of Main Street were lined with bright, beautiful flowers and the town bordered on the river. There was a real estate office wedged in between a lawyer and an insurance broker, and a new garden store that took up most of the block. You could get a very soggy oversized sandwich, potato chips and ice cream at the Crazy Dog and down at the very end of town, you could gas up and buy lottery tickets. Clarissa half expected to see tumbleweeds blowing down the street it seemed so quiet and desolate.

The Fine Fettle, however, was busy and her window seat was taken. She was only able to grab a small table near the kitchen but the large plate glass window in front was still visible and she assumed that if the little hellion came tearing down Main Street on her blue bicycle, Clarissa would know it.

"Hey, how are you, are you all right now?"

Clarissa looked up, it was the waitress that had waited on her last time she was in.

"I saw that fall you took," the waitress said.

"Fall? I was run over is more like it."

The waitress laughed. "Well, yeah, looked pretty brutal. You survive?"

"Barely," Clarissa said.

"Well, let's see, a few months ago Pleasant ran into a baby carriage, knocked it right over."

"My God," Clarissa said, "was there a baby in it?"

"Yep, but no harm done. The kid cried for a good hour but no broken bones."

"Who was that kid?"

"Oh, it was Doris Luellen's baby."

"No, not the baby, the girl on the bike."

"That'd be Pleasant Day." The waitress made a face, raised her eyes up, put her lips in an odd position.

"That's her name? Pleasant Day?"

"Yep, not a bad kid, mind you. She's just, well, she's opinionated."

"Where does she live?"

"You going to tell her parents how she ran you over?"

"I just might. She'll be driving in a year or so, now there's a horrible thought."

The waitress smiled broadly and held out her hand. "I'm Sandy Hoover."

"Clarissa Blackwell," she said as she shook the hand extended, feeling an immediate pull in the area of her chest, she'd been tapped. Lots of emotional pain, she thought as she stared up at Sandy Hoover.

"So, where does Pleasant live?" Clarissa asked.

"On Balsam Lane, right across from the jelly stand."

"Homemade jelly?"

"Sure is. I heard Old man Wiley has Boysenberry this year. Cantankerous old bastard but his wife's preserves are out of this world. Worth putting up with him."

"Think I'll walk on over there and get me some Boysenberry Jelly."

"Walk? It's a couple miles out."

Clarissa shrugged her shoulders. "That's good. After

a great breakfast two miles is nothing."

"I guess that's what keeps you so thin." Sandy smiled.

Clarissa opened her menu and ordered the whole wheat French toast with a side of fresh grapefruit and organic coffee all the way from Maine.

～

The road was straight for most of the walk and then it curved so sharply you couldn't see around it. Clarissa imagined that most people went right by the little jelly stand. Drivers would have to have so much focus on the curve that they'd go right by it, Clarissa thought. But being she was on foot, she couldn't miss it. The old man had a table out and he sat behind it on an old kitchen chair. He smiled as she approached. She couldn't help but smile as well, he was wearing a bowtie, must be taking his retirement job very seriously. She noticed the cane that was leaning against the table. It had a fancy ivory handle. The table was filled with fruit preserves, jellies and jams. The little sign told her that everything was six dollars.

"Do I get a special if I buy more than one jar?" she asked.

He nodded his head. "I know you, don't I?"

She stared at him, tried to recall his face but nothing came to mind. "I don't think so."

"Never forget a face."

She picked up the Boysenberry. It had a little ribbon around it. She read the labels off the jars as he stared at her carefully. All natural ingredients, she was pleased to read.

"My wife gets them ready for the season. She likes to make them pretty."

"Very good presentation, tell your wife I said that."

"I will."

"I'd like the cherry and the Boysenberry."

He got out a little brown bag and set them inside. "Ten dollars for both."

"Sounds good." She fished inside her pocket for a ten dollar bill. She looked around.

"Do much business here? It seems so quiet."

"I do."

"You could probably sell these in town, you know? Local stuff. People like that."

"If they like it they have to come get it, right where it's made. I'm not a delivery boy."

Clarissa looked across the road. "Who lives over there?"

He might have answered her but coming around the bend, peddling fast, came Pleasant Day. When she noticed Clarissa she slowed down and finally came to a stop. Clarissa stared at her.

"You might have just knocked me down again," she said. "Thanks for stopping."

"I wouldn't have."

"Stopped?"

"No, knocked you down."

Clarissa watched as the girl walked across the road with her bike.

"My name is Clarissa," she yelled out.

All of a sudden she saw the girl duck.

Clarissa looked back in horror. The old man was tossing pebbles at her.

"What are you doing?" Clarissa said.

"Cute, isn't she?"

"You can't throw rocks at her, put those down." He frowned and threw the pebbles down. Clarissa noticed that the girl had run behind the fence and was sitting cross legged on the ground. Then she noticed that the old man had a bucket of pebbles next to him.

"You see her? You do see her, don't you?"

Clarissa nodded her head. It was obvious he was off his rocker. "Yes, I do see her, and you are not to throw pebbles at her."

"She's from heaven. Must be. People go to heaven they come back with dimples, people go to hell they come back with pimples."

Clarissa stared at him carefully. Ramblings from an old man could be dangerous. She walked across the road.

"He won't throw anymore pebbles," she said. "You can get up now."

"You come here to tell my parents what I done to you, that I knocked you down?"

Clarissa studied her face, the resemblance to Chloe was less acute. The girl looked more like herself, whoever that was. "No. I just walked out here to buy some of Mr. Wiley's jellies."

"Walked?"

"Yeah, I like to walk."

"Funny coincidence you showing up here. You sure you're not going to tell my parents?"

"Do your parents know that that old man throws rocks at you?"

"More like pebbles."

"Whatever. He's not to do it anymore. I want you to tell your parents."

"He just lies and says I'm crazy."

"They don't believe that, do they?"

"I don't know what they believe. What are you doing here?"

"Well, I wanted to buy some jelly. I didn't know I'd find you living across the road."

The girl eyed her with distrust. "You didn't, huh?"

she mumbled. "I gotta go."

Clarissa watched as Pleasant ran up the drive with her bicycle. At the porch she turned and stared back. Clarissa wondered what she was thinking. She put her hand up to wave but Pleasant didn't return her wave. She just stood there staring, willing Clarissa to leave. After a moment, Clarissa turned around and started walking back toward the little town of Hollow Creek.

Chapter Seven
Pleasant Day

I got to thinking, not all women are innocent. Hell, look at my Mama. I've seen her scale a fish and skin a chicken without so much as a flinch. She doesn't smile much either, only when Sawyer is around. She looks real delicate, the type to cry at sad movies but she never does. Sometimes she even laughs when someone dies at the end of a movie, and when I look at her like she's missing marbles she tells me she knows how to separate and I should learn the skill.

I got to thinking that woman out there on the road was up to no good, the one I ran over. I don't trust people that walk around all the time, it's like they're lurking. She looked a little too interested in me and my house as well. I didn't believe she just happened to show up across the road from me to buy jelly from Mr. Wiley. Maybe she was going to do me in like she did in Millie. Maybe me and Millie have something in common that I didn't know anything about and it's cause for murder.

Once I saw that woman disappear around the bend I hightailed it over to John Peter's. I wasn't sure his mama was going to let me in so I planned to climb the tree by his window. John Peter's mama was real protective of him. He didn't have a father so I guess she felt that he was going to be completely adrift out in the world with no role model teaching him aggression, so she'd just have to smother him and teach him a different kind of aggression.

I didn't have to climb the tree up to his room. He was out in the front yard sulking. If John Peter wanted to sneak out at night he could do it real easily with that old tree just begging to be climbed. It was growing right up against the window to his bedroom. I wouldn't mind a tree like that in front of my bedroom window, not that I was sneaking out any time soon but I figured there was going to come a time when someone would be down there wooing me, sort of like Cyrano de Bergerac wooed Rosalind, and I'd want a tree I could slide down real easy. I just knew I was going to be a pushover for sweet words.

Me and John Peter walked out back 'cause his mama was home cooking dinner and I didn't want her over hearing us.

"You look upset," I said.

"My mama is about to kill me."

"Why?" I asked.

"I don't want to talk about it."

Truth is I didn't really want to know about it, I had more important things on my mind and John Peter always thought his mama wanted to kill him.

"John Peter, that man you saw at your door could have been a woman."

He looked at me like I was nuts.

"It was a man."

"You said he was tall? Well, I just seen me a tall woman, perfectly capable of doing in Millie."

"Pleasant, you're nuts. I saw a man, not a woman."

"You sure?"

"Yeah, I'm sure."

Well, I wasn't. I think there's something awfully suspicious about a grown woman walking around the back roads of Hollow Creek. Only people coming out here live on the road and they stop at the jelly stand 'cause they know it's there. Hell, no one makes a trip out here just for jelly.

"Well, I gotta go," I said.

"You just got here."

"I know, but it's getting late. You think I want to be biking these roads at night?"

"Yeah, I wouldn't."

"Gee, thanks for sharing, John Peter." I hopped up on my bike and started home. I heard him yelling behind me, "don't take the back roads, Pleasant. Stay on the main roads."

Well, of course, I didn't listen to him, took the road behind Piper Hill because it was a short cut. If I stayed on the main roads I really wouldn't get home till dark. The road is nice up on Piper Hill, just a little narrow dirt road, can't drive it but you sure can bike it. There's only one section where it's woody, lots of trees but then it fans out pretty quickly and you can see the valley below. You can even see the creek winding its way down toward the Saluda River.

It wasn't night yet but there was a deep blue sky over me looking just about to turn dark. I could hear my tires on the dirt and birds up over head were flying, their perfect formation looked like a monogram against the sky. I could even hear their wings in the air. I was thinking about the strange woman I had knocked to the ground so I didn't hear the other bike right away and when I did hear another set of tires I figured it was John Peter, come to protect me from whatever monster was out there. I figured I'd scare holy shit out of him so I ducked back behind some brush and crouched down. When I heard his tires get close I jumped out into the road and started screaming and waving my hands like a crazy woman just got spooked by a mouse on her kitchen counter.

Immediately, I saw the bike he was riding flip up. The next thing I saw was Bodean Frasier on the ground and the only thing I was thinking was, holy shit.

I tried jumping on my bicycle so I could high tail it out of there, the whole time praying he'd been hurt and couldn't follow me.

"Hold up, hold up," he yelled as he came toward me. The next thing I knew he had me by the arm. I guess he hadn't been hurt at all. He was too goddamn big to get hurt.

"What you gonna do, Bodean, rape me?"

He started laughing. "You are a conceited little thing, aren't you? I don't' need to rape a girl."

"You going to hop at me like a bunny with your hands up your crotch, 'cause if you are I'm going to puke."

"Oh, that, pretty stupid of me, huh?"

I released myself from his hold. "Your self- awareness is touching. I'll be taking my leave now, then."

"I followed you from Brandywine Road."

"Why?"

"'Cause you shouldn't be out on your own after dark."

"What the hell do you care if I get murdered?"

He stepped back a few feet like he wanted to get a better look at me. "Whoa, you sure don't think much of me, do you?"

"Why should I? You almost drowned my brother the other day. You're a bully, Bodean. You know that about yourself? You pick on everybody. You're a goddamn bully."

"I sure as hell don't like little faggots who sell themselves at the Sheraton hotel in Augusta so they can buy designer clothes and think they are better than everybody else."

"You shut up." Of course I knew about that but I had no idea everyone else did too.

"What do you think, I was going to kill him or something stupid like that?"

I wanted to take a punch at the son of a bitch but I restrained myself due to the isolation of my present location.

"He's a snob," Bodean said, like that justified torturing him.

"What the hell do you care what my brother is or does?"

"I don't, he just makes my blood boil."

"Why?"

"I don't know."

"I didn't think you did, your head is too empty to know anything."

"I know I've just been insulted."

"Perhaps you're jealous of him?"

"Why? I don't want to be pretty."

"You could have drowned him."

"I wasn't going to drown him, Pleasant."

"Now, I'm going to turn around and get on my bike and go home and I want you to leave me alone."

"I'm taking you home, Pleasant, whether you like it or not. It's not safe on these dark roads. I'd never forgive myself if something happened to you."

I noticed that the deep blue sky was turning black as charcoal and I could start to see stars."All right, let's go."

Bodean took me straight to my door. As he stood there looking as goofy as a jack in the box, I looked him right in the eyes, noticing they were kind of pretty, greenish, like muddy water gets after a rain. The porch light was making his eyes shine like the stars. He had very dark lashes, looked like brooms, they were so thick.

"Please don't pick on Sawyer," I said.

"Okay, okay." He nodded his head up and down. I had never seen this side of him, he was soft as cotton candy and there was a pinkish glow to his cheeks. "Will you go to the movies with me sometime?"

I was shocked as all get out. Bodean was not my idea of poetry in motion but he did have pretty eyes.

"I don't think my daddy would like it."

"Well, if he okayed it, would you?"

"If I do will you stop picking on Sawyer?"

"I will."

"I'll have to think about it," I said, and at that point my daddy came out on the porch.

"Good evening," he said.

"Just wanted to get her home safely, sir," Bodean said and jumped back on his bike so fast I saw the dust kick up around him.

We watched him ride off then Daddy turned to me. "Isn't that Bodean Frasier? He the bully almost drowned Sawyer the other day?"

I nodded. "That's him."

"Don't worry," he said, putting his arm around me and leading me back toward the kitchen. "Nothing like a pretty girl to knock a bully down."

≈

The next morning I came out on the porch after breakfast and found Daddy sitting in the rocker.

"I should have said something to Bodean about picking on Sawyer," he said. "I think I'll have a talk with him."

"Yeah, might help."

"Looks like your instincts were right, Pleasant." He seemed lost in what he was reading. "John Peter didn't do it."

"I knew it." I grabbed the newspaper right out of his hand and read it over quickly. It seems that John Peter was not a suspect. The article said that there were no scratches on his body, no defensive wounds and the police were quite sure that John Peter didn't have the strength to carry Millie up to his room. There were no drag marks on the grass and they deduced she was carried from the back yard, where she was killed. They were able to pinpoint where the murder took place because of the scarf they had found at the end of the yard. They deduced she'd been strangled with it.

"I know all this, Daddy, John Peter told me 'bout the scarf, 'bout the police thinking he wasn't strong enough to carry her, 'bout there being no drag marks."

"I don't think you should read anymore of that," Daddy said, reaching out for the paper. "It gets a bit gruesome."

I shot back fast so he couldn't get hold of it and continued reading—didn't take but a moment to make me sorry I had. The article went on to report that Millie had probably fought for her life and the killer was sure to be scratched up as a result of that, which I knew because John Peter had told me, but I didn't know that the killer had broken Millie's nose and had knocked out a tooth. The papers were calling it brutal and senseless. They said the murderer must have gone back into the house after he strangled Millie because he wanted the large garbage bag to hide her body in. Millie had been found inside the bag that was inside the box spring, with her legs outside of the bag.

I felt sick to my stomach. "Oh, my God," I felt Daddy

take my hand and squeeze it.

"Please don't read anymore."

But I couldn't help myself, I had to get to the end of the article, I had to know everything.

"This can't be," I said as I scanned the last two paragraphs.

"What's that, honey?"

"The article is saying she wasn't a virgin?"

Daddy blushed and looked up at the sky. He better get more articulate talking about sex with me because if he thought Mama was going to clue me in about the birds and the bees, he was sadly mistaken. Besides, that conversation should have happened years ago. I was beyond the age of innocence.

"Yes," was all he said.

I knew Millie and John Peter hadn't done anything yet so that was news to me.

"They weren't sleeping together, Daddy. Millie never slept with John Peter, not yet anyway."

"And how do you know that?"

"He told me."

"Then he lied. Someone emailed photographs to John Peter's mother of the two of them naked together. Did you read that?"

"Where'd it say that?" I asked, scanning the article again.

"Second paragraph, I think. Seems someone with a camera was spying on them, a kid no doubt."

"That's disgusting. You think the same guy that took the photographs also killed her?"

Daddy shrugged his shoulders and looked away. "The whole thing is disgusting. I'm sorry it happened to your friend, Pleasant, real sorry."

"It doesn't say anything about them being in the act, just being naked."

Daddy raised an eyebrow. "Well, what does that imply, Pleasant?"

"Well, it doesn't prove they actually slept together." I was getting angry now. Daddy was too eager to believe any cruddy thing about John Peter without proof of it.

"Well, you're right, it doesn't. Personally, I think that Millie was followed to John Peter's house by whoever killed her. John Peter must have been out and the murderer saw an opportunity to kill that little girl. Afterwards, he must have shoved her in the box-spring because he didn't know what to do with the body. Maybe he was coming back for it."

"What's the motive?" Daddy shrugged his shoulders."I think a woman did it," I said. "And I met her. I know who she is."

Daddy looked at me like I was as dumb as fake ice cream. "A woman? And what reason on God's earth would a woman have to kill that little girl?"

"You see a hump on Bodean's back?" I asked, wanting to change the subject as quickly as possible. Besides, when I had more evidence about that strange woman I'd be more verbal. I was getting tired of Daddy asking me to prove everything anyway. I knew any woman lurking on back roads for no other reason than to buy jelly was up to no good.

"Bodean seemed kind of sweet on you."

"What?" I started feeling angry again. "He acts like an ass around me and besides, he's a bully."

"Well, bullies do like girls." He smiled wide. "I had a crush on a girl when I was his age and I acted like the biggest fool on earth."

"Bet you didn't."

"I did."

"Tell me about it."

"Well, I grew up with her, the two of us used to play

together as little kids. She lived down the block. But then, when we became teenagers, it suddenly dawned on me that she was no longer a little kid, she was beautiful, like a princess, or a movie star. It got me kind of stupid, I guess. All I did was act like an idiot in her presence. I even made fun of her, bullied her something terrible. I used to tell her she didn't have any brains."

"Why?"

"Self protection, I guess."

"Self protection?"

"Yeah, well, I figured that if she thought I didn't like her she couldn't hurt me by rejecting me. So I was safe from getting hurt."

"That doesn't make sense."

Daddy shrugged again.

"What happened then, you ever get together?"

"No, not for a while. You can't treat someone badly and expect them to like you. Maybe Bodean is just protecting himself against your rejection. He may think you're just too beautiful, too good for him."

"Yeah, right."

"Well, could be why he acts like such a jerk. You've got to try and understand people's behavior, Pleasant."

"That girl you liked marry someone else?"

"Well, yeah, she did, at first, but after I got myself a job and a convertible the tables turned. I drove into town one day and saw her on the street so I pulled my car to the curb and whistled at her."

"What'd she do? I don't like when boys whistle at me."

"Well, she liked it. We took one look at each other and it was like cannons going off. We fell in love."

"Right then and there?"

"Yep, right then and there but she was married."

Daddy got silent. Maybe he'd been married too.

"Young love is very special," he said.

I tried to think of my Daddy falling in love and acting like a fool, which wasn't really too hard to do. I mean, Daddy was a ladies' man, that was for sure.

"You see a hump on Bodean's back?" I asked again.

Daddy shook his head. "Nope."

"You sure?"

"He doesn't have a hump on his back, tall for his age, maybe he stoops a bit." He looked at me, his grin so wide it was about to fall off his face. "He's actually kind of cute, nice eyes."

I looked off. The fact that I was even contemplating Bodean as the object of my affections was as disgusting as stepping into cow dung, and it being so slippery that you fell in the damn shit face first.

"What happened to her?" I asked.

"Who? Chloe?"

"That her name, Chloe?"

"Yeah."

"Well, what happened to her?"

"She ah…died."

"Died? Daddy, that's a sad story."

"Yeah, it is, it is, baby doll, very sad."

Angus showed up on the hill early that day, while I was lying in the sun trying to turn that healthy color Millie used to get.

"You read the paper?"

"Yeah, Daddy gave me the article. Pretty frigging gruesome."

"I guess the son of a bitch was getting it." Angus sighed and sat beside me. "Guess I ought to try harder."

"They weren't sleeping together, Angus."

He looked at me like I was nuts and shrugged his shoulders. "Well, we don't have to prove nothing anymore, John Peter didn't' do it. He's off the hook."

"But we have to prove who did, for Millie."

"Oh, right," he said and lay back on the ground.

"Does Bodean have a hump on his back?"

"I don't think so."

"I thought you said he did."

"I never said that. Besides, you got eyes, if he had a hump you'd see it."

"I'm not so sure."

Neither one of us heard John Peter approach, didn't even know he was there until he started talking. Angus must have had his eyes closed too. I sat up and opened mine.

"I snuck out," John Peter told us.

"You look like you been crying, John Peter." I gave Angus a look, he was sitting up now, looking at John Peter like he was some sort of hero for talking poor Millie into having sex with him.

"Hey, John Peter, you're off the hook, what the hell is the matter with you?" Angus asked. "You look suicidal. Why the long face?"

"Your bipolar swing heading south?" I slapped his shoulder.

"Lay off, Pleasant." I told you my mama was about to put my head in boiling water, didn't I?"

"Well, you said something to that effect but doesn't' she always want to put your head in a pot and serve you up for dinner?" I laughed but I could see John Peter did not find that in the least bit funny. Angus, on the other hand was nearly spitting up his tonsils.

"Some son of a bitch sent her photographs of me and Millie naked as newborns."

Of course I already knew about that 'cause I'd read it

in the paper so I kept silent. I figured that was embarrassing enough and I didn't need to make him feel worse.

"Yeah, it was all over the papers. Now it's all over town," Angus said and I shot him a look dirty as three day old underwear.

"Some bastard must have climbed the tree at my bedroom and took pictures of me and Millie fooling around. My mama was fit to be tied. I thought she was going to kill me."

"Wow, I wouldn't want my mama getting any photographs of me naked with a girl. Shit." Angus fell back down on the ground. "Shit,"

"Cops asked me if I slept with her and I had to say no, 'cause I hadn't'. We'd come close but we did other things, you know?"

"I sure as hell don't know and I hope your mama doesn't either." I looked away; I did not want the image of a naked Millie and John Peter haunting my waking hours.

John Peter blushed and looked at the ground. "The bastard got me getting...." He looked at Angus.

"Yeah?" Angus said.

"Shut up, John Peter, I don't want to frigging know." I put my hands over my ears.

"Tell me later," Angus whispered.

"The newspaper said she wasn't a virgin." He hung his head and shook it. "Now the whole town knows she wasn't a virgin. But it wasn't her fault she wasn't."

"What are you talking about?" I asked.

"Nothing, just that she wouldn't be happy about her business being all over the place."

I shimmied in close to him and put my arm around his shoulder. "The important thing is, John Peter, you're not being charged with her murder. We have to find the real killer and make sure he or she gets her do."

"You still on that kick, Pleasant, that some woman did it?" John Peter seemed to think that women weren't capable of anything but cooking and nagging.

I looked back at the two of them. I knew I didn't have the sharpest knives carving my Christmas turkey but I had what I had.

"Everyone is under suspicion until I say differently." I gave them both my fiercest look.

John Peter scowled back and nodded his head but then I heard him mutter, "it wasn't no woman."

I ignored him. "Now, let's think about this. Who had it in for Millie?"

Chapter Eight
Clarissa Blackwell

Clarissa awoke with a start. My God, why had it taken two whole days for it to finally come to her, and in her sleep no less?

She knew who the jelly man was.

When she got out of bed it was the moon shinning in her window and not the sun. She went into the kitchen and made herself a cup of tea. She tried to picture his face the way it was twelve years ago but she hadn't really paid much attention to him at the time. He was simply the attorney who was defending Randall Holmes, a man accused of killing sixteen women over a period of two years.

Randall Holmes was sentenced to life in prison and Clarissa had played a role in his capture, not as Dennis would like to believe, in some voodoo fashion, but with her visions, which had, none the less, certainly proved to have merit. After all, it had been her description that had led police to one of the crime scenes where a victim's body had been discovered.

Everyone knew about the serial murders in the surrounding counties of Edgefield so women began to travel in groups when they weren't out with husbands or fathers. A profiler had determined that the killer was a married man who no one would suspect, probably had a decent job with flexible hours. Ten of the women he had killed had been blonde but six of them had not been. Randall Holmes didn't seem to care how old his victims were either for at least three of the women had been over fifty. The only thing the women had in common was that they were all single, working women. Each of them had been sexually molested and then strangled to death. The killer severely disfigured his victims with a knife that he used to cut up their bodies before discarding them in the woods, buried in remote shallow graves.

It was actually at the end of the first year of this grisly murder spree that Clarissa began to have visions of this monster. She was sure she could describe the face of the man she kept seeing in her head. She would certainly recognize him if she ever passed him on a street. She went to the police in the hopes that they could hook her up with a forensic artist but they kept sending her home. She knew they thought she was a kook looking for publicity. But at the end of the second year Clarissa's visions became like a movie reel in her mind and she actually saw the location of one of the murders.

Luckily, Dom Sacco, who had recently been assigned to the case, agreed to see her. Detective Sacco had Clarissa give details of the man's appearance to a forensic artist. The sketch was plastered all over town. Clarissa was able to describe the most recent crime scene so clearly that police located the woman's body based on her account.

Randall Holmes was apprehended in a roadside diner and his DNA proved to be a match with DNA found at the scene. He was convicted of that murder and later of another one in which his DNA was found under the nails of the victim. It wasn't that Clarissa solved the crime but Dom was convinced she had a rare gift. He contacted her about other heinous crimes after that, but unfortunately Clarissa did not always have anything to offer.

Clarissa's god-daughter, Chloe Rappaport, had been found brutally stabbed to death in her home five days before Randall was charged with two of the murders. After he was apprehended, Randall confessed that he had been the one to end Chloe's life and he purposely did not mutilate her body because he wanted to confuse the police and get them off his trail. But Chloe had not been sexually molested like the others, nor had she been strangled. When asked what he had done with Chloe's one month old infant he said there hadn't been any baby present. He also told them that Chloe's murder had been spontaneous, not planned like the others had been. He was subsequently charged with the murder of Chloe Rappaport despite the fact the pieces didn't fit.

After his confession, Clarissa stormed Dom's office and insisted that they keep the investigation of Chloe's murder alive, that Randall Holmes had nothing to do with it. But Dom closed the case and no one would listen when Clarissa insisted that Randall was lying. She eventually accepted that she had to lay her suspicions to rest, especially when everyone around her felt vindicated by Randall's several life sentences. It was Philip Wiley, his defense attorney, that got the death penalty knocked down, the punishment that most people thought he deserved.

The profiler had been correct for the most part. Randall Holmes was a middle aged married man with no children. He worked as a food inspector and lived in a modest house. It was later learned that his father had abused him as a child and his mother was a hotel maid with five children. His mother eventually abandoned her family and all five children were put into foster care. Their father wanted nothing to do with them and Randall never heard from him again. Clarissa did not believe that wretched childhoods necessarily created serial killers but she did believe that serial killers were born with the evil within them, and if she could get close enough to them she could sense out their damaged souls. Problem was she couldn't walk around town trying to solve Chloe's murder with nothing to go on but her sixth sense.

After Randall's conviction, it would seem that it was all over, but for Clarissa, not entirely. When one has doubts then part of the whole story is missing, like a puzzle with one irregular piece of it forced to fit where it didn't.

She hadn't seen Dom Sacco in nearly twelve years and had to get his address from his ex-wife, who lived not far from her in Summerford. It seems that Dom had recently retired and had moved to Augusta to be close to his sons. She had his phone number, she could have called him but she didn't like speaking on the telephone. She really wanted to see his expressions. Clarissa didn't like speaking on the phone to anyone; she felt that the phone was too much of a barrier behind which people could get away with lying far easier than if you had a face to stare down.

As she pulled into Dom's driveway she was happy to see the little compact SUV in the drive. She wasn't sure he'd be home. Clarissa drove an Escalade, the latest extravagance she'd accepted from Dennis, though there had been other gifts far less costly. She thought those little baby SUVs were for people who liked to think they had room to haul things of any importance but really didn't. Couldn't get much in them besides flowers and groceries, maybe a small ladder or two but it sure didn't work for hauling antique chairs and tables.

Dom lived over on River Bluff Drive with great views of the Savannah River. It seems he hadn't done badly at all in retirement and Clarissa wondered if he'd remarried. Harriet, his ex wife, hadn't mentioned that.

Dom seemed pleased to see her and gave her a rather ferocious hug. She noticed that his few years in retirement had put a few pounds around his middle but he still had that handsome demeanor, the one that might have made him a film star if he'd decided he wanted an easier life instead of the one he had.

"Come in, come in, Clarissa Blackwell." He swung open the door and she stepped into a cream colored marble foyer.

"I hope you don't mind, I know I didn't give you much warning. Actually I didn't give you any warning, did I? I'm so sorry, Dom."

"No need to apologize, I'm happy to see you."

He led her into the living room and she sat on a large, sectional couch that ran the length of the wall. It was the color of faded roses and everything around it was blue.

"Brandy?"

"No, no, beer if you have it. Cold as it comes."

"Gotcha."

She watched as he walked back toward what must have been the kitchen, though she couldn't really see it. She imagined another marble floor and sleek track lights extended from the ceiling.

"What a lovely house," she said as he returned with her beer and a bowl of pretzels. She was glad her lies didn't show as readily as his might. The house seemed cold, more like Harriet, his ex-wife than him. She wondered if Harriet had a hand in decorating it.

They went through a half hour of pleasantry and gossip until he brought the conversation back into focus.

"So, why are you here, Clarissa, is it really just to see me?"

"Well, it's nice to see you, Dom, but no, that's not the entire reason I'm here."

He sat back and crossed his legs. "I thought not."

"Well, I'll get right to the point."

"Sounds good."

"I saw a girl in Hollow Creek." She laughed. "Almost killed me, ran me over with her bicycle."

"Glad she didn't hurt you, Clarissa. She didn't, did she?"

Clarissa laughed. "Oh, no, not really."

He sat back and eyed her. "Well? That it?"

"The girl looked like Chloe Rappaport."

He cocked his head a little. She knew he was curious but not curious enough, at least, not yet.

"Must be a lot of men in this town that look like me. So what's that mean?"

"You never found the baby, Dom."

"Chloe's baby? That's what this is about, Clarissa? That's old news. Randal killed it and buried it in the woods somewhere. We'll never find it."

"The man killed women, not babies." She noticed his expression, he didn't look at all convinced to her. "Get him to tell you what he did with her then. What's he got to lose now?"

"Randall? He's not cooperative, there's no reason for him to be. We've got nothing to offer him. Besides, he said there wasn't a baby there so he's not admitting to killing the infant, but I think he did."

"He was the one who wasn't there, Dom. I always told you how I felt, that Chloe's murder had nothing to do with Randall's killing spree."

"He confessed to it."

"He lied. Another notch on his belt. Ask him now."

Dom looked off. He clearly didn't want to be bothered. He didn't want to get his hands dirty anymore. He was living the good life, it seemed to Clarissa.

"Not sure what you're getting at, Clarissa."

She wondered why it mattered. If Pleasant Day turned out to be Chloe's baby what difference would it make now? The girl didn't need to know, didn't need to have her life turned upside down by that little bit of news. But maybe her parents had been involved, were guilty of something. She never believed for a moment that Chloe was Randall's victim. She decided to change the subject, but only a bit.

"Who was the defense attorney on Randall's murder case?"

"Philip Wiley."

"Philip Wiley? What happened to him?"

"Retired."

"Where?"

"I'm not sure. Why?"

"He was always a bit eccentric, wasn't he?"

"He was. Hell of a defense lawyer though."

"I think he's living over in Hollow Creek."

"So?"

"Well, I don't know. He sells jelly now, on the side of the road. I didn't recognize him right away, came to me in my sleep who he was."

Dom looked completely puzzled. "I heard he has a bit of dementia."

"Well, that might explain why he throws pebbles at this girl across the road, the girl that looks like Chloe."

Dom sat forward and looked at her with a pinched expression. "What's this all about, Clarissa?"

"I do not believe that Randall murdered my god

daughter, Chloe. I told you that fourteen years ago."

"It's over, been over for fourteen years, twelve since the trial. Randall is sitting in prison for the murder of those women."

"He murdered sixteen women we know of. Got off easy."

"Seventeen counting Chloe. He's paying for all of them."

"Listen Dom, he didn't strangle Chloe, didn't bury her body in the woods, didn't sexually molest her like he did all his other victims. Whoever murdered Chloe stabbed her to death and walked off with her baby."

"We don't know that."

"What happened to that month old infant then?"

"We assume Randall murdered it and buried it in the woods. I'm sorry, Clarissa, but the case is closed."

"You wanted it closed fourteen years ago because you'd had it, two long years and how much money spent on finding that bastard? So his last victim didn't fit the profile? You assume he did it anyway? He confessed? Case closed? Not so fast, Dom."

Dom sighed and sat back. She could tell this was making him uncomfortable.

"Look," he said, "I'm sorry we couldn't get him fast enough...before he murdered Chloe. She was random. He knew we were on to him and he wanted to throw us, that's all. He wanted to change his pattern. That's why it doesn't fit. He wanted to shift our attention onto someone else and get it off him."

"Bullshit."

She had startled him and his body jolted back into the cushions.

"You spent nothing, no time, no resources on finding out what happened to that baby." Clarissa realized she was pointing her finger at him.

"For God sake, why are you bringing this up now?"

"Because I think that little baby grew up in a town called Hollow Creek and someone got away with my goddaughter's murder."

"You must be having visions about it, but you have no proof, do you?"

"No, no visions and no proof either. But I saw Chloe's daughter and I spoke to her. I want the murder of my god-daughter reopened, Dom."

"On what evidence?"

Clarissa finally took a sip of her beer and made herself comfortable on the large, oversized faded rose sectional while Dom stared at her.

"I have none."

"Bring me something, anything, and I'll use it but I can't reopen this case based on what you're telling me. Besides, I'm retired."

"Then I'll hire you to investigate it."

"Randall confessed to the crime."

"Sure he did, one more victim to claim. He was caught, why not? The son of a bitch was proud of murdering women, bragged about it. He's probably still bragging about it."

"It should be easy to prove that this girl isn't Chloe's daughter. Maybe I can look into that for you."

"Okay, okay, that's a start."

"You ever suspect anyone of Chloe's murder?"

Clarissa thought back. She wished she could say the husband did it, how easy that would be but Chloe's husband, Martin Holly, had bitten the dust shortly after the baby was born. Clarissa thought he was not worthy of Chloe at the time. He looked like his name, so vanilla, his hair and his skin and his eyes seemed to be all one color, very pale. Apparently he had gotten wind of Chloe's affair and of course that's reason enough to kill your wife, at least in the minds of some men, but Martin was English and had moved back to his homeland, probably with a broken heart. She remembered the police telling her he wasn't even in the country at the time of Chloe's death. Clarissa had heard that he had recently returned to America and had settled somewhere around Summerford but she'd never seen him, not sure she'd even recognize him if she did see him.

"I can't think of anyone who'd want to murder Chloe," she said. "But Randall didn't do it. I know it in my heart. Some kind of horrible disturbance has been kicked up inside me since I saw that girl. Maybe Chloe is trying to tell me something."

"The dead don't speak, Clarissa."

"Perhaps you're not listening hard enough."

Clarissa had wanted it all to be over fourteen long years ago. It was just too easy to believe that Chloe was simply one more victim of a madman. Perhaps by not dwelling on it she could heal. Besides, no one was on her side. The fact that she didn't believe Randall had murdered Chloe didn't seem to be important to anyone else, so why should it be to her? Dom was finished with it and Chloe's own mother, Savannah, was done with it. It was as if Chloe had never existed.

Despite everything, Clarissa had tried to reach out but Savannah wouldn't answer the door or return her phone calls so she had no idea if it was over for Savannah or not. But knowing Savannah the way she did she assumed she would put up a good front and suffer in silence, keep her doubts to herself and let sarcasm take care of her anger. Someone had murdered her daughter and that person was sitting in jail for it, case closed.

It never made any sense, it should have been the other way around, should have been Clarissa not taking Savannah's phone calls. After all, she was the injured party, Savannah had stolen Dennis from her, so what was Savannah's beef? There was no reason for Savannah to reject her and yet, Savannah acted like Clarissa had done some terrible harm to her. The vast wedge that had fallen between the two of them had never weakened, not even after Chloe was gone, and it had not weakened in all the years since.

Perhaps they should have been brought together by the tragedy but they sat rows apart in the courthouse and did not comfort each other with Randall's murder conviction. He was found guilty of Chloe's murder, and he got a life term for killing all the other women as well. The bastard was never getting out of prison. But for Clarissa, the pieces didn't fit. Someone other than Randall had gotten away with killing Chloe, maybe even killing her baby.

Clarissa wanted to call Savannah the evening of Randall's conviction and rant and rave into the phone about how preposterous the justice system was. As long as someone paid it didn't matter who. What did she think? Did she really believe Randall had been the one to murder Chloe? But of course she couldn't call Savannah and she'd never know the answer to that question.

Where was the reason in distancing and blaming when there was no cause anymore, when all cause had evaporated to time? Rejections could be stubborn and senseless, refusing to bend; Clarissa knew that all too well. All it took was time so that now the glue that kept their rejection of one another alive was fused with the emotional petrol of lethargy, not even anger anymore, just the stasis of habit.

Clarissa poured herself a glass of wine and sat, cradled by the comforting arms of an old antique chair that she'd just had lovingly restored in Augusta. Memories that cease to be painful are still nostalgic and nostalgia made her sad, always about a loss of time. She thought about Savannah in a way she hadn't thought about her in years, without all the anger. She recalled the young rebel rouser, the beautiful blonde whose southern charm wrapped everyone around her finger, the puppies she made of men. The girl on the bicycle was bringing it all back. Savannah and Chloe, the two people she had loved most in the world.

"Why my husband, Savannah?" Clarissa whispered. It was still a shock after all these years, a betrayal with an endless sting.

They'd grown up together, she and Savannah, hop scotching their way up the block, giggling so loudly in movie theaters they were asked to leave. When they were older Clarissa fondly remembered their walks down Main Street arm and arm, fragments of conversations charged with emotion, about boys, parents, a bit of seventies politics- the war was right, the war was wrong, marijuana should be legalized, no of course it shouldn't, Bob Dylan was just so cool. What? He's a straggly bore, etcetera, etcetera. They argued about everything, especially who was sexy and who wasn't but even about antiques, for God's sake. Savannah wouldn't buy anything old unless it was in excellent shape, she refused to lay out the money for restoration, even though her family had more money than a Federal bank. Clarissa would buy anything with good bones and pay good money to bring it back to life and each one thought the other was being stupid.

They argued constantly, but always in good humor, about the answers to everything on earth, about the lyrics to old songs, what actors had starred in what old movies, and especially, directions. Turn right here, Savannah. Turn where? Turn, turn, oh my god, we're lost, I said turn right. I thought you meant left. Why aren't you more clear? They usually wound up in each other's arms, laughing hysterically and calling the other one wrong even when the other one had been proven right.

They'd both pursued a degree in English at the same college, and both returned to Summerford four years later to settle down in their hometown. They bought houses in walking distance from each other. They were as inseparable as young women as they had been as children. When Clarissa got a Masters in education, Savannah followed in her footsteps, to cover her ass, as she put it. Though Savannah had published at least fifteen works of fiction over the years, she wound up spending thirty years teaching English at Andrew Jackson High School, alongside Dennis Haworth and her best friend, Clarissa Blackwell. Truth was, Savannah never had to work a day in her life but she chose to, believing she was doing some kind of good, instilling her passion for literature into the minds of students far too indifferent to words. Clarissa could almost hear her saying: U r swell will never replace thou art good, children.

"Where did it go wrong, old friend?" Clarissa whispered as she reached to switch on a light and watched as the last vivid rays of sunset faded.

Clarissa barely remembered Chloe's father, a man by the name of Jeffrey Black. Clarissa thought he was incredibly handsome but she couldn't stand him. Good looks never made up for a black soul, she used to say, but only to Dennis. Yes, he was named correctly, she would tell him, Jeffrey Black, black like the devil.

No one was surprised that Jeffrey Black skipped town and everyone was relieved that Savannah had never married him.

"I want you to be the baby's god-mother," Savannah had said after Chloe was born and Clarissa was so happy she couldn't stop beaming, as if she had been the one to have given birth.

And Clarissa had been so content to take the baby on weekends and on trips, oftentimes introducing her as 'my daughter.'

And then everything changed and her fifteen year marriage to Dennis was over. What in God's name had it been about Dennis that had captured Savannah Rappaport? Of all the men she could have married she chose the one that was married to Clarissa. Clarissa always wondered what could have possibly gone through her head. Dennis was a very ordinary man. Clarissa had fallen for him for just that very reason. Anyone extraordinary would have intimidated her and probably exhausted her but Savannah thrived on interesting and convoluted men, not Mr. Nice Guys like Dennis Haworth.

Clarissa had gone from a crush in college to loving Dennis as deeply as she would ever love anyone, but that love quickly evaporated after his affair with Savannah. She went from loving him to hating him to being completely indifferent to him. She realized she'd had no idea who he was, never thought in a million years he was capable of cheating on her. They'd had a good marriage for as long as it lasted. They had been compatible partners, married for fifteen years and expected to be married a good deal longer. Then out of nowhere Dennis admitted to being in love with Savannah and before she knew it, she was divorced and Dennis was out of the house and married to the one friend she never would have suspected of betraying her.

Dennis remained married to Savannah for about eight or nine years. Then one day he appeared on Clarissa's doorstep. "She threw me out," he said. Clarissa hadn't been surprised, their marriage never appeared happy. She didn't feel vindicated, she just felt empty. She thought it was odd that their divorce happened right after Chloe was killed, as if her murder might have been the cause of their divorce. Sometimes grief does come between people, so maybe it was too much grief that had hurt their marriage.

Clarissa didn't know how she felt about Savannah any more, she was beyond hating her, but when she was being honest with herself she realized she missed her a great deal more than she deserved to be missed. Yet a door had slammed on their friendship and it looked as though it would never open again.

Dennis, on the other hand, was like a flu she couldn't shake. She barely enjoyed his friendship, too much resentment between them, but she tolerated him. He had become like an old sweater, full of holes but never to be discarded, too many cold nights to find it in the back of a drawer and pull out.

It's funny, Clarissa thought often, how life reveals that which we may never have guessed, that some people are so undeserving of us.

Clarissa reached over and picked up Chloe's photograph from the table beside her. In it she was laughing. Clarissa remembered so clearly, she'd been caught by surprise. Clarissa had taken the picture right after Chloe had admitted to being pregnant, so many years ago, just seven months before her murder. She had been so happy. Clarissa assumed she was going to work on her marriage and end the affair she was having, that her life was finally getting on course. Clarissa had told her that an extra martial affair was not a good idea, especially with a baby coming. "You should try and make your marriage work," Clarissa had said and Chloe had agreed. "Yes, yes, you're right." Clarissa thought the matter would be settled, but then she had a disturbing thought. "It is Martin's child, isn't it?" she'd asked but she never got an answer to her question, Chloe had been distracted by something, perhaps her cell phone. Clarissa had assumed an affirmative answer without giving it a second thought.

Chapter Nine
Pleasant Day

The whole process disgusts me, just put me in the goddamn earth and walk away. I don't want to lie on a cold slab in some old house waiting to have my innards drained and embalming fluid put inside my poor dead body, just put me in the goddamn earth and walk away.

Everybody says the dead don't know what's going on, the hell they don't. How the hell does anybody know what the dead are aware of? I had the oddest feeling sitting in that church, looking at Millie inside that coffin, I felt she was trying so hard to communicate with me but she couldn't 'cause the goddamn funeral people had sewn her lips together.

By the time we got out to the cemetery I was shaking. Millie was in that goddamn coffin and how the hell did anyone know she wasn't afraid. I sure as hell don't want to go underground, I'd want to scream and holler that if one more son of a bitch throws dirt on my face I'm raising holy hell.

I felt Daddy's arm over my shoulder. Mama was standing there looking bored and Sawyer was checking out the crowd. He was always looking for blonde boys, he liked blonde skinny boys. I guess he would have liked

Angus if he wasn't so poorly dressed. I saw John Peter across from me. His mother's face was wet with tears and John Peter was so distressed he looked sick, like at any minute he might die himself.

Poor Mr. Grady was crying, grown men crying makes me nervous 'cause they're really not supposed to be doing it. It's an unnatural act. It's natural on women but when men cry it seems to me that they're pretending something hurts somewhere, or maybe someone is back there pinching 'em so hard it causes tears.

I took Daddy's hand, felt his long fingers. His face was sad, but he didn't even know Millie. Mama had met her but she didn't even care enough to remember. I wanted to hit my mama in the back of her legs with the side of my palm, right at her knees. You do that to a person they'll fall over. I wanted her to fall, right in the hole they were putting Millie in. Then maybe Millie would find the goddamn hole was too crowded and jump out.

"You okay, Sweet pea?" Daddy asked as he bent down to my ear.

"How long that preacher going to talk, Daddy?"

"He's got to give your friend a proper goodbye."

"Sure enough." But I knew I didn't want a crowd of people standing over my sorry self locked inside some pine box. I didn't consider this a proper goodbye at all. I kicked the dirt under my feet. I knew I looked angry. The anger started rising inside me until I wanted to scream. If I couldn't have any control over my goddamn dead body then I'd bring my ghostly form back here and haunt that crazy preacher for the rest of his life, that would be a start, and anyone else I didn't like, I'd haunt them too. I mean, how does that crazy preacher know where the dead go and how the hell does he know the dead like being there? He's trying to make it sound like the only reason we get born is to bite the dust.

"Daddy," I said as we walked back to the car. "When I go, I don't want a proper goodbye. You hear?"

After I ditched my stupid church clothes I ran up to the hill hoping I'd be alone, no Angus and no John Peter. I put my head back and all I saw was Millie's face. I knew she'd suffered, how could you not suffer when someone is strangling you to death? I wanted to help her and I couldn't, I was a useless piece of shit, living in this world, on this sorry earth while my friend was under it. I couldn't do nothing but cry. I cried until my face hurt and I could barely open my eyes. Why is this a world in which evil is done, I wondered. What justification is there to rip open a sky of blue, a sky of moon and stars, and leave it empty, and leave it listless as an echo, devastating as a lifeless battlefield.

When I finally lifted my head, it hurt like hell. I felt like I'd been through a war. I was lying in a field of daisies. Hell is empty and all the devils are here I thought, wondering which play that was from, not remembering. It was Shakespeare, of course, maybe The Tempest. I wondered why I had thought of it. Maybe I was beginning to see that they are all here, the devils. That's why there is no hell. They're here, the sadistic artists who paint in black, disfiguring form and masking themselves behind some cloak of semiotics. Semiotics was a word I'd learned from Nana and I thought it was the coolest word I'd learned so far. Nana said that Jack the Ripper had been a sadistic artist, leaving clues like shadows in his work. Clues are what I had to find if I wanted to solve Millie's murder. I had to see what I wasn't seeing. I had to know who killed my friend and when the truth came clear, I'd see that son of a bitch boiled in oil.

~

I awoke to Fredo's licks all over my face. He knew where to find me and I guess Mama had let him out. She hated that dog, said his high pitched barks were giving her high blood pressure. She would have given him away if it weren't for Sawyer. He liked the dog, liked sitting with him in all those open air cafes 'cause Fredo demanded attention. My brother craved attention so much he'd do anything to get it. I told Daddy he was hyperactive and should be given a sedative but Daddy just said he was having growing pains. He was almost grown for God sake, he was seventeen years old, old enough to stop screaming every time someone told him his lip gloss had faded.

When I got back home I saw Daddy out in the garage and I could hear the old, rock and roll coming off of Mama's CDs, the ones she played on Saturday nights and sang along to. I watched as Sawyer led her around the living room. They looked kind of sweet dancing together but it made me sad. I don't know why. Maybe I just wanted to know what it would be like to hold Mama in my arms and dance with her. When I walked out back to the porch I saw Daddy coming toward me. He was smiling and holding out his hands.

"You know how to dance, young lady?"

"I was born knowing."

We started dancing to some old song. Daddy said it was called "Unforgettable" by Nat King Cole. You might have thought I had on a long dress that trailed the floor and my daddy was in tails, the way we danced, cheek to cheek. He taught me years ago. Daddy loved it. He was so light on his feet I felt like I was moving on a cloud. Then we'd spin around. We never tripped up, not even once. Two more songs came on. One was a Lindy. Daddy did that real well and I loved it, thought it was more fun dancing like that then just standing around shaking, trying to look sexy. Daddy said kids today wouldn't like doing the Lindy 'cause it meant learning how to do it, takes too much effort, he'd said. The next song was real pretty. "How Long Has This Been Going On" by Peggy Lee. It was one of Daddy's favorites. He liked sultry singers like Peggy Lee, he always said, and I got to like 'em just as much being that I grew up with them and all.

When the song ended Daddy kissed me on the cheek. "Make yourself pretty after dinner. Real pretty. We're going for a ride. I've got a surprise for you."

I noticed that Mama had caught the tail end of our last dance. She was staring at us and had an odd smile. Sawyer had disappeared.

"Still cut the rug better than any man I've ever known, Graham." Mama laughed.

A rare night, I'd say.

~

When I got to my room after dinner, Sawyer was going through my things. "I don't remember inviting you in here," I said.

"You didn't, Daddy did."

He pulled some clothes out of my closet, made a horrible face and put them back. Then I noticed he had a skirt in his hand. "Not bad," he said.

"What the hell are you doing?"

"Daddy told me to make you pretty. If it was left up to you you'd walk out of here looking like a boy. You need my magic touch, little sister." He opened up my dresser drawer and took out a sweater. " I was happy to see you owned a skirt, at least. Here, wear this with it."

"What the hell is it, my birthday or something?"

Sawyer shrugged his shoulders. "Beats me. Get yourself into those nice clothes. I'll be back to do your make-up."

"Don't you think I can do my own make-up, Sawyer? Besides Mama doesn't want me wearing make-up."

"It'll look natural as can be. Now listen here, Pleasant, you're a challenge so you just do like I tell you and I'll have you looking like Kate Winslet, who is just sooo beautiful." He took himself a little spin at my door before he closed it.

"Oh, brother."

The skirt hit my thigh at a good place and the sweater was a pale shade of yellow that seemed to go well with my hair. I noticed he had found sandals with a three inch heel. I was beginning to wonder if I was about to be victim to an arranged marriage.

~

By the time Sawyer was through with me, I just might have been able to fit my foot in a glass slipper and win me a prince. He had sat me in front of the mirror and had gone over my face with little brushes that tickled my skin.

"Don't worry none about what Bodean and Ike did," I said. "They're just awful. They tease everyone."

He took a comb to my hair. When I looked up in the mirror I noticed he was smiling.

"You like being picked on?" I asked.

"Listen here, little sister, Ike is as queer as a midget running a marathon."

I looked at him like he was crazy. "Are you out of your mind?"

"Hardly."

"You better not let Bodean hear you say that."

"Bodean is an idiot, thinks Ike doesn't want to stick it to him. He better watch his ass, literally."

"You're nuts, Sawyer."

He shrugged his shoulders. "Believe what you want. I went over there to meet Ike in the barn. Not the first time I been there either. He likes me better than any girl he's ever going to know." He winked at me.

"I don't believe you."

"Well, we almost got it on before we heard Bodean drive up. Party pooper. Ike grabbed me by my collar and dragged me outside, told Bodean I was hitting on him. I mean, how else could he explain me coming out of his barn?"

"And you let him get away with that?"

He shrugged.

"You say anything to Bodean?"

"Are you crazy? I protected Ike, why not, he and I got a thing, you know? It's casual but satisfying." He grinned salaciously like some old man eying a pretty girl.

"You're disgusting." I scowled. "I don't even want to think about what you two do."

"Then don't."

I couldn't believe it. I was so shocked I could barely keep my lips together for the color he was brushing on my mouth.

"Pucker, Pleasant."

"Learn something every day, I guess."

"You've got good bones," Sawyer said as he bent

down to kiss me.

Daddy let his mouth fall open. "Wow, I think you overdid it, Sawyer. That skirt a little short?"

"They would be if her legs were fat, but they're not, so they're perfect."

"What did you do to her eyelashes?"

"You ever hear of mascara?" Sawyer raised his eyes.

"You are the prettiest little thing I have ever seen," Daddy said.

Mama came out from the kitchen drying her hands on a dish towel and staring at me like I was there to hand her a tax bill.

"Looking good, Pleasant," she said.

"You think her skirt is too short, Martha?"

Mama shrugged. "She's got a chaperone. Girls these days don't hardly wear a thing anyway. So all things considered I guess she's just showing skin like all the rest of them."

"Humph," Daddy said as he led me to the car.

"What's up, Daddy? You entering me in a beauty contest?"

"I should be." He grinned at me. "You look so much like your mother."

I looked at him like he was crazy. "I don't look like her at all."

He nodded his head. "You do, you do."

"I look like Nana. I know we're not blood or anything but don't you think I look like her?"

I stared out the window, waiting for Daddy's answer

which I never got. I guess Daddy felt he had to say that about me looking like Mama. Girls should look like their mothers.

"How come Mama didn't join us, or Sawyer?"

"'Cause this is your night."

"It's not my birthday."

"Every day is your birthday, honey."

"We're not going to Buck's?" I asked as he made a turn he didn't usually make.

I watched my Daddy in silence as he drove on, a smile was plastered on his face like he was up to no good.

"Where we going? I don't know this road."

It was still light out but the sun had faded and the wind was warm. I loved this time of day, like everything was just about to close down, bringing on a night of expectations. And there I was, about to be surprised by something or other, maybe a steak dinner, but then I realized Mama had already fed me.

"There he is," Daddy said. "'Bout time you had a date."

Nothing on this earth could have prepared me for Bodean Frasier in a suit and a smile and a shine on his shoes that almost blinded me. He was standing in front of his house waving at us.

"Let me out of this car right now," I shouted. "I should have known you had something nasty up your sleeve."

"Now, now, honey, listen to me, I went over to talk to him about picking on Sawyer. He's really a great kid, told me how much he likes you. I thought you two should get to know one another. He's not such a bully, he's really a sweet boy and he thinks you are the prettiest girl in the state. Not to worry, I told him I'd break his legs if he disrespected you."

"I'm going to kill you," I said through my teeth.

"Evening, Mr. Day," Bodean said as he came around and hopped in beside me. "Where we going?"

I sat there fuming the whole time Daddy told him he was taking us to Buck's where the cherry pie was homemade and some day we'd be able to appreciate the beer.

"You don't really expect me to spend time with him? He's homophobic," I whispered in Daddy's ear.

Daddy pinched my cheek. "Everybody has got to hate someone, human nature."

~

Well, of course, Daddy took a side trip to apartment Six leaving me there with Bodean who kept telling me I oughta wear skirts more often.

I noticed how light his eyes looked, how the freckles across the bridge of his nose were most appealing. He had muscles too. I wondered if he was born that way.

"Where did your Daddy go?" he asked me.

"He's got a friend in apartment Six, back behind Buck's."

"Oh."

"You do anything to get your muscles that big?"

"You think they're big?" he asked and I nodded.

"I don't do anything." He flexed a bit and stared at his arms.

"Uh-huh," I said.

He leaned over the table and looked me right in the eyes. "I'm changing my life. I wanted you to be the first to know. Mr. Dempsey told me I'd never get into Clemson U if I didn't become a better citizen. So that's what I'm going to do."

"Cows can't change their spots."

He laughed. "This cow can."

"I'll believe it when I see it."

"There are some things I don't like about myself. I think a man has to take stock, realize what's important to him and what isn't. Mr. Dempsey said I've got real potential."

"Potential for what?"

"Being a better person."

"Well, for one, you can stop being a bully. How's that for being a better person?"

He smiled at me. "Guess I can, doesn't get me anywhere."

"Except hated, no one likes you, Bodean."

"Yeah, I know."

"You can stop being homophobic too while you're at it."

He seemed to blush. "I guess."

"You trying to get me to like you?"

"Would there be anything wrong in that?"

We stared at each other 'till I got uncomfortable and looked away.

"I'm not hanging out with Ike anymore," he said, kind of out of the blue.

I laughed to myself. Maybe it had dawned on him that Ike had a thing about his knees, he liked getting on them.

"I'll believe that when I see it."

"That all you can say about anything?"

"Appropriate, isn't it though?"

He cocked his head at me and took himself a few moments of silence, then he leaned in. "Sometimes when things are wrong, you know, when someone does something you know is just so wrong, you've got to take a stand against it. I cannot be instigated or controlled by someone else."

"By Ike, you mean?"

He nodded his head.

"What did Ike do?"

"I'd rather not say."

I figured he had gotten wind of Ike's shifting tides. That was fine with me, I could care less. The cherry pie came and I watched how quickly Bodean ate it, smiling at me in between bites.

"You going to get another piece?" I asked.

"I just might."

Life is kind of crazy 'cause this kid was getting under my skin. It wasn't anything he was saying, it was more the way I was feeling when I looked at him. At one point, he caught my gaze and I felt something shoot through me, like a shock. He pushed his pie away and wiped his mouth, then he did the unexpected, he reached over and took both my hands in his.

"Pleasant, you make me feel like my life has to be good, has to be based on integrity and making the proper choices. I just looked at you the other day and my heart took a flip. It was unexpected 'cause you're really just a kid but it floored me. All of a sudden, whether you like me or not means everything and I don't want to do anything stupid to turn you off, the way I been doing."

"How do you know I'm in the least bit turned on?"

He smiled that wide smile, showing off his white teeth and his light eyes seemed to twinkle. "When a cannon goes off not everyone has to hear it, but the point is, it's gone off."

Now in normal times he wouldn't have made a lick of sense but that night I knew exactly what he was talking about. Hadn't Daddy said a cannon went off with him and that girl, Chloe, and they knew they were in love? Oddest thing but a cannon was going off between me and Bodean. Who would have ever guessed that?

"One day I looked at you and it was like I was seeing you for the first time, I just wanted to be around you," he said.

I kept wondering if this was going to be my first experience of love or if this was going to be my first experience of being sweet talked into parting with my virginity.

"I swear Bodean, if you compare me to a summer's day I'm going to fall into your arms."

Lucky for me, he was at a complete loss.

Chapter Ten

Clarissa Blackwell

"Take the first left at the end of the block and keep following the road. You're going to see a little sign that says Piper Hill. Take that road. It'll be off to your right."

"That will take me straight up to the hill?" Clarissa asked.

Sandy started clearing away the dishes. "It's real pretty up there but it's hilly." She smiled at Clarissa. "But I guess it won't be much of a challenge for you."

"If I follow the road where will I wind up?"

"You'll find yourself on Balsam Lane if you take the road all the way to the end."

"That's where Pleasant Day lives?"

"Yep. Her house is the first thing you see when you come down from the hill."

"Well, I'm sure to get some nice pictures today; it's so clear out."

"Are you a professional photographer. That camera looks kind of serious."

Clarissa had borrowed the camera from Dennis. It looked more important than the little digital one she'd had for years and she figured it would appear more impressive, especially to teenagers.

"Ah, no, I just like to take pictures."

~'

As Clarissa followed the road she wondered why she hadn't come to Hollow Creek more often. She had a boyfriend once named Alex, they had loved packing up a picnic lunch and finding a spot on some remote farm to spread out a table cloth. They'd bring fresh meat and cheese, some fruit and chocolate. They always brought wine, which made them tired and they'd nap in the shade. For the rest of the afternoon they'd read and talk, usually until three or four. Clarissa always thought she should have married Alex but he married someone else because she hemmed and hawed for so long. He would have loved Piper Hill though, Clarissa thought, as she sighed, remembering the one that got away that probably shouldn't have.

She stopped by the stream, watched it flow, idyll, as if too lazy to run. Everything around her was filled with color: purple, red and yellow flowers, grass so green it taunted her to dance barefoot through it. She remembered Savannah in her youth, gliding shoeless through the grass, carrying her sandals at her side. "No cow dung yet," she'd called and Clarissa had sat and laughed with her, watched as moments later Savannah ran screaming to the stream to wash her feet. "Never trust grass," she'd yelled out, "too many hidden dangers."

~'

Sandy had mentioned how much the kids liked playing on Piper Hill, especially Pleasant, who lived so close. Clarissa decided to go up there and wait, take her chances on such a nice summer day that Pleasant would show eventually, but she didn't have to wait long at all. She heard them before she saw them, distant sound of laugher and voices raised, a bit too high pitched for her ears, especially the barking dog who sounded like one of those little terriers you wanted to muzzle. Eventually they were visible, three teenagers, and she'd been right, one frenetic fox terrier, barking and running around the kids like an over wound Ever Ready bunny.

She watched as the girl spotted her, watched the expression that came over her face. They walked toward her, each obviously curious. She assumed they usually didn't see adults up on Piper Hill. The dog kept running in wide circles, until eventually they were all not more than a few feet away. The girl stood firm, as if Piper Hill belonged to her and poor Clarissa was going to be shot for trespassing.

Even from a distance she had known it was Pleasant, the hair color for one. Both Chloe and Savannah had it too, a golden blonde full of waves and an unruly tendency to fall every which way, leaving the impression of mischief, the impression being that if the hair was wild, the girl under it probably was too.

"What are you doing here?" Pleasant asked.

Clarissa stared at the boys, who seemed friendly enough. "She's allowed," one of them said.

Pleasant kept her stance. She kept her gaze on Clarissa as if she were staring down an outlaw.

"Taking pictures," Clarissa said.

"Wow, a Nikon." One of the boys bent to examine the camera until his face was upside down.

"Here," Clarissa said, handing it to him, "before you hurt yourself."

"Can I take a picture with it?" Angus asked.

"How rude," Pleasant said.

"No, really Pleasant, he can. I don't mind."

Angus stood up and walked around with the Nikon. He looked through the lens and pointed it out toward the field.

"How about us? Take a picture of us," Clarissa said.

The three of them sat in a huddle, the dog made himself comfortable in Pleasant's lap. The boy did not smile for the camera, and neither did Pleasant.

Angus came back and joined them. He handed the Nikon back to Clarissa. "Who are you?"

"Clarissa Blackwell. I'm from Summerford. I walked over."

"Walked?" John Peter asked.

"Yes, I like to walk."

"You walk a lot?" Pleasant shot John Peter a knowing look and put her eyebrow up.

"I do, good for the soul, the body, too." Clarissa noticed the way Pleasant's eyebrows were now meeting over the bridge of her nose.

"What do you do in Summerford?" Pleasant asked, in quite an accusatory way, Clarissa noticed.

"Well, I'm retired now but I used to teach."

"Teach?" Pleasant seemed surprised by that and stood to her feet.

"Yes, English."

"English?" Pleasant looked as if someone had poked her.

John Peter glared at her. "Why do I get the feeling you think she's the one did it just 'cause she walks?"

"Shut up, John Peter," Pleasant said quickly.

"Did what?" Clarissa asked.

"The Great Gatsby's Daisy Buchannan." Pleasant stared at her and waited patiently.

Slowly Clarissa seemed to get it. She was supposed to respond. The girl was playing Jeopardy with her. Pleasant kept staring, kept waiting for her reply.

"Are we playing Jeopardy?"

"Come on, English teacher, The Great Gatsby's Daisy Buchannan."

"Who is the woman Gatsby loved?" Clarissa smiled and quickly retorted. "In Wilde's novel, Basil Hallward paints his portrait."

"Who is Dorian Grey?" Pleasant grinned at her. "Okay, one more."

"Your call or mine?"

"Here's one, The Girl With The Dragon Tattoo has a name."

"Easy. Who is Lisbeth Salander?"

"You're right, too easy. One more, in Ulysses by James Joyce he had quite an appetite."

"Much too easy, Pleasant. Who is Leopold Bloom?"

"I got one for you… Miss Brooke had that kind of beauty which seems to be thrown into relief by poor dress."

Clarissa laughed. "Isn't that a bit long for Jeopardy?"

"You two are crazy," Angus said. "You can't play the game with any other categories but literature, not when you're playing with Pleasant anyway."

"Keeps me up on things," Pleasant said and smiled at Clarissa. "Well?"

"What are the opening lines from the novel Middlemarch by George Elliot?"

"Wow," Pleasant said, smiling broadly, "I've met my match."

~

Even Chloe hadn't been that good, had never really been that into books though she'd always gotten an A in English. But it was Savannah who had known every admirable work of fiction ever written. It would seem that Savannah's granddaughter was very much like her. Savannah could recite every Shakespearean sonnet by heart, and she was an expert on Henry James, Jane Austin and Virginia Woolf. Clarissa had the impression that Pleasant would not be far behind, perhaps maturing into analytical readings of Henry James or Proust. She might also become a writer of fiction like her grandmother. Clarissa wondered if they'd ever meet but of course she'd have to be absolutely certain of Pleasant's identity before she let that happen. If she ever would let that happen.

"How did you get so smart?" Clarissa said.

"She doesn't know anything about anything else," John Peter said.

"She just likes to show off," Angus piped in. "Ask her anything about math or chemistry, even history. She doesn't know shit."

"I know all I need to know," Pleasant said and made a face at both boys. "There's wisdom in literature."

Clarissa could tell they were all good friends and they joked around affectionately for the next hour or so. John Peter was a troubled boy, in Clarissa's opinion. He seemed deeply distressed, even though he joined in the fun. She could feel sadness in the pit of her stomach, it was a hollowed out feeling. It seemed to join them together somehow. She was being tapped by John Peter's distress, like a pull on her soul.

Pleasant had made a three hundred and sixty degree turn about getting her picture taken and she posed like she was getting money for it. After John Peter and Angus left, Pleasant stayed, which surprised Clarissa. Pleasant seemed to want to talk to her, to tell her all about her family, mostly about her father and her seventeen year old brother, Sawyer.

"He's going to be famous. He's just so out there."

~

By the time the afternoon came to an end Clarissa had invited Pleasant to come see her in Summerford. She didn't want to hurt this girl with her curiosity about her past but she had to look under every rock she could find. Being with Pleasant had brought back the closeness she'd had with Chloe. She always thought that there was something so special about having a friendship with a younger person. That's why she had loved teaching so much. But Chloe had been so special, she'd been family, and she owed it to her to find her missing daughter and to bring some closure to her murder. Despite everything, she even owed it to Savannah.

~

Clarissa had loaded the digital photos on to her IPAD and had scanned in a lot of old photographs of Chloe at the age of fifteen. It had been a week since she'd seen Dom but she was so excited by the likeness between the two girls and she wanted him to see it as well.

"I was going to call you, Clarissa," he said as he opened the door for her.

"Good news or bad?" she asked.

He ignored her question and pointed to her IPAD. "What you got there?"

Clarissa quickly flipped to the photographs of Pleasant and Chloe. She reached over and handed him the IPAD. "See for yourself."

"What am I looking at besides a pretty girl?"

"The first photograph is Pleasant, the one following is Chloe. Look at the resemblance. Pleasant, Chloe,

Pleasant, Chloe, like that. There are five each, ten altogether. If you split the screen it will be even more jarring."

She watched as he looked at all of the photographs one by one and then went back and looked at them again.

"Remarkable resemblance."

"Can't you see they're related?"

Dom sat forward and put the IPAD on the table before her. "I was going to call you about this... but Clarissa, there is a birth certificate for Pleasant Day. She was born to Graham and Martha Day in 1992 at the Lexington Medical Center."

Clarissa's face fell, she had been so certain. For a moment she felt terribly confused.

"Are you sure of this?"

"I've got a copy of the birth certificate," Dom said. "I'll get it for you."

"No, no, Dom, no need." She sighed deeply. "I guess I was wrong about Pleasant. It's just that they look so alike and I felt tapped."

"Tapped?" He looked at her with an amused smile.

"It's what happens to me when I feel that something out of the ordinary has happened, is happening, something that's been fated to happen. It's not always a bad feeling, sometimes it's a good one. Sometimes I just feel how other people feel. I feel what they carry around with them, in their hearts and in their souls."

He nodded his head a few times but didn't say anything.

"I feel so embarrassed." Clarissa sighed and started for the door.

"Oh, really Clarissa, it's perfectly all right. I know how much you loved Chloe. Of course if you don't believe Randall murdered her you'd want to know who did. I understand that."

Clarissa felt a bit weak at the knees. "I didn't will that girl into my life, she came to me as if she were sent to me. I'm not sure what this is all about, Dom, but I just feel...Oh, I don't know. There's more to this than we can understand right now. I don't know what it's all about but I still feel I need to unravel it."

Dom nodded his head again and remained silent.

~

Clarissa was deeply disturbed about Pleasant Day. She had the feeling that nothing was as it seemed. Yet the girl had legitimately been born to a Graham and Martha Day. Dom had the birth certificate to prove it. Perhaps Clarissa had to let it go, if she could, if her uncertainty didn't continue to eat away at her. But she wasn't wrong about the disturbance she felt. Pleasant Day was Chloe's daughter. She felt too strongly about it. Three days passed without her being able to think of anything else but how to prove it.

Clarissa was sitting in her favorite chair at sunset when it hit her like a rock had crashed through her window and had knocked her to the ground with a note that said, wake up, stupid. She literally jumped up, as if pinched. "Oh, my God," she said.

She ran to the phone and dialed Dom's number, all the while her heart beating like it might come popping out of her chest. He finally picked up.

"Dom," she yelled. "What took you so long?"

"I was outside. Clarissa? What's wrong?"

"That baby that was born to Graham and Martha Day was born in 1992?"

"Yeah."

"Well that would make that child seventeen years old,

Pleasant Day is not seventeen years old."

"What? How do you know that?"

"She's in the tenth grade, Dom, only going into the eleventh, only going on sixteen."

"Well, maybe you're mistaken."

"I'm not mistaken. She has a seventeen year old brother but she is fifteen. She told me the other day. Chloe's baby would have been fifteen."

She could hear him thinking on the other end of the line. "Well, I'll dig a little deeper, Clarissa but I can't promise anything. You could be wrong about her age. As a matter of fact, you probably are wrong about her age."

"I'm not wrong. Something is disturbing me, Dom. You hear me? Something is not right about that birth certificate. I think it's wrong."

She heard him laugh. "I highly doubt that but I will look into it."

"Thank you, Dom."

Chapter Eleven
Pleasant Day

"You going to lay it to rest now, Pleasant?" John Peter stared at me and shook his head. "How many times do I have to tell you it wasn't a woman, it was a man that came to the door."

I had no recourse but to believe him now, that teacher woman was no murderer.

"Well, it wasn't that particular woman, I was wrong there, but it could have been anyone, male or female." I noticed that his face looked contorted and he gritted his teeth at me.

"It was a man."

"Okay, okay."

Me and John Peter were up on Piper Hill with Fredo. We didn't know where the hell Angus was but I was glad he wasn't there, he didn't have the patience for meditation. Meditation cleared the mind and I was sure going to take advantage of the peace and quiet without Angus's taunts raining down on us like hail stones. It was the perfect opportunity to get John Peter in touch with his memory through the deep mind relaxation I was going to lead him through.

"Lie back," I said.

"I don't think I want to do this," John Peter whined like a five year old. I was annoyed enough to slap him.

"We have to do this, now lie on your back and close your eyes."

The minute John Peter was prone Fredo jumped on his stomach and started licking his face all over. John Peter laughed like he was being tickled and pushed the dog off, but pushing Fredo off only meant to Fredo that he was being engaged in some sort of game.

"Get outta here, Fredo. Get outta here, we're not playing with you," I yelled. I chased the dog all the way down to the creek. I couldn't see nothing but his ears dancing over the weeds when I got back.

"He won't bother us anymore, he's chasing bugs."

"I don't remember anything, Pleasant. How many times I have to tell you that?"

"Shish, lay back. Close your eyes and relax, like you're on a cloud and the cloud is drifting across the sky. You've got no worries, your mama is far away, she's not yelling at you. You are at peace."

"This is stupid."

"Concentrate, John Peter. Concentrate until you can see that man at the door. You see him?"

"I see him."

"What's he wearing?"

"A polo shirt, I think."

"What color?"

"I don't know, green maybe. Maybe blue."

"What color pants?"

"Black, I guess. But they might have been brown."

"What color hair?"

"I don't remember. Maybe he was bald."

"C'mon, John Peter, what color hair?"

"Shit, Pleasant, I don't frigging know." John Peter jumped up and Fredo shot through the weeds and started barking at him all over again.

"You're not concentrating."

"I'm concentrating. I'm concentrating." John Peter's cheeks were red with rage. "You trying to get me murdered too, huh, Pleasant? You won't be happy until I'm dead in the ground."

"John Peter, what are you talking about? We're just trying to catch this guy and I need your cooperation."

John Peter was jumping up and down like Rumplestiltskin and Fredo was all over him, leaping up as high as his mouth. John Peter was yelling at the top of his lungs. "I can't tell you anymore. I won't tell you anymore. Get this goddamn dog off me, Pleasant."

"Calm down, John Peter."

"How do you know he's not here, listening to every word I'm saying? How do you know he's not going to follow me home and strangle me to death too?"

Before I knew it John Peter was running off and Fredo was in hot pursuit, nipping at his ankles, barking like a maniac. By the time Fredo decided to return to me he was in a drooling pant. I couldn't see where the hell John Peter had gone off to but this I will tell you, his reaction dismayed me.

"Fredo, that boy is keeping something from me. He overreacted. He overreacted something terrible."

Poor Fredo collapsed in the grass and went to sleep.

~

I finally agreed to let Bodean take me to the movies on Saturday afternoon and I sure was glad the cinema was in Summerford. I didn't want Angus or John Peter seeing me out with Bodean.

"I like you in tight little blue jeans too," Bodean said as I hopped into the passenger side of his should be banned from the road Ford. His car looked like an old rusted piece of tin, but it ran, like a faulty washing machine, but it ran.

"Well, this isn't a real date, if it were a real date I would have dressed up more."

"What do you mean it's not a real date? It sure is a real date to me."

I noticed when his feelings were hurt his eyes glazed over.

"My daddy said he was letting me go to the movies with you, not go out on a date with you."

"That's what he meant, he was letting you date me."

"That implies more than one, to date is to definitely see a person more than once. Daddy says I have to wait until I'm sixteen before I can see any boy more than once."

"He's messing with you. Besides, you look sixteen." His eyes traveled to my breasts, which had blossomed quite nicely, as Sawyer liked to say. I felt myself blush.

"So I kind of figured we'd make a thing of it, see how we like one another. So I say we're dating."

He took my hand and I felt the electric shock again, all through my body. Now If I had any say in this, that shock would not have been there. It was way too soon to feel my virginity was flirting with a sudden death.

~

As we sat in the movie theater together I could feel him next to me. His arm was over my shoulder and at some point I heard him breathing like we were meeting each other's flesh on a windy beach and all the stop signs had been knocked to the ground and were buried deep within the sand so you didn't even know those stop signs were there.

At one point he kissed me, quite unexpectedly, I might add. I had my mouth full of popcorn and couldn't get it swallowed fast enough to get it out of the way of his tongue. I would never be able to tell you what movie I saw that day but I do recall quite vividly his hand falling into my lap like it had a right to be there. I poked him in the ribs.

"Ow," he said.

"I find your fingers exploring my inner thigh again, I'll break 'em," I whispered fiercely.

He sat back. I knew he was smiling though I couldn't see his face. He took my hand again and held it. At one point he brought my hand to his mouth and just grazed his lips over it. I liked that a whole hell of a lot better than his kiss, which he had done with too much fervor, so much in fact my mouth felt like it was going to swell up.

"It's dark in here, I didn't know my hands were in your lap."

"Bullshit."

~

While we sat in the coffee house after the movie, I noticed he was staring at me like I had just been announced Miss South Carolina.

"Boys are going to try and get into your pants, Pleasant. You do know that, don't you? It's just the way boys are."

I scowled at him. "I suggest you don't try to."

"I'm not going to be able to help myself. You're as cute as a puppy pen, Pleasant."

"Cute does not necessarily imply sexy."

"Every girl I like looking at is sexy to me."

"If you want to keep dating me, Bodean, you better

learn the meaning of the word no."

He slumped back in his seat. "Okay, I do respect you, Pleasant, I always will."

"You better."

"You like me any more today than you did yesterday?" He looked at me with his pretty eyes, almost coyly.

"I do. And I'm glad you aren't hanging out with Ike anymore. He must have been a bad influence on you. You're so much nicer without him around. I had no idea you could even be nice."

He slurped some chocolate ice cream off his spoon and stared at me. "Are we friends?"

I nodded my head. "You got to get there before you can get anywhere else. Friendship matters first and foremost."

"You want to know why I don't hang around with Ike?"

I knew I'd cocked my head at him. I guess I was going to be let in on what he thought was a secret—Ike walked on his toes when no one was looking. Well, I already knew that.

"I think I know. Sawyer told me."

He looked surprised and sat back. "He told Sawyer he took those photographs?"

"What?" I was stunned. "What photographs?"

"The ones of Millie and John Peter. He climbed the tree by John Peter's bedroom and spied on them. He wanted me to and I wouldn't. Well, I did once but I didn't want to do it again. It was pretty gross. They were just poking each other and John Peter had a hard on big as a Chiquita frigging banana. I didn't need to see that."

I looked away. "Well, why blame Ike for spying, you were doing it too."

"Only once, and besides, I didn't send the frigging

pictures to his mother. That sucked. I respect women, Pleasant, mothers especially."

"It was Ike that did that?"

Bodean nodded his head and went back to his ice cream sundae.

"Did Ike tell the police it was him sent the photographs to John Peter's mother?"

"He didn't tell the police a thing."

"He might have been a witness to the crime."

"Look, Ike is going to do what Ike is going to do. I can't force him to go to the police."

"You can go to the police and tell them what you know then the police can find out if Ike saw the murderer. You are both withholding information from the law."

Bodean shook his head from side to side. "I'm not getting involved."

"Take me home. You are a coward and you have no integrity at all. I take back every good thing I ever said about you."

Bodean gave me a pathetic look but he paid the check and fished in his pocket for his car keys.

Of course I didn't say a word on the ride home. Bodean dropped me off without saying anything either. But just as we got in front of my house he cut the engine and reached for my arm.

"That information about Ike is just between you and me. Don't go telling anyone."

"You are withholding information that could be important. Ike could have seen the murder in process. Don't you get that, Bodean? I suggest you fess up to the police."

"You ever going to let me kiss you again?"

"Hell, no!" I ran up the walk.

I watched Bodean's car until it vanished from sight then I grabbed my bicycle from the garage and headed out, hoping Ike would be home. When I got to his house Ike's father told me he was out back watering in the garden. I should have known he liked flowers, pansies the most, I'd bet.

"Hey, Ike," I said as I walked up to him.

"What the hell are you doing here?"

I almost gasped, his face was a mess. He had scratches and red marks all over him.

"Just came to say hello. You aren't happy to see me, Ike? I would think that any sister of Sawyer's would be sure to be given a better greeting than the one you're giving me."

His face fell just a little. "I don't give a rat's ass if you're Sawyer's sister."

"You saw who killed Millie, didn't you?" You were up in that tree and you saw the whole damn thing."

He turned completely white and his muddy eyes grew huge. "What the hell are you talking about?"

"I know you climbed that tree to spy on Mille and John Peter getting it on, didn't you?"

He stared at me but he didn't speak, not until after I did.

"You don't tell me what you saw I'll tell everyone in this town that you'd rather eat a hotdog than a cupcake, you hear me, Ike?"

He looked confused. "I don't know what you're saying. As usual, you speak like you're from another planet."

"You're queer, Ike. My brother will attest to it."

He sat on the ground, the little bastard was defeated.

"Your brother is a liar, wishful thinking is all. I'll

deny it."

"People would rather believe you're a fruit than not, just the way people are."

I sat beside him and put my hand over his. "Look, Ike, if you cooperate with me your secret will be safe, I swear."

He met my eyes and I could tell how angry he was. "It shouldn't matter, should it? Nothing wrong with it, is there?"

I shook my head. "Some of us born to hide, some of us need not to. You make your own choice, I'll respect that. But I would think you wouldn't want it spread all over town, not when your father's got a shotgun long as my arm and a sign in the garage that says God hates faggots."

He stood up and motioned for me to join him and we started walking together back behind his property. After we got so far away from the house we couldn't see it, he pushed me down hard on the ground.

"Don't ever say anything, you hear me?" I noticed his fist was raised above my face.

"Okay."

"I'm not gay or anything, I just get it where I can, you understand. You know how girls are, they don't' give it up."

"Sure, Ike."

"How do you know I saw anything at all?"

"I don't but you might have."

"I didn't."

"How'd you get so beat up?"

"Okay, okay, I did see it. Damn tree scratched the shit out of me. Look, I'll keep my part of the bargain. I'll tell you what happened and you keep your mouth shut."

"Deal."

"Okay. I was up in the tree. I'd been spying on them

for a week or so. I wanted to get them in the act. It was a joke, just a joke. I was going to show the photos all over school, send them to everyone on my email list, put it on my Face Book page. So anyway, I could see them in the bedroom, both naked. They might have done it that day for all I know, looked pretty close to it. Then all of a sudden the doorbell rang and they freaked out."

"Did you see who was at the door?"

"Yes, I did, but I never saw him before. I mean, he looked kind of familiar but no one I said hello to, you know what I mean?"

"Then what happened?"

"John Peter and Millie threw their clothes on and went down stairs. I couldn't see anything anymore but I was afraid someone would see me so I stayed in the tree. They let the guy into the house. I heard the door close behind him. I heard his voice."

"What? They let him in?" I couldn't believe my ears. That meant John Peter was face to face with the killer.

"Yeah, the man was in the house. After a while I heard yelling and I heard the door slam. The man ran after whoever it was that left the house, turned out it was Millie. She started running down the street and he pulled her back into the yard. Then I heard the door slam again, must have been John Peter. He ran off in the other direction."

"Why didn't he get help?"

"I don't know but I did hear the man yelling a lot. He was yelling at the two of them so maybe John Peter was too scared to do anything but run."

"What happened then?" My voice was shaking. I noticed that Ike seemed to be getting some kind of warped pleasure out of telling me what he saw.

"He strangled her. I saw it happen. Then he went in to the house by the back door. A moment later he came back out with a big trash bag and stuffed her in there. Problem was she didn't fit and her legs stuck out the end."

The color in his face had returned and he was so red I thought he was going to pass out.

"When did you leave the tree?"

"I stayed there until dark. I was too afraid to move. When John Peter returned I finally climbed down and scratched the shit out of myself doing so. I ran home fast as I could. That's it."

"Would you recognize the man you saw?"

"I might."

"I think we should tell the police." I stood to my feet and faced him.

He came up close to me and put his hands around my neck. "You keep your mouth shut or you'll never be able to open it again. You hear me, Pleasant? You say one word of anything that came out of my mouth this afternoon I'll beat the shit out of you."

"Don't threaten me, Ike."

He started putting pressure on my neck and I swear to God, I thought he was going to strangle me and I was getting ready to jam my knee into his groin but he finally released his hands and pushed me back.

"Get the hell out of my face," he said.

"I'll tell everyone about you," I yelled as I ran away.

"And I'll slit your neck, make your choice, Pleasant."

≈

I was pretty shaken up about everything. I didn't appreciate almost being choked to death but at least I now understood John Peter's behavior. He'd seen the murderer and he was surely petrified he'd be next on the killer's list. I realized the danger he was in, he could identify the man that killed Millie.

I wasn't really that afraid of Ike. I knew my Daddy would send him to hell if he laid a hand on me, but I didn't want to go to the police and put John Peter in danger. I didn't want this story getting out because John Peter might pay for it with his life. The killer might find out he'd opened his mouth. So I wasn't sure what to do. I didn't even know why Ike emailed the photographs on to John Peter's mother, just to cause trouble, I guess.

I didn't know what to do with the information I had. Daddy would only make me go to the police and Angus would tell me to stay the hell out of it. I realized there was only one place I could go, one person I trusted just enough to give me the right answers and it might have been Nana if she lived closer but it wasn't Nana. Unfortunately, she lived an hour away by car, too far for me to travel. But biking to Summerford was no big deal.

Chapter Twelve
Clarissa Blackwell

Clarissa heard the car. She'd been in the kitchen trying out a new recipe for vegetable lasagna and had just slipped it into the oven when she watched, with a certain amount of excitement, as Dom drove up her drive. She quickly fixed her hair and checked her lipstick.

He was all apologetic when he entered. "Didn't want you driving all the way over to see me this time, thought I owed you this information. Besides, I was on my way into Summerford anyway."

"Well, come on in and have a seat. No need to explain, Dom."

"This place is like something out of a magazine," he said, looking around. He stood at the entrance to the living room. He looked uncomfortably out of place with all the delicate, ornate chairs, his frame seemed so huge in comparison. "You live here during the trial?"

"I did indeed."

"Something smells good."

"I just slipped dinner into the oven, not three minutes ago."

"I smell tomato sauce?"

"You sure do, I'm making lasagna."

"Yum." He smiled at her and she noticed that he appeared all spruced up, sports jacket, a nice pair of pressed trousers, good shoes."

"You look very dapper tonight," she said.

"Well, I'm calling on a good looking woman."

Clarissa blushed and felt foolish. Did he mean her or was he seeing someone in Summerford, she wondered.

"What did you find out, Dom?"

"Something very interesting, let's sit down in the living room, if that's okay."

"Of course." She led him to the couch. "Can I get you something?"

"No, no, I can't stay long."

She sat opposite him and watched his expression. "Okay, what's up? I feel you're the bearer of bad news."

"Well, it might be bad news for someone but it's good news for you."

Clarissa nearly held her breath. "What is it?"

"You are an amazing woman, Clarissa, almost spooky."

"Exactly what my ex-husband calls me but I'll take that as a compliment, though I'm not sure how you meant it."

"Well, listen to this." He fished in his jacket pocket for a piece of paper and handed it to her. "That there is a copy of a death certificate for Pleasant Day, who died in 1995. She was the child of Graham and Martha Day. She accidently drowned in their pool."

Clarissa sat forward with a sudden jolt. "I'm confused. How could she have a death certificate? Pleasant is alive."

"Unless she isn't."

She stared at him incredulously. "What are you saying?"

"Graham and Martha lost a child in 1995. That little piece of paper proves it. They might have kidnapped Chloe's baby three years later." He looked at her with a raised brow. "They might have given this new child their dead child's identity."

"But their baby was older by almost three years."

"Their baby was born in 1992. They could have doctored the baby's birth certificate later on in life, when they needed it, probably made a copy of the original and changed the two to a five, not difficult to do, just run a line at the top of the letter. That would have made Pleasant look her age when it was time to send her to school."

"I don't understand."

"You should, you were right about all of this. Graham and Martha somehow got their hands on a baby that wasn't theirs and raised it as the baby they'd lost, never even bothered to change her name. Maybe they thought they wouldn't have been able to get a birth certificate if they did change it, so they were kind of stuck. They moved from Summerford abruptly, three years after the death of their daughter and the appearance of a new baby. I suspect they didn't want anyone noticing in Summerford that the stork had blessed them right after Chloe's baby turned up missing."

"Who could do that?"

"Grief stricken parents."

"Do you think they killed Chloe because they wanted her baby?"

"I don't know what to think, Clarissa, but I do think it warrants an investigation. I've taken my findings to the chief of police. The courts might take another look at Chloe's murder based on this odd bit of news. I can't promise anything but they will look into it, that I can assure you."

"Good God, I feel like crying."

"Your instincts are good, Clarissa, or whatever you call it, your tappings?"

"Thank you, Dom."

"Do you remember Chloe ever mentioning a man called Graham Day?"

Clarissa thought back. "Chloe was having an affair back then but I never knew with whom. She knew I would have frowned on it so she didn't discuss it with me. I do know she was terribly in love with whoever it was. She was discreet, I imagine, because they were both married."

"Well, I won't keep you," he said, slowly getting to his feet. "But I thought you'd want to know about this new development."

"Yes, of course." Clarissa turned toward the kitchen. She assumed it would be impolite not to ask him. " I would invite you to join me for dinner but I see that you have a date."

"A date?" He looked at her oddly and after a moment he laughed. "Well, I do have a date, with my daughter. She lives here in Summerford." He smiled at her as if he'd suddenly realized she'd been jealous.

She blushed a great deal more deeply than she had the first time. "Oh."

"But I'll take a rain check on the lasagna."

"Deal," she said with a smile.

～

It wasn't even three minutes after Dom's departure that the doorbell rang. Clarissa immediately hoped that Dom had changed his mind, or perhaps his daughter had cancelled their plans, but when Clarissa opened her door she found Pleasant staring up at her.

"Hope you don't mind," Pleasant said.

Clarissa was taken off guard but delighted to see the girl. "No, of course not, I invited you any time."

"Nice place." Pleasant peeked into the house."

"Come in, Pleasant."

It seemed as if Pleasant didn't know where to look first, her gaze darted everywhere.

"This place is old, isn't it?"

"It was built in the late 1800s."

"Wow," Pleasant said as she sat and moved her head to the left and then to the right and then to the left again, as if in the process of a neck exercise. "I like it. My mama wouldn't, she doesn't like old things but Daddy says there's value in yesterday's possessions. He drives a '69 Camaro. He tells me all the time that age is the ambrosia waiting to be sipped, the compliment hiding in the wings, waiting to be given to that which is too young today to value the character it will have tomorrow."

"Your Daddy said that?"

"Sure, he's wise."

"I guess he is."

Clarissa had not yet taken a seat. She was amused by the girl, almost too small for the chair that embraced her, and she was hardly small.

"You are so much like someone I used to know," she said softly.

"Daddy says that one day all I'll think about is people I used to know."

Clarissa laughed. "Your daddy sure does say some very interesting things."

Pleasant smiled. "That your husband just left?"

"I'm not married anymore, Pleasant. No more husband."

"Oh. That your boyfriend then?"

Clarissa shook her head. "I'm afraid I don't have one

of those either."

"I have a boyfriend. Well, at least I did. I don't want to see him anymore, he doesn't have integrity."

"Good choice then, I'd say. Come into to the kitchen, Pleasant. I'm going to make you a smoothie."

"I like chocolate ice cream, just so you know," Pleasant announced as she followed Clarissa into her kitchen.

"My smoothies aren't made with ice cream, Pleasant."

"That sounds boring."

"It's a fruit smoothie but I can make it with chocolate yogurt."

"Oh, I guess. I never had chocolate yogurt, but I guess."

~

By the time Pleasant admitted that there was purpose in visiting Clarissa she'd finished two tall glasses of a banana, strawberry mixture that she compared to cough medicine.

"You must like cough medicine then, you finished two glasses."

Pleasant smiled. "Chocolate yogurt in there?" she asked.

Clarissa nodded. "Some."

"That must have been why. Chocolate is chocolate, yogurt or not."

Pleasant sat back on the banquet and stared out the window for a bit. Clarissa waited patiently; she knew it wouldn't take Pleasant long to get to the point.

"We have to talk," she finally said. "I need advice."

"Okay."

"I'm trying to solve a murder." Pleasant turned back to Clarissa, her soft hazel eyes suddenly sad.

"What did you say?"

"I'm trying to solve a murder."

Clarissa thought to say, so am I, but stopped herself. It was uncanny, this bit of news.

"You hear about what happened to Millie Grady?"

Clarissa thought a moment. She recalled reading about the gruesome murder of a young girl.

"You knew her?" Clarissa asked. "I thought she was from Summerford."

"Yeah, but we went to the same school. She was my best friend aside from Angus and John Peter."

"I'm sorry for you, Pleasant."

"They didn't like her, Angus and John Peter, but I liked her. I liked her a lot."

"Why didn't they like her?"

"Because she wasn't like anybody else, she was different."

"How so?"

"She only had one arm, lost her other arm in a car accident."

"Hardly reason enough to dislike someone."

"I know but Angus isn't very mature. John Peter… he's just weak, said he didn't like her but then I found out he was having sex with her. I think he was embarrassed because she only had one arm and the other boys would have laughed at him, told him he couldn't do better."

Clarissa was a bit startled and sat back. Sex? These kids were hardly passed their toddler stage. She wanted to say, I hope you're not having sex, but decided not to.

"Kids can be very cruel," she said instead.

"Ike, he's this horrible bully at school. He told me that John Peter saw the man who murdered Millie."

"How could Ike know that, Pleasant?"

"'Cause he was up in the tree spying on them. He

even sent pictures of John Peter and Millie naked to John Peter's mama. He saw the murder, saw the man that did it."

"Well, did he tell the police?"

"No, he won't tell the police."

Clarissa reached out her hand and covered Pleasant's small, delicate one. "Then you have to. I'm afraid you can't withhold this from the law."

"But it would put John Peter in danger if I told the police. The murderer would find out and come back and murder John Peter for opening up his big mouth."

"The police will protect your friend, don't you know that?"

"John Peter doesn't usually lie to me, he must be scared shitless."

"You've got to tell the police, Pleasant, this is very important. Do you want me to go to the station with you? I can drive you over."

"That man could get wind, could come back to Hollow Creek and kill John Peter. That's what he's so afraid of, that's why he won't talk truth. And that's what I'm afraid of too."

"Pleasant, withholding information from the very people who can help John Peter isn't smart. Besides, this man, whoever he is, won't know John Peter told the police anything."

"So you think I should go to the police and tell them Ike was in the tree and saw what happened?"

"I do."

"Let me think about it."

Clarissa nodded. "I'm sure you will do the right thing."

"Don't say anything to anybody."

"I give you my word, Pleasant."

"Maybe me and you together can find out who this

man is and he can be arrested before he becomes any kind of threat to John Peter."

"We didn't see the man, Pleasant. We don't have a clue as to how to find him. But John Peter saw the man. Likely Ike did as well. You've got to tell the police that. With a police composite they may be able to pick him up."

"I'm squealing if I do that."

"I don't think trying to save John Peter from harm is squealing, it's being brave, and smart." Clarissa got up and sat next to her. "Pleasant, why didn't the man kill John Peter as well?"

"He ran."

"He didn't kill him because he didn't know where he was, he ran away, but the killer knows where John Peter lives so he could come back at any time and harm him. We need to protect your friend from that."

"You think?"

"I do. So it's best to let the police catch this man first."

Pleasant left quietly without another word, just a slight nod back over her shoulder.

~

What strange parallels there are in the world, Clarissa thought. Here was Pleasant trying to solve the murder of her friend. How extraordinary. Clarissa saw so many coincidences between them. She sensed how deeply both she and Pleasant had been drawn to each other. Surely their meeting one another was meant to happen, perhaps it had even been some sort of divine intervention. Clarissa felt that it was all too coincidental to be happenstance, a murder each between them. Their sudden friendship was surely fated.

"This is meant to be, isn't it?" she said softly. Capturing one murderer might lead to the discovery of another, was that it, she wondered? Was it possible that the murder of little Millie Grady could somehow open up a roadmap that would lead her to the vindication she so desperately needed for Chloe's murder? She finished off a pot of coffee as she sought to understand it.

Clarissa certainly wasn't going to bother Dom while he was out with his daughter but she felt she had to tell him about Pleasant's friend, that he'd seen the murder of that poor little girl and he could probably identify the killer. Clarissa was excited by the information she had and she knew that Dom would be as well. He would know the detectives on the Millie Grady case and he'd appreciate her for letting him in on that. Clarissa waited until a respectable hour, eleven was good, most people were home by eleven.

"Hello, Clarissa."

"So, my number came up and gave me away, did it?"

"That it did," he said.

"Did you have a good time with your daughter?"

She could tell he was sitting down. She heard him sigh and bend.

"Yes, for once we had a good time."

"You usually don't?" she asked, making herself comfortable against the pillows on her bed.

He seemed to chuckle a bit. "On a good day we have a good time and on a bad day, we don't. Tonight was a good day."

"Dom, I wouldn't bother you at this late hour if it wasn't important."

"What's up?"

She realized she was about to betray Pleasant. Yes, her information was critical but Clarissa had promised to keep her mouth shut. She decided then and there that she couldn't really do that to Pleasant, she'd promised the girl she wouldn't tell anyone. She had to give Pleasant just a bit more time to force John Peter into telling the police that Ike may have seen the murder and he may have seen the murderer's face. She quickly changed her mind about saying anything, at least for the moment.

"Chloe's husband, Martin Holly, was he questioned?" she said the first thing that came to mind. Well, she'd been thinking about Martin lately, thinking how he never even showed up at the trial to see his wife's killer pay for what he'd done.

She could feel Dom's puzzlement. She was just making up an excuse to speak to him and maybe he knew it too. She had nothing important to say and it was obvious. She'd just wanted to hear his voice. That's the way it must seem. All of a sudden, she was embarrassed. But she wasn't going to tell him what Pleasant had told her. She'd made a promise. She had to give Pleasant a chance to do the right thing herself.

"Of course. He was the first one we looked into. He had left the country a week before Chloe's death, and he hadn't returned, not until recently. He doesn't live far from here now, I believe."

"Yes, of course." She felt like a school girl. Why the hell had she called him, she asked herself. "I'm just thinking of everything. Everyone and anyone who might have hurt my Chloe."

"Of course."

"Sorry to bother you."

They both paused for a moment and she thought it best if she just got off the damn phone. She was making a fool out of herself. Calling him had been a stupid idea. Once she decided not to betray Pleasant, it was obvious she'd had nothing really important to say.

"How was the lasagna?" he asked.

"You must try it, it was delicious."

"I'm waiting for my invitation, Clarissa."

"And you're going to get it, Dom. Well, goodnight."

She realized her hand was shaking as she hung up the phone. She had a crush on him and she hadn't wanted to admit it to herself. Out of the blue, there was someone she found attractive. "Will wonders never cease?" she whispered.

Clarissa didn't really suspect Martin Holly of Chloe's murder. He'd been out of the country the night Chloe was murdered but she decided that he might be able to tell her something important. It took Clarissa all of five minutes on her computer to find an address for Martin. He lived in Fairmont now, only ten miles away. As she drove up his drive-way she thought that the house looked exactly like it should, like Martin Holly himself, plain and unobtrusive, barely noticeable.

It was Saturday and she assumed she would find him home but she did not expect to find his wife and three children there as well. She hadn't even thought that his life would go on after Chloe's death, but of course it had. Chloe had hurt him, had cheated on him, why shouldn't his life go on?

He was surprised to see her, rightfully so, she surmised. The color seemed to drain from his face as he stood there gaping at her. He stared at her as if she were a visitor from heaven, perhaps even hell.

"I'm Chloe's godmother, Clarissa Blackwell. Do you

remember?"

He shook her hand. "Yes, of course, now I do." He seemed to be waiting for her to speak, his body seemed frozen in motion, as if wrapped in a sheet of ice. He kept staring at her and said nothing more. She looked past him, at a woman who must have been his wife. She gave Chloe a partial smile and stood behind her husband.

"It's for me," he told her, "someone I used to know."

His wife moved on to another room without a glance back at Clarissa. A set of twin girls followed after their mother and a boy of about ten looked to be building a model boat in the living room.

"I wonder if I might have a word with you," Clarissa said.

"Of course." He led her toward the stream at the side of the house. "We can sit here, my house is a bit over run at the moment, with my children… they ah don't start school for a few weeks."

It was a pretty spot and Clarissa sat back in a wooden chair and watched the water run. She sensed she made Martin nervous.

"You remarried?"

"Yes."

"I'm happy for you, happy you found someone."

She could feel his eyes on her though she continued to stare at the stream.

"Thank you."

"You didn't attend the trial?"

"No, no, I had returned to England."

"Did you get word that Randall Holmes confessed to Chloe's murder?"

"Yes."

Neither of them said anything more as they watched the water, it was soothing and strong, with a language of its own, indifferent and rhythmic. After a moment,

Clarissa spoke.

"I don't believe Randall did it."

"Really?" he said, turning away from her, but she had felt him stiffen beside her.

"No, I don't."

Martin slowly turned back to her.

"I know she was cheating on you," Clarissa said, meeting his gaze. She watched his expression, the slight twitch to his jaw.

"That she was."

"Do you know with whom?"

"Of course, she told me."

Clarissa was surprised and wondered if she should ask him who the man was, if he would tell her anything at all, but before she could ask he offered the answer.

"Graham was the only one for Chloe, just the way it was. The child was his, you know."

"Graham? Graham Day?" It seemed to make sense now that Graham had raised the baby, or perhaps more appropriately, had stolen the baby. It also seemed obvious that Graham murdered Chloe, he must have. All the pieces were beginning to fit. It was Graham's baby, Graham's and Chloe's. Of course he would take the child after murdering Chloe. He'd lost his own child, he would want this one.

"She lied to me at first but one night she told me everything." Martin turned to stare at her and Clarissa noticed his eyes, they were like indifferent tides, shielding knowledge of an impending storm. "She asked me for a divorce that night."

"The baby was presumed dead. They never found her."

Martin shrugged his shoulders. "I didn't take her, if that's what you're thinking."

"No, no, I wasn't."

"I try not to think about that part of my life."

"I'm sorry to bring it up to you then, but I have to ask, could Graham have killed Chloe?"

He kept his eyes on hers. Clarissa remembered why she didn't like him, he was astucious, an ambiguous villain in a gentleman's three piece suit. Even on a weekend by the stream his pants were pressed and his shirt was starched.

"Why? Why would he kill her?"

"Well, I think I remember Chloe telling me she was going to work on her marriage. That could have made Graham angry."

He laughed. "That sounds like Chloe, she appeased people to keep them from getting upset. To Chloe, lies held purpose."

"That's motive, if it were true."

"It wasn't." She detected the bitterness in his tone.

He got to his feet quickly. "I must move on with my weekend and my life, but it was nice of you to come. Your theory is most interesting but if I were you, I would let sleeping dogs lie. That serial killer, he confessed to it."

Clarissa felt her insides turn over and she wasn't quite sure why. "Yes, that he did. Thank you for your time," she said as she left.

Chapter Thirteen
Pleasant Day

I had a sensitive task to perform. Clarissa was right, the police had to know the truth. I had to get John Peter to fess up.

"Good morning," I said to Mrs. Clottey as I walked into John Peter's house. "I'm here to see John Peter."

Mrs. Clottey smiled at me and I noticed it seemed haunted, like it was an effort to stretch her lips into upward lines. The minute her facial muscles relaxed the creases around her mouth fell past her chin. I felt she was a wreck after finding Millie's body in her son's box-spring and she might never smile natural again.

"Go right upstairs, Pleasant. John Peter is in the front room now."

So John Peter was no longer in his old room, the one with the tree out front and the body removed from his box-spring.

"I guess your old room is still a crime scene," I said as I walked in.

John Peter was sitting on his bed just staring at the floor. I sat myself in a chair across from him after I took the clothes that had been on the seat and tossed everything at his feet.

"You need a maid, " I said, looking around.

"What do you want, Pleasant?"

"You and me got some serious talking to do."

He lifted his head and stared at me. "I'm not in the mood to talk."

"Listen to me, get hold of yourself. You've got to start doing the right thing, the smart thing."

"That's exactly what I am doing."

I sighed before I started speaking. "I know Ike was in the tree when Millie got murdered. I know that the man that came to the door was inside the house yelling at you two. What about?"

I never seen his eyes get so big in my life. He looked petrified. "Get out," he shouted. "Get out of my room."

I jumped up and went over to him. I put my hand over his mouth. "Shut up, John Peter. I don't want your Mama running in here."

He grabbed my hand and glared at me. "You're going to get me killed."

"I'm not going to get you killed," I said and sat down next to him. "Listen to me, John Peter, you've got to go to the police and tell them who that man is. They'll protect you. They won't let anything happen to you but you've got to tell them."

"You don't know what you're talking about." He stood up and started pacing.

"Ike told me everything."

His eyes got big as golf balls. "Ike didn't tell you shit," he said. "You're lying. You're bluffing me."

"Yeah, Ike told me everything." I stared him down.

"Not everything I would imagine."

"Told me that man that came to the door came in the house."

"He told you the man came in the house?"

"Please don't be afraid. I'll come to the police station

with you. I'll demand police protection for you, John Peter. I'll tell my daddy too, he won't let anything happen to you."

"Go home, Pleasant. And don't hang out with Ike, You hear me? He's a bad seed."

"Listen, I got something on Ike. I can control Ike. I can make him tell the police everything he told me."

"You're deluding yourself, Pleasant."

"He's gay, John Peter, Ike is gay. You think he wants the whole town knowing that? I got his arm twisted behind his back and he's screaming monkey."

I saw the shock come over John Peter's expression and then he looked confused.

"Ike is gay? How do you know that?"

"Sawyer."

John Peter kept shaking his head. "God damn son of a bitch."

"Please come down to the station with me, 'cause I'm going. I'm going to tell them that you and Ike know who that man is that murdered Millie. I have to do this, John Peter, for Millie's sake."

"I don't know anything, Pleasant. I didn't see anyone. There wasn't anyone there."

I stood there staring at him, trying to let compassion rule when all I felt was that I wanted to take a punch at him, he was being so hard headed.

"You're lying."

"Not lying."

"No going back now, John Peter, you can't retract anything you said any more than Ike can. You either follow me out this door to the police station or you don't but you're going to have to fess up and stop being such a little coward. I have lost patience with you."

He turned his face to the wall and went stiff on me, like he froze up.

"You coming?" I asked but he kept standing there like an ice statue.

I marched out of his room praying I'd hear him behind me but I heard nothing. I stopped at the foot of the stairs and listened but John Peter had not followed me. I called his name once before I walked out of the house. I was hoping he'd catch up to me on his bicycle so I slowly pedaled down the road. I was peddling so goddamn slowly I fell off the bike twice. When I got to the police station John Peter was nowhere to be found.

Miracle upon miracle, Bodean Frasier had come to the police station of his own accord and told them that Ike had been in the tree taking pictures of John Peter and Millie. I didn't have to tell them anything significant after that, I figured they'd go on over and interrogate Ike and get the whole story out of him without me having to open my big mouth. I started to tell them what Ike had told me, that he witnessed the murder, I really did, but truth be told, Captain Crawford put his hand on my head and patted it and I shut up fast.

"Go on home, Pleasant," he said. "Your friend Bodean has told us all about Ike being in the tree taking pictures of John Peter and Millie. We're going over there to question him now. He might have some serious information for us."

I nodded my head. "Yeah, he might have seen the murder."

Captain Crawford smiled at me like I was just a kid who didn't know shit. I didn't say a thing about John Peter lying to them and not telling them that the man that came to the door had been inside the house. I couldn't. I figured it was all going to come out and either

John Peter or Ike was going to have to tell the truth about that man. I was thinking one of them knew the guy, that's what I was thinking, and he'd threatened them both something bad. But it wasn't up to me to spill the beans, but if I got wind they hadn't told the truth I'd made up my mind that I was going to.

~

When I got home Sawyer was on the porch looking through some magazines of fancy houses.

"Don't you read anything with a story to it?" I asked as I plopped beside him.

"Good decorating is a story, Pleasant. It's a story of taste. It's a story of personality, of character. Look at any good decorated room and I defy you to tell me it doesn't have a story to tell. When I see a well painted room I want to meet the storyteller behind the color chosen. I truly do. Show me a man with taste and I'll show you a man with character."

I couldn't help but laugh. He was probably right.

"Where you been?" he asked.

"I was at the police station." I looked at his face, one eyebrow was up, one perfect brown eyebrow.

"The police station. What were you doing there?"

"It's a long story."

"I'm listening."

"Well, I know it was Ike up in the tree by John Peter's bedroom when Millie got murdered and I was going to tell them that but they already knew."

"How'd they know?"

"Bodean told them."

"Let you off the hook."

"For now it does. But it's my duty to make sure Millie's murder is solved, to see whoever did it punished.

I don't want anything to happen to John Peter but I have to see justice done, you understand? I'm not keeping my mouth shut for very long."

"Maybe you shouldn't get involved, little sister."

"I won't have to get involved if Ike tells them that he saw the guy. If Ike tells the truth then I won't have to tell them John Peter lied to them. I won't have to rat on him." I looked to Sawyer for reassurance but the only thing in his expression was amusement.

"So Ike had been spying on John Peter?"

"John Peter and Millie were having sex, or about to. He was taking pictures of them naked."

I heard Sawyer laughing. "Doesn't surprise me."

"What doesn't surprise you?"

"That Ike would spy on John Peter. He was probably furious that he was having sex with that one armed girl."

"What are you saying?"

"Ike had a thing for John Peter, little sister."

"Ike had a thing for John Peter?" I was astonished.

"You bet he did, bored me senseless with his infatuation, probably climbed the tree to watch John Peter undress."

"He sent those pictures to Mrs. Clottey."

Sawyer went nearly hysterical. "Hell hath no fury like a faggot scorned."

All I kept thinking was how furious John Peter would be if he knew Ike had a thing for him. John Peter was nearly as pretty as Sawyer with all that curly hair of his but he was as straight as any piece of thread you'd pull through a needle.

~

Bodean showed up on my doorstep the next day, while I was sitting on my front porch trying to digest the information of the last few days. I figured they had Ike in an interrogation room and were on their way to pick up the killer. I hadn't gone back to John Peter's house, even though I could safely say it wasn't me that told the police a damn thing, it was Bodean, I've- turned- over- a- new- leaf- Bodean.

"Afternoon, Pleasant," he said.

I just looked at him. His light eyes looked intensely green in the sun and his hair had recently been cut. I could smell whatever he had greased it back with. It looked shiny and slick and the one dimple he had on the left side of his cheek was deep enough to wade in. Only problem was he had a black eye, not too bad but definitely bruised.

"Afternoon."

"I did the right thing."

"I know you did, the police told me."

"Deserve a kiss for that, I'd think." I stood up and kissed the dimple. "What happened to you?"

He held out his hand. "Let's walk," he said.

We walked the far end of Piper Hill, where it was the most woody and you had to side step wayward branches that kept scratching up your arms.

"So what's with the black eye?" I asked.

"Ike."

"He hit you?"

Bodean nodded. "Said I was the only one could have told you anything, I was the only one that knew anything about the picture taking. Told me you came to talk to him." He looked at me like I was a fly he was about to swat.

"That I did."

"Remind me not to tell you anything in confidence again." I knew he wasn't that angry at me 'cause he started whistling.

"Does it hurt?"

Bodean laughed. "It does, a little." He turned to me. "I beat the shit out of him though. He should have known not to mess with me."

"Then you went to the police?"

"I did."

"Have they interrogated Ike yet?"

"About taking the pictures?"

I felt him take my hand. I didn't pull back. He had, after all, done the right thing. "Ike saw the murder, saw Millie being strangled." I looked at him to see if he knew about that too.

Bodean turned white. I saw the color drain from his face and it was obvious he didn't know anything about that at all.

"What, he saw it?" he said, his eyes still round as Saturn's rings.

"He saw the whole thing, saw the man that did it too."

"Holy shit."

"Yeah, that's why I went to the police but I didn't tell them that. I figured they'd get it out of Ike and I could steer clear of being a big mouth."

I saw him grin. "You are a big mouth."

"Millie was my friend and so is John Peter so I'm going to do anything I can to help them, even though I'm too late to help Millie." I almost started crying thinking about Millie being helpless to protect herself.

"Okay, okay, the police will get the truth out of Ike for sure. They'll catch the guy, Pleasant."

We hadn't stopped looking at each other. I think my gaze kept going to his mouth, I know his kept going to mine. Our bodies were very close. I felt the electric shocks moving between us.

"What's that scent you're wearing?" He took a huge step toward me and started sniffing my neck.

"You're tickling me, Bodean." I turned my face around. I could feel my chest on his. I could feel his belt against my stomach.

Next thing I knew his lips had found my lips. I couldn't tell you who kissed who first, all I do know is that Bodean must have taken kissing lessons since the movie theater when I was sure he had bruised me with his fervor. But not now, now was soft and sweet as honey being poured on a biscuit.

It wasn't 'till we pulled away from each other that I realized we weren't alone. Angus was there, gaping at us like we'd been caught with our pants down, which might have been the case if Bodean had kissed me any longer.

I quickly stepped away from Bodean. "What the hell you want, Angus?" I asked, feeling myself turning red as a hot house tomato.

Took him a while to answer, he was still gaping, standing there speechless, obviously in shock.

"I thought you might need me, saw you from a distance walking with him and I followed, just to make sure you're all right." Angus stared at Bodean like he was a grizzly and Angus had a gun he was about to employ. "He isn't safe to be alone with, you do know that, don't you?"

"I don't like what you're saying, Angus," Bodean said.

Angus turned to me. "Did you hear?" he asked. "Or have you been otherwise engaged?" He gave Bodean the look of death.

"Hear what?" I asked.

"John Peter is missing, hasn't been seen for two days."

"What?" I felt my heart race.

"Nobody has seen him. Police have been out combing the fields, they think he might be dead, I guess."

Angus glared at Bodean again but Bodean was too busy leading me off so he didn't see the hate in Angus's stare.

"C'mon Pleasant, let's see if we can find him." Bodean kind of yanked me down the trail away from Angus. But I felt Angus right on our heels. "We can join the search," Bodean said to me.

"We don't need him, Pleasant," Angus called. "He don't give a damn about John Peter."

"I don't," Bodean shouted back, "but I like a little excitement in my life."

"That all this is to you?"

At that, Bodean stopped walking and turned to look right at Angus. "If anyone is going to find John Peter, it's going to be me so you best follow my lead. Got that, Angus?"

Angus was sweating and out of breath but he wasn't taking shit from Bodean. "If anyone is going to find John Peter it's going to be me and Pleasant. He's our friend, you wouldn't have a clue as to where he'd hide out."

"I have tracking skills."

Angus raised his eyes up and looked at me pathetically, "yeah, right," he said.

I didn't stop to break up any bull shit going on between Angus and Bodean, I just wanted to find John Peter but half way down the trail I felt Angus pull me back.

"What the hell are you doing with him?" he whispered fiercely.

I pulled my hand away. "Nothing. Nothing I'm going to be telling you about any time soon."

Chapter Fourteen
Clarissa Blackwell

Clarissa hated bars, never much cared for them when she was younger either. She hated the smell of stale beer, rancid and sour, like cat boxes that hadn't been cleaned soon enough. But that's where Graham had agreed to meet with her, and she supposed it was the best place. She had suggested The Fine Fettle but that didn't go over well, he said he'd never be able to find anything stronger than chamomile tea at The Fine Fettle, so he insisted on buying her a beer at some little roadside bar called Buck's, and that was fine with Clarissa, lots of people around. If she was meeting up with Chloe's killer, she certainly didn't want to be alone with him.

Clarissa realized within five minutes that Graham Day had not murdered Chloe. Maybe it was sixth sense, or maybe it was the way he looked when he mentioned Chloe's name.

"Hello, Graham," she said.

She realized immediately that Graham was familiar and the familiarity comforted her. The recognition told her that he was no threat, nor was he a killer.

"Do I know you? I could swear we've met before."

Clarissa strained to be heard over the music, country, which she liked but not when she wanted information.

"We do. It came to me the minute I saw you. You used to play with Chloe when you were kids. You used to come over and the two of you would be back climbing trees and swimming together, having the time of your life." She laughed at the memory. "I didn't remember your name but you look the same as you did back then."

"Ah, yes, Chloe."

Graham had the kind of smile that instilled trust, she thought. He'd smiled like that as a young boy too, the kind of smile that always made her want to hug him. She remembered that. He'd been a little mischievous kid with brown hair that fell into his eyes. Graham was a fond memory, no one to fear or to hate. Yes, he had stolen a baby but that baby was half his.

"You're Clarissa Blackwell, used to live down the block from Chloe? Her Aunt?"

"Her godmother. You do remember."

"What do you want to talk to me about, Clarissa? Chloe's been dead fourteen years."

"I still want to talk about her."

"We drifted apart, Chloe and I."

"But apparently you drifted back together at some point."

Graham seemed a bit startled that she would know about something like that. "Yes, we drifted back together, you could say that."

"When did you fall in love with her, Graham?"

"So, you knew about us then?"

"She never mentioned your name but I knew about you, knew there was someone in her life that was threatening her marriage. I never dreamed in a million years that it was that little boy that used to come over with enough quarters in his pocket to buy her an ice cream cone. You were a very considerate little boy, Graham."

"I loved her. I think I was always in love with her, but it wasn't for years that I owned up to it. Unfortunately it was while we were both married."

Clarissa was well aware she was about to dive into deep water but she couldn't solve Chloe's murder unless she took risks. She wondered what Dom would say if he knew she was questioning Graham Day. She brushed the thought aside and leaned over the booth.

"Did you accept Randall Holmes as her murderer?"

He seemed shocked for a moment but then he shook his head. "No, I never believed he did it but it was a slam dunk back then. You had to accept it."

"You ever suspect anyone else?"

He looked off and took his time answering. "I don't know."

"You did suspect someone, didn't you? I can feel that you did."

"I knew everything about Chloe, things nobody else knew." He looked at her like he was about to betray a confidence that was years old, too old to matter, perhaps. "Look, I'm not accusing anyone but... there was someone might have been threatened by her."

"Who?"

He leaned in to her and whispered softly, as if still protecting the confidence. "Chloe was molested as a child. She was thinking of exposing the man right before she was killed. It always bothered me, that there might have been a connection between her murder and this son of a bitch. But I couldn't say anything. It would have opened up a whole can of worms for me. I couldn't put my family at risk. Blake's got a lot of power."

Clarissa felt as though someone had taken a two-by-four and hit her on the forehead. She lunged back.

"Molested? What are you saying, Blake molested her?"

"Yes, she was molested by her uncle until she was about thirteen years old."

"That bastard." Clarissa felt the shockwaves moving through her. She remembered Blake so well, handsome, blonde Blake, who could charm anyone into believing he wasn't the bastard he was. She remembered that one date she had with him when she was sixteen and he was nineteen. He had tried to force himself on her but Savannah had come home and interrupted what very well could have turned to rape. After that she had kept her distance from him. She never told anyone about that incidence, it had made her feel dirty, like she'd done something to make him act that way.

"Did her mother know?"

Graham shook his head. "I'm not sure, she might have told her later on, after she was an adult. Chloe was ashamed of it and damn angry at having to be ashamed of it."

Clarissa put her head in her hands, "my God, why didn't she tell me?"

"Look Clarissa, that doesn't mean Blake killed her."

"Why was she going to expose him right before she died, why did she chose that moment? If she was ashamed of being molested why would she go public with it?"

"He was running for some state government office. That put a fire under her. She didn't think him worthy of serving the people of South Carolina. Nobody would have disagreed with her, but even if no one believed her, it would have ruined him politically."

"He's our state senator."

"Yes, he is, isn't he? Look, I tried talking her out of saying anything but she was on this warpath against him. I always felt he was a really dangerous man, completely ruthless. I was afraid for her, but she was right."

"My God, I never suspected anything like that, not ever."

"I imagine nobody else did either."

Clarissa felt like she wanted to just get up and leave. The information he'd given her had infuriated her and her head was reeling, but she had to let Graham know he'd become a suspect in Chloe's murder.

"Graham, the police are going to question you about Chloe's death," she said quickly and quietly, feeling guilty for being the cause of that.

His head shot up and she saw the confusion, the disbelief.

"I don't understand. Her murder was solved years ago, according to them. And they questioned me years ago, nothing came of that."

"But you must have been there the night she died, you took the baby, didn't you?"

She saw the shock in his expression that morphed into fear right before her eyes. She felt how deeply thrown off his feet he had been by that bit of news.

"I didn't kill Chloe," he finally said. "I loved her more than anything."

"Perhaps, but you took her baby."

"Our baby. I took our baby. I couldn't leave her there. She was mine. She was my child, Clarissa."

"You found Chloe's body, didn't you?"

He put his head in his hand and nodded. She noticed how long his fingers were. Pleasant had them, their only obvious resemblance.

"I think I frightened him off. I heard something as I came in. I heard someone struggling to get out the back window but I was so shocked by what I'd walked into. There was blood everywhere. Chloe was just lying there on the floor and the baby was crying."

"Did you see anyone?"

"No. I heard him but I didn't see him. I didn't follow him either. I couldn't. I didn't know if Chloe was still alive or not at that point. I was praying that she wasn't hurt badly but there was blood all over the room. The baby was so distressed. I could hear the murderer shoving on the window frame, forcing it up but I had to comfort the baby. I had to clean her. She had her mother's blood all over her."

As he spoke, Clarissa saw a clear vision of it, saw what Graham was describing, but she couldn't see the man at the window. She only felt Graham's anguish, the horror of what he was witnessing and experiencing. She saw the blood every-where in her vision, saw Graham reach for the child. She almost cried out but she stopped herself. She took a deep breath and went on.

"The police know you took the baby. I'm sorry but it does make you a suspect. They're going to look into the case, perhaps reopen it."

"Knowing what I knew what would you have done? Would you have left that little infant to be exposed to Blake Rappaport?"

"I would have taken her too, Graham, if it makes you feel any better."

"How did you know that I have her?" He looked at her in such a way that she reached out and put her hand on his arm.

"Your daughter ran me over on a bicycle, came into my life like a little cyclone. She is so much like Chloe, looks so much like her, I couldn't help but want to put the pieces together, appease my own curiosity. How could anyone resemble another person that much unless they were related?"

Graham's distress showed, but so did his love for his daughter. "Yes, she is a mirror image of Chloe, isn't she?

She's smart as Chloe, too. I should have moved further away than Hollow Creek, it would seem."

"I know about the little girl you lost, Graham. The police do too."

Graham looked off. "That isn't why I took her, I took her because she was mine and Chloe's. I wasn't going to leave her, to subject her to her perverted uncle. I couldn't."

"Didn't your wife question you?"

"Yes, she questioned me. I told my wife that I purchased the baby for five thousand dollars from a woman that needed money and sold her to me. What else could I say, that she was the result of my affair with the love of my life?"

Clarissa was shocked, stunned by his wife's acceptance. "Your wife didn't force you to return her, she believed you just purchased her? It was all over the paper that Chloe's baby was missing."

"She didn't put the pieces together, maybe she didn't want to. She believed what I told her because she was still so distressed over the loss of our daughter, even though it had been three years. She wasn't getting over it. She would have believed anything I said. I never told her the truth, of course." He looked at her sadly. "I guess it will come out now, all of it."

"It will, Graham. You've got to make a lot of things right, with your wife, and especially with Pleasant."

～

Clarissa didn't hesitate a moment when she got home. She picked up the phone and called Dom even before she took off the new shoes that were killing her. Heels never made a lick of sense to Clarissa but every woman's legs looked better when elevated by three inches or more and she was no exception.

"Chloe was molested, Dom."

She heard the pause. He didn't respond. It sounded to Clarissa that he was at a real loss for words and maybe put off by everything she was coming up with. Maybe he was angry that she had called him the other night for no reason at all. She had shown him her full deck and she was still feeling like a fool because of it.

"Are you there, Dom? Chloe was molested by her uncle. That's motive. She was going to expose him."

"How do you know that?"

"Graham Day told me."

She heard the pause. "What were you doing speaking to Graham Day?"

"I had to."

"You've got to stop that Clarissa. Leave it to me to question people."

"Yes, I promise, I will."

"Who is her Uncle?"

"Blake Rappaport."

She heard the breath that Dom let out from the back of his throat.

"Blake Rappaport?"

"Yes. Don't sound so surprised. I know Blake, he's capable of it. He doesn't have any sexual boundaries. He thinks he's doing women a favor by forcing himself on them. I never knew he liked little girls though. That bit of disgusting news was new to me."

"Can you prove it?"

"Of course not."

"If they decide to open the case all roads are going to point to Graham Day. Rappaport is a senator. It's unlikely he killed anyone."

"Oh, come on Dom. You know better than that."

"You are not to talk to Rappaport. I'll talk to

Rappaport but it's going to be hard to prove he molested a dead girl who isn't here to accuse him."

"Maybe he's got a history of it."

"Maybe, but I still say it's going to be hard to prove. There are no allegations of sexual misconduct about Senator Rappaport as far as I know."

Clarissa found it impossible to sleep. She tossed and she turned, got up three too many times to use the bathroom. When she finally did fall back to sleep she had a deeply disturbing dream that she couldn't even shake off the next day. She tried analyzing what she had dreamt but she was not coming up with any solid interpretations, just guesses. For Clarissa, dreams were a language, not necessarily profound and not necessarily prophetic but they always had merit when understood correctly, even the ones that seemed most ridiculous.

This dream was far from ridiculous, and it was difficult to interpret, with its eerie and nebulous shadows, offering no clues to its dark images. She kept seeing a man with two heads murdering Chloe. Clarissa couldn't see any features on his face, just sparse hair and the erratic movements of his hands. He was angry, furious and he stabbed Chloe over and over again, long after he'd killed her, he just kept stabbing her.

She didn't want to see this, she didn't want to remember the dream but she couldn't get it out of her mind. She could see the murderer stopping by the infant's crib, putting a pillow over the child's face. But something startled him. She saw the two headed man run out the back window. That was all, all she could remember. But it was enough. She couldn't interpret it but it was exactly what Graham had told her of that night. She must have been so susceptible to his experience. But Graham hadn't seen any two headed man. But then again, maybe the two heads signified the two sides of Blake, the side he showed the world and the perversion he hid from the world. If Blake had been the killer. Yes, of course that would make sense, but still, that seemed too obvious.

Graham's news had devastated her, the fact that she never knew, never suspected that the little girl she had loved so much had been subjected to Blake's advances. It wasn't like Chloe to keep anything in, yet what does a child do with an experience so confusing and disturbing? Clarissa realized only too quickly that Savannah would have to be paid a visit. Clarissa had to know if Savannah knew what a bastard low life her brother was. She also had to know that her granddaughter was very much alive, very much like her. Clarissa was so angry at Savannah, not only for ruining her marriage but for rejecting her. The last thing in the world she wanted to do was contact the woman, and give her a great gift, the return of a missing child. She didn't owe Savannah anything so important.

Clarissa's hand shook as she reached for the phone, her voice shook too as she began to leave the message she was forced to leave because Savannah never picked up the phone to her. Savannah had not picked up the phone to her for years, and she never called her back either. Clarissa was sure that nothing had changed, but she had to start somewhere. She gathered strength as the little beep sounded.

"Savannah, this is Clarissa, do not ignore me this time. This is important. We need to talk. I am coming to your house in fifteen minutes and I want you to answer the door. You have a granddaughter, Savannah, guess it's 'bout time you….."

The phone was picked up quickly but there was no voice, no greeting.

"Savannah?" Clarissa said, listening to the echo.

"Hello, Clarissa."

Clarissa might have cried hearing Savannah's voice come back from the dead, how many years had it been, twenty?

Clarissa sighed. "I think it is about time we got together, Savannah. There's a lot to say. I need to talk to you, about Chloe, about her baby, about Pleasant."

"Pleasant?"

"That's her name now, the baby's name."

"I see."

"She's your granddaughter."

Savannah laughed, which Clarissa found odd. "Have you proof?" she finally asked.

"Yes, I do."

"Still meddling in my affairs."

Clarissa felt stung, what an odd thing for her to have said, she thought to herself. After all, it had been the other way around.

"Just be there when I get there because I'm not leaving until you show up."

~

Savannah no longer lived fifteen minutes away but forty minutes outside of Summerford. Clarissa had forgotten that Savannah had moved years earlier, probably to get farther away from her. Well, it had worked. As far as Clarissa knew, they'd never seen each other again. It was a very large world when one wanted to disappear.

Clarissa had looked up Savannah's address and then programmed it into her GPS because she had no idea where it was. The directions led her onto roads that were endless winding pathways filled with enchanting farmhouses that were half hidden behind towering trees and flowering bushes, looking intoxicatingly gorgeous. After forty minutes of driving on roads that were nearly a monotony of beauty, the little flag on her GPS finally appeared and the anomalous technology announced her arrival on the right.

Savannah now lived in an understated but still regal yellow Victorian farmhouse with sweeping vista views of valleys and farmlands. It was fitting for Savannah, a perfect retreat and Clarissa imagined her walking the property with her walking stick, the way she used to do as a younger woman. "A walking stick gives me so much character, don't you think?" she'd say.

Clarissa smiled as she got out of the car, the young woman that was once her friend had died a slow death. Clarissa had come for Pleasant's sake and Chloe's sake, not Savannah's. Pleasant would want to know she had a grandmother, now that her father might be put on trial for the murder of her biological mother. Clarissa shuddered, she hated herself for bringing this all up, for subjecting a young woman to such painful and disturbing news.

She almost ran away, turned around and drove off, never to be seen or heard from again but before her legs could reverse themselves Savannah was there, standing before her, speaking her name.

"Wish I could say it was good to see you," Clarissa said as two large beautiful blonde Labrador Retrievers wagged their tails around her.

Savannah did not smile, though Clarissa had been sure she would. Savannah had always smiled after an insult. Now she saw the expression that drifted across her face like a large adumbration that had appeared to diffuse the light.

"Please come in," she said.

Clarissa followed Savannah through to the sun porch where coffee and scones had been placed on a table brightened by yellow place mats and apricot cloth napkins.

"I thought you might be hungry, "Savannah said, sitting in the chair that faced out over the road and the sweeping trees that graced the porch with their long, wistful branches. "I know I am."

Clarissa thought the house looked beautiful though Savannah had not offered to show it to her, as she would have in the old days. She'd have taken her hand and led her into every room and pointed out every nook and cranny. Well, Clarissa thought, perhaps she would show her the house after she finished her scone, had a cup of coffee or two, asked to be forgiven for stealing Dennis, and thanked her for discovering her granddaughter long thought dead.

"So what's new, Clarissa?" Savannah said. Clarissa sensed her sarcasm. She poured the coffee from a silver pot that had kept it hot and steaming.

"I have cream. I remembered how much you like cream in your coffee." Savannah smiled, the charming, southern mask that shielded whatever the hell she was really thinking.

"I'll be brief," Clarissa said staring at the still beautiful woman, with her mostly grey but thick hair that framed her face in a stylish cut. She wore jeans and a simple shirt. She looked as if she hadn't gained a pound in the last fifteen years.

"You look good," Clarissa said.

"For my age?"

"Yes, for your age."

They sat in silence staring at the trees and the road

that had a poetic curve, like stanzas leading off in playful rhyme, ending somewhere magical, ending at a place where all feeling was caught up in rhythm and nonliteral language.

"Where does the road go?" Clarissa asked.

"Nowhere." Savannah took a sip of her coffee. "And what is your opinion of this…Pleasant?"

Without turning to Savannah Clarissa answered. "I like her, she's so much like Chloe."

"And she came into your life on a cloud, I imagine? In one of your images, taps or whatever you call it?"

"Not quite. She ran me over on a bike in Hollow Creek."

"Ran you over?"

"Yes."

"And because you have this gift, this psychic gift of yours, you knew without a doubt that she was my granddaughter?"

Clarissa turned to stare at Savannah, she was being factious, of course. "Without a doubt."

"I have doubts."

"I imagine you do but you wouldn't if you saw her."

Savannah picked up a scone. She picked off the blueberries one by one and ate them.

"Maybe we should let sleeping dogs lie."

"She doesn't know anything."

"All the more reason to let sleeping dogs lie, I'd say."

"Her father is about to be charged with the murder of a woman she doesn't know was her biological mother. So it's all going to come out. That child is going to be very hurt, very confused. In many ways I feel terrible about this, exposing that girl to the truth, but I don't believe the correct man was charged with Chloe's murder and I can't sit by and not do anything about it. I can't imagine you're not as angry as I am."

Savannah looked as if she'd been shot with a laser gun. "Just who have you spoken to, Clarissa?"

"A friend of mine, a retired detective. He's helping me. Feeling the way I do I have to do something, find closure somehow. I'm sorry about Pleasant but for god's sake, Savannah, Chloe's murder was never solved."

Clarissa noticed that Savannah's expression was almost frightening and now she appeared quite furious. "Feeling the way you do? You don't really know anything, do you? You just feel."

"What I feel is all I know."

"And now Graham Day is to be charged with killing my daughter?"

Clarissa was startled and sat back. "How did you know it was Graham? You knew about Chloe and Graham?"

"Yes, I knew about them, and he didn't kill her."

"He took the child."

"Really?"

"He took her and raised her. She is over in Hollow Creek as we speak and she looks exactly like her mother."

Savannah sipped her coffee. She appeared to be deep in thought.

"If he's charged he's going to need a very good lawyer. I imagine this is all your fault, yours and that detective friend of yours. Just how many lives are you going to ruin?"

"Savannah," Clarissa said, ignoring her comment. "Did you know that Chloe was molested as a child?"

By the look on Savannah's face, Clarissa had her answer. She turned to face Savannah head on for the first time. "You did know, didn't you?" she said. "Please tell me I'm wrong."

"Is this what you feel? Is this one of your taps, or

what you know?"

Clarissa ignored her comment. "She never told me about it. I just found out. Graham knew, and now it seems you did as well."

"Children fabricate these things all the time."

Clarissa could tell, could deeply feel the rage inside Savannah, the rage that had begun to boil and bubble.

"Blake molested your daughter," she said slowly.

She met Savannah's gaze, it was as if the bubble had reached its point of eruption and Savannah could not control her emotions anymore. The cup in her hand shook as she brought it to her lips.

"You think Blake killed her, is that it, Clarissa?"

"I don't know what to think, Savannah."

"It's all too late. It's too late to do anything about anything. Leave the girl in peace. Go away and stop interfering in everything. Just get lost, Clarissa." Savannah voice was soft, but Clarissa knew she wanted to scream.

"Get lost? Chloe was your daughter and I'm the only one that gives a damn that her murder was never solved?"

"It was solved." Savannah got to her feet. "You've said what you wanted to say, now I think it's time you left."

Clarissa stared at her in disbelief. "How many elephants are there in the room, Savannah? Chloe? Pleasant? Blake? Dennis? You want to ignore them all, shoo them all away?"

"None of them matter anymore."

Clarissa walked up close to Savannah. "What happened to you? Or were you always this shallow and I never saw it? Maybe no one matters to you. Maybe you are just a cold hearted bitch without any feelings for anyone, and the only thing that has any value to you at all is your own ego and what lengths you'll go too to protect it."

"Get out of my life, Clarissa. Stop meddling in my affairs."

"As if you didn't meddle in mine? As if you didn't screw up my marriage?"

The two women confronted each other, their faces red with anger. Clarissa finally turned on her heels and walked out. Her hands shook so much she could barely get the key in the ignition. Finally, she started her car and drove off. The tears started when she got to the end of the drive and she had to pull over and have herself a good cry.

This isn't worth it. That damn woman was never worth it.

Chapter Fifteen
Pleasant Day

Bodean had met up with some men his father knew and they took him out to the farm fields over by Thistle Down Road to search for John Peter. Angus said he knew where John Peter would hide up on Piper Hill. Lucky for John Peter Angus was too excited to think clearly so he was up there with the sheriff's men acting like he knew what he was talking about. Either that or he was too afraid to turn John Peter in for breaking and entering 'cause I knew exactly where John Peter was, if he wasn't dead. I didn't even want to think about that, but I knew it was a possibility. I was praying for John Peter's life the whole time I was pretending to search. I finally made up some lame excuse and said I had to get home. I knew that if John Peter was still alive, those people weren't ever going to find him. They didn't know where to look, but I did. Angus knew too but I was hoping he was too caught up in acting important up on Piper Hill and wouldn't remember all those getting out of the rain refuges we'd found in old houses for sale, sometimes even new ones, which we really liked best 'cause they barely smelled bad.

There was this little old house, been on the market

for sale nearly three years. We'd sure spent a lot of time there. The brokers who showed it were careless, left the door open or the windows ajar but it wouldn't have mattered if they'd been more conscientious, we could always get in, the key was always in the flower pot on the porch. Those brokers didn't hardly show it at all though, not anymore. And even if they did, John Peter could hear their cars coming up the drive and he could hide until they left.

It was a sorry little old house. The paint was peeling all over the place and the kitchen was a hundred years old. Those dumb brokers used to say that the kitchen was a charming original and should never be renovated, that you couldn't buy that kind of charm. We heard the things they used to say while we were upstairs hiding in the room we'd lock from the inside so they couldn't get in. They'd call the place a handyman's special, a showplace just waiting for the love and attention of the right buyer. Lucky for John Peter the right buyer hadn't been born yet.

I breathed a sigh of relief when I realized he was there. I came in through the back yard, hoping he wouldn't see me or hear me 'cause he could hightail into that room we used to lock, and I didn't want that. The day was hotter than a sauna room with one too many naked bodies sweating in a row. I noticed that all the windows were open and the front door was ajar. I guess he was choosing a breeze over the bugs he was letting in. I slipped inside quietly and spotted John Peter asleep on the floor. He had a knapsack by him that he was using as a pillow. I stood over him and kicked his legs, poor little bastard was so frightened he scurried across the room and hit his head on the wall.

"God damn it, Pleasant."

"What the hell are you doing, John Peter? The whole

town is expecting to find your dead body buried in mud. You are making a bad situation worse."

"I'm going to kill myself anyway, won't matter none."

"Not if I do you in first." I walked over to him and kicked him again. "Get up," I yelled.

"You don't understand, Pleasant. You don't understand anything."

"What don't I understand?"

"I can't tell you."

I bent down to his sorry body and put my hands on his collar and pulled him to me. "If you don't start talking to me, and I mean truthfully talking to me, I'm going to drown you in that old rusted sink, right in this house, in that shit hole of a kitchen that all those stupid brokers call charming."

John Peter started crying. "Okay, okay, Please. I need to tell someone anyway before I flip my lid."

"I'm listening."

"Ike did it, Pleasant." He looked up at me with so many tears in his eyes I could barely see the color. But I'm sure he saw the shock in my expression. "Ike strangled Millie. He got me to help him carry her and put her in the bag and then the box-spring." John Peter was crying so much he was gagging.

"Ike killed Millie?" I was reeling from the jolt of this news.

He nodded his head, his nose was running like a faucet.

"Why?"

"Ike jumped into the bedroom out of nowhere, scared the shit out of both of us. He started yelling and telling me I was useless and didn't know how to...to...."

"What? Screw a girl?"

He nodded his head. "He said he was going to show me how it was done and he pushed me out of the way and started coming toward Millie. She kept taking punches at him with that one arm of hers. That got him really mad."

"What the hell did you do, John Peter?"

"I didn't have time to do anything. She got away from him and ran downstairs. I heard him calling her a bitch. He was running behind her. He caught her right out front of the house and yanked her back in the yard. When I looked out the window I saw him beating the shit out of her. I didn't know what to do, I picked up the phone to call the police and then I decided not to, decided to run out back."

"Why the hell didn't you protect her?"

"I was going to, I was going to, that's why I ran out back but by the time I got there he had strangled her to death. She was gone. You know what a bully Ike is, how big he is. I don't even know if he meant to do it but it was done."

John Peter was bawling and hiccupping and drowning in his own snot. I was in shock. I couldn't believe it. I wanted to go find Ike and shoot him with my daddy's gun. I let John Peter cry himself out. I knew how badly messed up he was.

"Why did you put her in the box-spring?" I finally asked.

"Ike said we had to hide her, just get her out of the way, and he'd come by in the morning with his daddy's truck and we'd dump the body up near Fox Lake, in those woods up there. But he never came by and my mama found the body 'fore he could. Son of a bitch told me his daddy had taken the truck and it wasn't there when he got up."

John Peter began to cry again and I found myself holding his hand and putting my arms around him.

"So there never was any man at the door?"

"We concocted that story right after Mama found the body. We figured they'd blame the man and leave us alone. I couldn't let you think it was a woman 'cause we said it was a man. Ike wasn't supposed to tell you that he came in the house though. That idiot screwed up our story. I hate that son of a bitch."

"John Peter, you didn't kill Millie, Ike did. You've got to tell the police that."

"But I didn't help her. I wanted to help her but it happened so fast."

"You were confused, John Peter. I'm sure you were trying to help her in your own way."

"I was. I swear. I was going to call 911, but I ran out to get Ike off her first, and she was dead by the time I got back there. It happened so fast, so fast. The only thing he said to me was the stupidest thing, that I should be glad to be rid of her. He didn't even seem surprised or sorry that he'd killed her."

"He said that?"

"Yeah, and then he put his hand out to touch me and he said that we could be friends, me and him. I was so scared of him I fell back on my ass."

"I'm taking you to the police."

"Ike said he was going to kill my dog, my mama and then me if I told anyone."

"Sooner or later you've got to leave this house and go home. You can't live with this. Sooner or later you've got to get this off your chest."

"Not if you bring me food. I can hide out here. No one will find me, just bring me food."

I glared at him. "I am not bringing you food. You're leaving with me right now. You are going to tell the police what you told me and they will go get Ike so he can't hurt you."

"Can you promise me that, Pleasant? Ike said his

daddy had a rifle that would make a mess of me."

"I promise you, John Peter," and as I said it I was hoping that was one promise I could keep.

~'

They wouldn't let me stay with John Peter when we got to the police station. They told me to go on home and not to worry, that they'd take good care of him. I didn't know how they expected me not to worry, Ike was out there free and John Peter was probably going to be released 'cause he didn't do anything. And if Ike got word John Peter spilled his guts to the police, he'd shoot John Peter dead. So I decided not to say anything to anyone about John Peter being at the police station because I didn't want anything getting back to Ike. But before we walked up those steps to justice I told John Peter I was leaving it up to him to tell the police that Ike killed Millie and if he didn't turn Ike in, I was going to tell the police everything I knew.

~'

The search was called off and everyone was told that John Peter had been found safe and sound. They were all calling me a hero for discovering his whereabouts but I wasn't going to feel good or breathe any sighs of relief until I read in the papers that a seventeen-year-old boy named Ike Lewis had killed Millie Grady and was being put in jail for it. I felt in my gut that John Peter was going to do the right thing and turn Ike in. I think it was just eating him alive, keeping it all to himself. He couldn't spend the rest of his life with that buried up inside of him.

Daddy was out on the porch when I got back. I wanted to tell him all about it, that Ike had killed Millie, but I decided to keep my mouth shut unless or until I had to ask Daddy to give shelter to John Peter's dog and his mama 'cause Ike had threatened them.

"Where you been?" he asked.

"I was with the search party."

"Oh. They find your friend?"

"They did."

"Good, good."

"Where you going?" I asked, noticing that he was dressed up, which he only did when he visited Nana. Daddy never dressed up for Karlene McFaddy.

"I'm going to see Nana."

"You're not taking me?"

"Well, I have to talk to her about some important stuff."

"I don't care."

He looked at me long and hard and I put my lips in a pout. Nana would take my mind off everything, that was for sure. We could play Jeopardy for hours and hours, so I wouldn't have to think about what Ike did to Millie. I didn't want to remain home and sit on the porch by myself all day. That would make me crazy as a loon trying to sell me a calendar day.

"I don't want you to be bored while we talk."

"I don't care. You really weren't going to take me?" I gave him a hateful expression.

"Yes, Pleasant, I was going to, but you weren't here."

"Now, I am."

Daddy gave a resigned sigh. "All right, get in the car. Glad I waited that extra minute." I hate to say it but I heard a bit of sarcasm in that last remark.

~

I loved going to Nana's. She lived way out in the country, about an hour from us but I had been visiting her twice a month for as long as I could remember. She's another secret I have with Daddy that I don't tell Mama about. Daddy says it's because Nana and Mama hate each other and he never gives me more explanation that that. That's okay, I guess. He never tells me much about Karlene McFaddy either, so Nana is just another quirk of daddy's I just accept. Long time ago he and Nana told me to just think of her as my grandmother so that's what I do. I don't even know her real name, except from hearing Daddy call her Savannah, but you ask me her last name and I don't have a clue.

I can sometimes feel my daddy's moods, that's how connected we are. I knew he was worried about something 'cause he wasn't joking with me. He wasn't teasing me about Bodean or John Peter and he didn't make me dress up, the way he usually did when we visited Nana.

The story I got out of Daddy was that Nana was his friend and they went way back to his childhood in Summerford. I thought she was kind of uppity to be Daddy's friend but he used to say that friendship is a soul connection and has nothing to do with money or class.

Nana was the one that started me on loving literature from the time I could listen. She read me Wuthering Heights before I could read and I read her every Harry Potter book before I could lift a dictionary. I had to underline every word I didn't know and she'd tell me what every word meant and then I had to use the word in a sentence three times. I was about seven years old when we started teasing each other with jeopardy questions. I liked beating her so much at the game that I made sure I read everything out there so she couldn't trip me up. She did, every now and then, but I had to remember that Nana had been an English teacher like my friend, Clarissa, and knew more than I did.

Both Daddy and Nana used to say that Nana and I were such soul mates we had begun to look alike. That was okay with me. I could tell from old pictures that Nana had been a looker so I was proud of the resemblance, especially since I didn't look like anyone else.

~

Nana was distressed. I could see it in her expression, seemed to be in the same distracted mood as Daddy. She and Daddy hugged real tight when we first got there. It was like someone had died and they were consoling each other, and then I heard her telling him she was going to protect him. I guess they didn't think I could hear them because I was on the lawn playing with Nana's two dogs but I was listening hard. Why would Nana have to protect my daddy from anything? I wondered.

"And what are we reading now?" Nana asked as I jumped up on the porch and went to kiss her cheek. "Um, you smell like sweat," she said.

"Been on a search for John Peter."

"Who's that?"

"My friend, you remember? I brought him out here once."

"Oh, yes, sweet thing he was if I recall."

"Yes, he's sweet Ma'am."

"Well, I hope he was found?"

"Yeah."

"So?" she asked, handing me a book. "What are you reading?"

"The Time Travelers Wife," I said, looking at Daddy 'cause it had been the book he'd given me at Buck's but there was so much going on in my life I hadn't finished it.

I looked at the title she handed me. "The Art of Racing in the Rain?" I said. "I don't like racing, I won't like it."

Nana smiled. "Just trust me and read it. It comes with five stars in my opinion and you're going to love it."

At that point her two labs came up on the porch and jumped up on me. Nana laughed and went and sat in the white wicker rocker she loved, the one that creaked when she rocked. Always sounded good to me, those creaks. A country sound, just like cicadas and woodpeckers.

"Why don't you give my Button and Bo some exercise?" she said, tossing me a ball.

"Thought that's what I been doing. They wore me out."

"Go on now, Pleasant," Daddy said. "I have to talk to Nana."

"What about?"

"Now, go on and play with the dogs, like I said." Daddy looked at me stern and serious.

"But I'm tired of playing with them."

"Then go sit under the Oak tree and read a book." Daddy insisted.

I was pissed but I took my book out of my knapsack and sat under the tree. Nana and Daddy were into some real intense conversation but I couldn't hear a damn thing they were saying. Their heads were too close together, looked serious. They usually included me in whatever they were talking about, but I got the feeling they didn't want me around. I was always the center of attention at Nana's and Nana always fussed over me, but I could have been sitting there with Mama the way I was being ignored.

"She's a meddling old fool," I head Nana say. It seems they had forgotten themselves and were speaking up. Then they'd go back to whispering. They were frustrating the hell out of me.

Then Daddy said something real strange, "I'll have to tell Martha."

I thought he was going to give it up about Karlene McFaddy and I almost went running up on the porch with my advice to not do it. As I was about to get up, he said maybe it was too old to matter so I knew he wasn't talking about Karlene McFaddy.

They went on chatting and I got bits and pieces of what they were saying. I went on pretending to be reading but I couldn't concentrate. I felt something was off. When I raised my head up toward the porch, Nana waved but I went back to my book and ignored her. I wanted her to know I was pissed.

"Hope you have an appetite today," she called out to me.

We always had lunch when I went to visit Nana and so I was counting the hours till two 'cause Daddy had been right, I was bored being shut out of their conversation, which was probably some juicy gossip they weren't sharing with me. I expected them to stop their little conspiracy after lunch but I was wrong. Nana and Daddy finished their sandwiches in about ten minutes and went back into the house together. When I got up to join them Nana turned around and said, "Oh, no, Pleasant, homemade strawberry shortcake is on the way."

Well, when that strawberry shortcake came out onto the porch I have to admit, I didn't care where they'd gone.

I just had to sit out there for two helpings. When I finally went looking for Daddy and Nana I found that they had barricaded themselves behind the library doors.

I put my ear to the door and I overheard Nana saying she was going to get Daddy the best lawyer in the state. I assumed Daddy was in some tax trouble but I was still bothered by it. I was so bothered by it that on the way home I didn't even care that he'd know I'd been eavesdropping and I asked him what he'd need a lawyer for and he said just what I expected, "tax trouble."

"Why'd you and Nana go into the house and close the door behind you acting like you're heads of state at a summit?"

Daddy tried to smile, I could tell it was taking effort. "Nana said you were dressed like an inner city kid."

"I'm going to get a tattoo just to upset her. She pissed me off today."

"Told you we had to talk about something important."

"All damn day?"

Daddy laughed. "She'll disown you if you get a tattoo," he said and shook his head. "And so will I."

Well, I thought that was an odd thing to say. "How can she disown me? I'm not a relative."

Daddy reached over and held my hand. I got an uneasy feeling, not sure where it came from but it shut me up the whole rest of the ride home.

Chapter Sixteen

Clarissa Blackwell

Clarissa had another odd dream, similar to the dream in which the two headed man was stabbing Chloe so brutally. She was disturbed at how both dreams had not only been so violent, but so eerie. In her latest dream Chloe and Millie Grady were Siamese twins. They were trying to get away from each other but they couldn't. After Clarissa awoke at the ungodly hour of four a.m. she realized that maybe they weren't trying to get away from each other but from someone else, perhaps from the man who had killed them both.

Their murders have to be related. They must have been trying to get away from the same man, but could that really be possible?

Clarissa was outside the library doors the moment it opened and she was the first person inside. She knew that if she could find out how Chloe and Millie's murders were connected she'd have something to go to Dom with. She wished she could understand what her gut was trying to tell her but she couldn't get a handle on it. If she was being tapped, the taps were unclear, just riddles that angered her. She didn't want riddles she had to figure out, she wanted answers.

On microfiche, she found newspaper articles on Millie Grady, all about the car accident that had taken her mother from her and had cost her an arm. A fuzzy image of a little, brown haired girl stared back at her from the microfiche, a little girl with a haunted gaze. Clarissa stared at the photograph, it wasn't just about losing her arm, she realized, but there was something else that was terribly disturbing in the girl's expression. Clarissa felt herself falling into a trance. She went with it and closed her eyes. She held onto Millie Grady's image. As she did so, she felt such horrible distress. She also felt shame, tremendous shame. Clarissa realized that she may be staring at a child that might have been molested. But feeling someone else's trauma in her gut was no proof of it. Besides, she was so obsessed finding out about Chloe that it might be coloring everything she was feeling.

She read on, all about the murder. It was awful. Millie had fought back courageously but the killer had overpowered her. He had punched her several times in the face before he strangled her. She had angered whoever might have been trying to rape her, or simply just to hurt her. Again, Clarissa felt that Millie's murder was an act of rage.

She was merely going on instinct, feeling that Millie had been molested rather than knowing it. But, if she were right, and Millie had been violated as a child, then there was a connection between Millie and Chloe. But she needed proof, her feelings weren't going to mean anything to anybody else.

She began to gather her notes and put them away in her purse, but as she stood, she noticed one more article about Millie. The article was in a small community newspaper. She sat back down and started reading and as she did, her mouth dropped. There it was, just what she wanted to see. She was astonished to find exactly what she needed to tie the crimes together. In the very last paragraph she learned that Millie's father was the groundskeeper at Blake Rappaport's estate. He and his daughter lived in a cottage on Blake's land. Blake had given Mr. Grady a life estate and he and his daughter had lived there for years. Clarissa put the paper down. There it was. Chloe and Millie had been molested by the same man. Must have been. Child molesters don't have only one victim.

Clarissa needed to talk to Dom immediately. This information was critical. The distance to Dom's house was perfect for thinking it through. She could drive and sort her thoughts. She wondered how she could prove that Blake had killed both Millie and Chloe. Perhaps Millie was threatening to expose Blake as well? Clarissa knew that Graham had not killed Chloe. She knew that for sure. She also knew that Graham would be the one tried for it. She didn't want that. She had to convince Dom that Blake had murdered both Millie Grady and her goddaughter. She had to convince Dom to at least question Blake, to at least consider him as a suspect.

Dom did not look pleased to see Clarissa at his door. It only took a moment for her to understand why. Dom had a house guest, a pleasant looking middle aged women who was still at least twenty years younger than Clarissa. Clarissa stuttered at the door as she looked beyond Dom. This was an uncomfortable situation. The pretty blonde was lying on the couch in a rather suggestive robe sipping coffee from a mug and eating a croissant. She turned for a moment and stared at Clarissa. Clarissa quickly turned away.

"I'm so sorry. I didn't mean to disturb you. I didn't know you had company." Clarissa started back to her car. The other night she had to admit to herself that she was attracted to Dom. Now it must be obvious to him that she was jealous. She was acting too uncomfortable to be anything else. She felt Dom grab her arm.

"What is it, Clarissa?"

She blurted it out. She felt too awkward to present her findings in a dignified way.

"Blake Rappaport may have molested Millie Grady, the teenager that was murdered in Hollow Creek. We might just find a history of molestation."

He looked confused for a moment.

"Grady had a life estate at Blake's. Millie was raised there."

"I don't know what you're getting at. That's no proof of anything."

"There's a connection, Dom. He knew both girls. We know he molested Chloe. We know he molests little girls."

Dom shook his head. "No, we don't know that. We only have Graham's word and Graham is presently being investigated for Chloe's murder. There's no proof that Blake Rappaport molested anyone."

Clarissa felt herself nearly slip to the ground. "Graham didn't do it."

"Remains to be seen."

Clarissa realized that Dom was standing in his driveway in a bathrobe. What in God's name had she interrupted, she wondered.

"I'm disturbing you. I'd better go."

It looked to her as if he didn't know what to say. He seemed embarrassed. She got behind the wheel of her car and drove off quickly. She hoped he would take what she had told him seriously. She'd speak to him about it again, after the pretty blonde went back to wherever she was from.

Clarissa was letting her thoughts lead her, right to Philip Wiley. She drove toward Hollow Creek but not to visit Pleasant. What she needed to know could only come from Philip, if he was sane enough to remember anything that would help her exonerate Graham. She really didn't know how she could look Pleasant in the eye, knowing it was all going to be good ole Clarissa's fault if her father was charged with Chloe's murder. It was also going to be good ole Clarissa's fault when Pleasant discovered she'd been stolen and switched for another baby and her mother wasn't really her mother.

Clarissa was pleased to see that Wiley was not on the road selling jelly, probably the approaching clouds were keeping him inside. It looked like rain, maybe even a storm. That would be enough to keep Pleasant home and Clarissa hoped her car would not be noticed. Pleasant would easily recognize it, a big bomb, Pleasant called it, like a fat black beetle that had too much to eat, or was pregnant. Clarissa pulled the Escalade as far up the drive as she could to get it out of sight.

The house was impeccable. She noticed that right away, as soon as Mrs. Wiley opened the door and Clarissa looked beyond her into bright, sunny rooms. There was a clean smell in the air, she assumed it came from Mrs. Wiley's baking. It was a fresh smell, like there was bread in the oven. Mrs. Wiley was one of those pleasantly plumb women with cherry red cheeks who wore her brown hair in a bun, pulled back tight from her face. She smiled a lot and appeared to have a clear soul, Clarissa thought, free of negative thoughts.

"I'll get Philip," she said. "Would you like coffee?"

Clarissa declined the coffee and sat in the small living room staring at the Wiley's art collection. It was impressive and Philip and his wife clearly supported local artists. Beautiful scenes of trees and fields hung on the wall in oil and watercolors. Clarissa felt serene in the pretty blue and white room. There wasn't a television in sight, nor a radio, but Philip read newspapers as far away as DC and New York. She spotted them neatly folded on a chair.

Philip kept her waiting a good fifteen minutes. When he finally walked into the living room he looked as if he were trying a case in court. He had an air of assurance, quite different than his roadside manner where he appeared a bit wacky, or to put it more kindly, eccentric. He wore a grey three piece suit, his hair was neatly combed and parted. He smelled sweet, as if he'd bathed with a wonderful verbena flower soap.

"You here for more jelly?" he said with a scowl. "My home is not a store."

"No, no. I don't want jelly, Mr. Wiley. Actually, I came to tell you that we do know each other. I realized it the other day."

"So what?"

She was a bit startled until she realized he was most likely senile and should be forgiven his rudeness.

"Remember, you said you never forget a face? Mine, to be specific."

"Randall Holmes." He pointed his finger in her face. "You knew him or something like that. Right? I remembered too, after you left."

"Yes, yes. Well, no, I didn't know him but he confessed to the murder of my goddaughter. I was at the trial every day. That's probably why I look familiar."

"Oh, probably. Good deduction. He can't hurt anyone anymore, can he?"

"I don't believe he killed her."

"Killed who?"

"My goddaughter."

He looked up in an odd way, as if she needed consolation. "And your goddaughter was?"

"Chloe Rappaport, do you remember?"

He thought for a moment. "Yes, yes, committed that one too."

"He confessed to it but I don't think he did it."

"So what? He's serving time for it, isn't he?"

Clarissa sat back. "Did he ever tell you he didn't do it?"

"Nope."

"Well, do you believe he did?"

"Never thought about it."

Clarissa decided she would take Mrs. Wiley up on the coffee. This was going to take time and she wasn't even sure what she wanted from Philip. The only thing that would help Graham was to prove that Blake had murdered the girls. Wiley wouldn't know whether he did or he didn't but he might be able to tell her why Randall would confess to a crime he didn't commit. Maybe Blake had pulled some strings, offered Randall a payoff if he confessed to killing Chloe. Maybe Randall couldn't use a payoff but his wife would be taken care of.

"What do you think of the murder of Millie Grady?" She blurted out. She had been served the coffee and had spent about fifteen minutes complementing the art in his living room. Mrs. Wiley had included a biscuit with homemade boysenberry jam. It was delicious. Clarissa could not stop licking her fingers.

"Who?" Philip asked.

"The young girl that was murdered here in Hollow Creek?"

"Oh, that. Yes, some pervert did it of course. Was she raped?"

Clarissa shook her head. "I don't think so."

"Well, if she wasn't, some jealous boyfriend did it."

Clarissa smiled. "Well, do you think some jealous boyfriend killed my Goddaughter?"

"Who was your Goddaughter?"

"Chloe Rappaport."

"Husband did it."

"He wasn't here. He couldn't have done it. He was in England at the time she was murdered."

"He was the only one with motive. She was having an affair, wasn't she?"

"How do you know that?"

"Good guess. Having affairs is what gets women murdered."

"Well, her husband didn't do it. Like I said, he was out of town."

"Could have been a killer for hire situation."

"I doubt it, he wasn't in a position to find someone to kill his wife. Besides, there was rage in the stabbing. It was very personal."

"Good deduction. Are you a lawyer?"

"No. Why did Randall confess to the murder of my goddaughter?"

"I advised him to."

"But he didn't do it."

Philip shrugged his shoulders. "Does it matter? He'll never get out of prison."

"But my goddaughter's murder has gone unpunished." She felt ready to cry.

"Husband did it. They always do."

"Do you think someone could have offered Randall money to confess?"

"What the hell would he need money for?"

"Well, money to take care of his wife, perhaps."

Philip laughed loudly. "He hated that woman. Might have chopped her head off if we hadn't caught him and put him away."

Clarissa sighed. She wasn't getting anywhere with Philip at all. "Will you get him to retract his confession so the right man can be found?"

Philip started at her. "Let sleeping dogs lie."

"I'm getting sick of that advice."

"Then be done with it. Take it."

"But you advised him to admit to a murder he didn't commit."

"He did commit it."

"You just said the husband did it. You don't believe Randall did it either."

"Randall wanted leniency. He wanted an insanity verdict, wasn't going to get it so he made a deal. He confessed everything and the body of every woman he had murdered was found and the families were given closure. It's a gift, closure." He stared at Clarissa. "He wanted to give you closure, that's all. Should thank him."

She felt so angry she could have hit the old man."He didn't kill Chloe Rappaport. I've got to know who did."

"So who are you, an elder Nancy Drew?" He started laughing again.

Clarissa stood up slowly. It took all her effort not to take a punch at him. "Well, thank you for your time but you really haven't helped me."

"I sure as hell did, Ms. Drew. The husband did it."

Chapter Seventeen
Pleasant Day

I kept looking for news, kept hoping I'd read in the paper that Ike had been arrested for Millie's murder but there wasn't one damn word about anything anywhere. I was beginning to think that neither Ike nor John Peter told the police a damn thing and I'd have to be the one to see justice done. I'd given John Peter all the space I was going to give him and all the time he deserved. He wasn't calling me and he wasn't coming by. Every time I went to his house his Mama told me he was out and she wasn't saying where. I was getting the feeling he was avoiding me.

I was up on Piper Hill making up my mind to go camp out on John Peter's doorstep till he showed up. I couldn't believe that Ike had not been arrested for Millie's murder yet. I was deep in my thoughts when Angus appeared out of nowhere. He plopped beside me. I was not happy to see him, I didn't need Angus saying stupid things to me like he usually did.

Angus stared at me a good long while before he spoke. I just looked off but I knew he was staring at me. My peripheral vision was capturing his every expression which was fraught with confusion. I knew what about, of course.

"I can date whomever I want," I finally said.

"What do you see in him? He's a brute."

"I don't know what I see in him."

That seemed to piss him off. He jumped up. "You don't know what you see in him? You're supposed to know, Pleasant. You can't date anyone without knowing why you're dating him."

"A cannon went off between us," I said.

He looked more confused than ever. "A cannon went off between you? Huh? Well, then I guess one of you would be dead, wouldn't that be the case?"

I felt myself getting uncomfortable, having to explain anything to Angus at all. "You don't have a poetic nature," I said. "You do not get metaphors. That cannon is not an aggressive weapon, it denotes an explosion, the kind of thing that happens when people fall in love."

"Oh, really, well you know what it denotes to me, Pleasant?"

"What"

"A goddamn phallic symbol having itself a good ole time."

I stared at him in disbelief. "You are crude, Angus."

"You look at me but you don't see who I am."

"Who are you, Angus?"

"I'm a poet, that's who."

"Then give me some poetry."

"Okay." He sat right in front of me and stared in my face. "Roses are red, violets are blue. Both beautiful and you are too."

"Well, you can rhyme, Angus but you're not very original."

"I know how to kiss, too, same as Bodean. No girl in this county I'd rather kiss than you."

I guess I felt a little shocked. I stared back at him in

disbelief. I didn't quite know how to take this.

"You want a black eye?"

"I just gave you a compliment. Damn it, Pleasant, don't you know how I feel?"

"You really think I'm beautiful?"

"Yep, like starlight and rainbows."

"What are you saying, that I'm the one giving you wet dreams at night, Angus?"

"Talk about crude." He gave me a fierce scowl. "You leave me feeling like a balloon about to be pricked with a pin. I'm a glutton for punishment. I must be, to keep hanging out with you."

"I think I get it. You're jealous of Bodean."

"Damn right."

I was a bit unhinged. I never thought Angus had a romantic bone in his body. "All right, if you don't mess this up I'll consider going to the movies with you." I got to my feet. "Ready?" I figured going to the movies with Angus would be just like old times. We always went to the movies. It didn't mean I was going steady with him.

His whole face brightened up. "Try me." He stood up and faced me. His arms were crossed over his chest and for the first time since I'd known him he appeared to have an air of mystery about him, like who ever guessed he had an inner life? Who would have ever known that while he was looking at me, and saying stupid things, he wanted to kiss me and I'll bet he did.

"All right, Category, famous Williams. This is easy Angus, don't screw up. A master Elizabethan dramatist was he."

"Aw, Pleasant, how am I supposed to know that?"

"Come on, Angus, this is so easy."

"I'm not up on any of that stuff."

I started humming the Jeopardy music while Angus looked as if he'd eaten too many pickles at lunch and was about to puke.

"Come on, Angus. If you don't know this you got brains in your back pocket but not in your head."

I never saw him look so furious. His face turned all different colors.

"I'll give you a hint. 'Parting is such sweet sorrow that I shall say goodnight till it be morrow.'"

"Ah….."

"Shit, Angus. Ro, ro, ro," I said quietly, "me o and?"

"Wait, I got it, I got it. Romeo and Juliet. Who is William Shakespeare?"

"Won yourself a movie date, Angus." I grinned at him.

"We always go to the movies together, Pleasant, but this will be different, I'll get to hold your hand."

"We'll see."

"Damn it, Pleasant. You can't go out with Bodean anymore."

"Why not? I'm not beholden to any boy."

"Well, because you're the sunset that soothes my soul. When I look at you I hear country music that makes me weep. Damn it, Pleasant. I love you. I'll punch Bodean's lights out if I ever see the two of you together again."

I was speechless. I stared at him in disbelief.

"You have pierced an arrow into my heart. Bodean will never, ever feel for you as deeply as I do. He probably just wants to get laid."

I watched him walk off. I didn't like the way his Mama did his hair and I didn't like the dirt on his jeans but I sure did like the things he said. Angus had the soul of a romantic. Angus had a way with words. Maybe I ought to be looking at him in a whole new way, I thought.

It had been exactly three whole days since I had escorted John Peter to the police station, three whole days since he'd been pulling a disappearance act on me. I thought for sure it was going to be headline news that Ike was arrested for Millie's murder but zero, zilch on that. I dropped Fredo on back home after running with him on Piper Hill and went in hot pursuit of John Peter. I had to look all over town for that boy, but I finally found him at the high school where he was playing chess with Jimmy Downey. There he was, staring at the chess board like it was sending him messages from the dead. Jimmy sat opposite with his brow creased so much he looked like an old man. I always thought that chess was like yoga but instead of straining the body, it strained the mind, but Daddy said both took lots of concentration and effort. I didn't think either one was a whole hell of a lot of fun though.

"Get lost, Pleasant," John Peter said.

"You want me to get lost, John Peter, 'cause if you really do then I'm going to get lost behind a megaphone on top of Piper Hill and you know what I'm going to be yelling into that megaphone?"

He gave me a dirty look and moved his black rook toward Jimmy's white knight.

"What are you going to be saying?" Jimmy asked me.

"Checkmate," John Peter said loudly.

"You're a distraction," Jimmy said to me.

I grabbed John Peter's hand and pulled him back behind a building. "Don't touch that board," he yelled out to Jimmy.

"Why haven't you come by to let me know what the hell is going on?" I was fuming and he knew it.

"Nothing is going on. I told them everything and as far as I know they went over and talked to Ike."

"That's it?"

"Yeah."

"What did they do to you?"

"They told me they'd be back in touch, that's all."

"You still scared of Ike?"

"I can't live my life scared of Ike."

"Well, I'm happy to hear you say that."

He stared at me for a long while. "I'm sorry," he finally said. "About Millie. I'm so sorry."

"I think her death was an accident. I think Ike was really pissed off that she was punching him and fighting back, but maybe he was jealous of her."

He looked at me a moment, like he was trying to figure out what I meant. His expression told me when he had gotten it, when he knew exactly what I had meant.

"Ah, don't go saying that, Pleasant, I don't want to know anything about that."

"He had a thing for you. He probably hated Millie."

John Peter made a face. "Don't you ever tell anyone that he had a thing for me. Yuk."

"The police believe you had nothing to do with it?"

"I don't know. I told them I was there but I couldn't prevent it. You know cops, they were looking at me with their stone faces like I was Attila the Hun. They could see I didn't have any scratches on me. Ike told the police that coming down from the tree scratched him up, and after that, Bodean beat him up, but I heard they were going to check DNA so I don't know if they believed him or not."

"That'll cinch it, but checking DNA takes time I hear."

"Yeah."

"Look, don't worry none." I put my arms around him and hugged him.

"I'm going back to my chess game, Pleasant. It's the only thing that takes my mind off all this."

I glared at him, his mind shouldn't be anywhere else but on Millie's murder, but maybe he did need a reprisal, maybe we all did, and who was I to force him into feeling miserable?

But feeling miserable was about to swoop me up in its mighty arms and drop me on my head. I thought the worst day of my life was the day I heard Millie had died but it wasn't. I was living the worst day of my life and didn't know it, not yet, but soon enough. I could feel the darkness drifting over me and falling down, covering me in black ash, cutting off my air. I was about to die, the writing was on the wall. It was my epitaph I was about to read.

After I left John Peter I spent the afternoon alone up on Piper Hill finishing The Time Travelers Wife. I was planning on doing a book report on it when I got back to school. The house was empty when I got home. All except for Fredo, that is. He had gotten into Daddy and Mama's bedroom and was beating up on Handsome Howdy. When I walked into their room I could see that poor Howdy was about to lose a leg. I went over to save the poor dummy's life and I noticed that the closet door was opened. Mama never leaves the closet door open 'cause Fredo would eat all her shoes if she did. The closet felt half full. It wasn't like I was seeing it was half full, I was feeling the emptiness. When I turned to look, I realized that all of Mama's clothes were gone. I was staring into something that shouldn't look the way it did.

One of us was absent. I felt a strange sense of vertigo and I didn't know if Mama had disappeared or if she'd ever really been there. I ran over to her dresser and opened the drawers, throwing them to the floor. I found nothing but dust and old buttons and ribbons that had faded from years of not being used, from years of not enhancing anything or tying anything together.

Maybe that's why my dog was having a temper tantrum, Mama had left us. I was confused. If she'd died then why hadn't they told me? Why had they erased her out of my life so quickly? I sat at the edge of the bed and stared into space. That's when I noticed the bag, this little old purple cloth bag that Fredo had pulled out from under the bed. He'd been looking for Howdy, I guess, but I had kicked Howdy under a chair, not under the bed. Fredo finally found Howdy and sat there licking his face, staring up at me and daring me to come take Howdy away. But this would be no time for games. This time had higher stakes.

I had never seen that purple bag before. Mama must have hidden it from me, maybe from Daddy too. She'd left it behind, maybe on purpose, maybe not. I picked it up and put it on my lap. I guess I shouldn't have looked inside. It wasn't mine, it was Mama's. It contained Mama's secrets, Mama's dark secrets. I opened the bag, not knowing at first what I was seeing, but too soon I found the stranger I was, the absence I had become.

I pulled out a pink baby jumpsuit. It had certainly not belonged to Sawyer. It was mine, I assumed, must have been. Mama had saved it, I thought. That meant she loved me. I pulled out baby rattles and old dolls that I didn't remember playing with. It filled me with such sadness that Mama had loved me so much that she'd saved all my baby things and now she was gone, and couldn't ever tell me. I needed to hear her tell me that she loved me. I'd needed to hear her say that all my life. I'd never heard her tell me that. I pulled out old photographs, my eyes so filled with tears I could barely see. Had I really been that cute and chubby? I wiped my eyes until they were clear. I looked older than Sawyer. Sawyer was an infant, and there I was, held in Daddy's arms, big as a three year old.

It couldn't be, I told myself. Who was that child? Did I exist and only think myself to be the age I was? My hair was different, it was lighter. I was younger than my brother, not older. Who the hell was this imposter? I looked past the old clothes and the baby toys and pulled out a picture of Daddy with a young pretty woman. Mama was pretty but not that pretty. Someone had drawn a big x across it. Maybe it was Mama that done that. Maybe it was Daddy, and maybe I'd never know. On the back it said, Chloe and Graham, 1994.

I didn't remember right away, maybe it was a day later, maybe an hour, but it came to me. The day that Daddy had told me about the girl who died, the one he'd been a bully to. Chloe, the sad story, the name that made his forehead crease.

But that wasn't the only sad story. No, I was the other sad story. I had died, or had never been born. So I've dreamed my life. My death is a fog though. Guess I'm not ready for heaven. I must be in-between. I must be somewhere near where Millie is. I just can't see her yet.

Mama had saved a newspaper article, too. Pleasant Day had drowned in the family pool. I read the article through to the end, what a tragedy, little girl drowning like that. I don't remember that pool but must have been there if I'd drowned in it. I fell into the deep green water and no one had noticed until it was too late. Maybe that's why Mama is distant. I'm dead to her.

~'

Sawyer found me still sitting on the edge of Mama and Daddy's bed. He looked at the bed, then he sat beside me and took the bag from me. He picked up the newspaper article and read it.

"Are we both dead?" I asked him.

He didn't answer me. He took my hand and held it.

"I don't have much memory of her," he said. "But babies remember things. It's like a sense memory to me, that's all. Talk of an accident that made no sense, words that still ring in my ear."

"What accident?"

"Mama and Daddy had a baby. She was bigger than me, older than me. She fell in the pool and drowned, just like that article says. Mama was attending to me, maybe I caused it."

"Mama and Daddy had a girl baby that wasn't me?"

He nodded his head and the two of us just sat there staring out at the wall.

"Why was she named Pleasant?" I finally asked.

"I think, little sister, that the more appropriate question is why were you named Pleasant?"

"Why?"

"I don't know."

"She died?"

"Yeah. Next thing I knew there was another baby, younger than me. You."

"I'm not dead then?"

"No."

I wished I could have breathed a sigh of relief but I couldn't. "Where is Mama?"

"She went up to Sumter to be with Aunt Lou."

"Why?"

He turned and faced me. "I overheard them arguing. Mama kept accusing Daddy of cheating on her, said she couldn't take it anymore. Said he'd been doing it all their married life and she couldn't take it. She accused him of not loving her, never loving her. She accused him of never getting over some woman that died."

"How'd she find out about Karlene McFaddy?"

"It wasn't about Karlene McFaddy. It was about some woman he knew years ago that died. There were some men came by, police, I think, but they weren't wearing uniforms," he said. "They wanted to talk to Daddy so Mama and I had to leave the room."

"Why would they want to talk to him?"

"About that woman he knew. Mama seemed to freak out after they left, said Chloe's frigging ghost had never left and was never going to."

"Mama always knew about Chloe. Why should it freak her out?"

"I don't know."

I reached in the bag and pulled out the photograph of Daddy and Chloe. I handed it to him.

"He dated her before Mama and Daddy married, I would guess."

He ran his fingers over the photograph where the x was, then he looked back and studied my face. I couldn't tell what he was thinking.

"Look, it will be all right," he said.

But I wasn't so sure it would be. It was a feeling I had, like a fork in the road had been reached, but both roads led nowhere so I might as well take either one. I mean, it didn't matter.

Nothing mattered.

Chapter Eighteen
Clarissa Blackwell

Clarissa almost spilled the coffee on her Persian rug. The news was so jarring that the cup nearly slipped from her hand. There it was in black and white. Clarissa brought the paper closer to her face and read the article again. Ike had given the police a name, Blake Rappaport. Blake Rappaport was now under suspicion for the murder of Millie Grady and he was being questioned in the fifteen year old murder of Chloe Rappaport.

Clarissa was astonished. That meant that Blake Rappaport must have been the man who had come to John Peter's door that day, the man Pleasant had told her about. Apparently, John Peter had done the right thing and had told the police that his friend Ike was in the tree outside the window and he saw what happened, saw someone come to the door and murder Millie. Ike must have been able to give them Blake's name. But as Clarissa read further she learned that Millie had confessed to John Peter that Blake Rappaport had molested her when she was a child because he needed to know why she wasn't a virgin, being her boyfriend and all.

Clarissa wished she felt a sense of relief, but she didn't. She felt unsettled, as if something was amiss. John Peter would have recognized Blake right away. Why didn't he tell the police right away that Blake had come to the door? Well, maybe he was afraid of him. Still, Clarissa felt as if things weren't adding up. Why would Blake be stupid enough to strangle a teenage girl to death in broad daylight?

When Clarissa was about to have a vision she had to sit in the most comfortable chair available. It was as if the vision was about to pull her down. Her eyes had to be closed and she needed absolute quiet. There was always a bit of a warning that she was about to see something in her mind's eye that was psychic and clairvoyant because she'd feel faint. Clarissa began to feel the warning, the weakness in her knees and the queasiness in her stomach.

She made her way to the reading chair with its plush cushions and muted colors. She closed her eyes and as she did so, the vision slowly materialized. As she stared into it the vision became more and more clear, like fog slowly lifting. She kept her eyes closed and after only a second, she saw Millie on the ground, so frightened. She was trying to get away from something or someone. She heard boys laughing in the background. They were laughing at Millie and pulling on a red scarf. They were pulling tightly and Millie kept trying to scream for them to stop.

Clarissa called Dom, but not right away. She wanted to think about what she had read in the paper and what she had seen in her head.

She should be happy, she had connected the two dots between the two murders. Blake Rappaport had known both girls and had molested both girls. But had he killed both girls? Was the right man really going to be indicted? Instead of feeling good about it, Clarissa gave way to her instinct and the vision that had come to her, Blake was not responsible, at least not for Millie's murder. All the pieces only seemed to fit together but they really didn't. She kept her eyes closed and the vision reappeared. It was like watching a movie flit across her brain. In the images, Millie was on the ground, but she was stuck and she kept trying to get away, and the boys kept laughing.

~

"Good morning, Dominic," she said.

"How do I know you're smiling?" He took a sip of something, most likely his morning coffee.

"I wish I could feel good about this but I don't, not altogether. Dom, something is not right about it."

"What's that? You're the one told me that Blake was the killer. You change your mind?"

"Well, I didn't say that in so many words, did I? I mean, I'm not sure now that he's the killer."

"Clarissa, I don't understand you."

"Listen, Dom, John Peter told Pleasant that he didn't know the man that came to the door. Why would he say that, wouldn't he want the killer apprehended? But Ike recognized him weeks later, under questioning? Blake Rappaport is well known. His picture is all over the news. He's a big mouth, a loud southern politician who wants to ride every liberal into hell. It's impossible that they wouldn't have known him."

"Ike told the police that it was Blake Rappaport that came to the door. So he did recognize him."

"But not right away. Why the hell didn't the boys tell the police who they saw right away? Ike could have gotten that information about Blake from John Peter afterwards because they needed to take the attention off themselves, so they concocted a lie. How perfect, blame the murder on her molester. They could have come up with the idea to frame Blake days after the murder. They needed to save themselves, they were desperate. Blake was the perfect scape-goat, he had harmed Millie when she was a child. Listen, why didn't John Peter tell the police that he saw Blake at the door? It doesn't make any sense to me at all that Ike would be the one to tell them way after the fact. And why would Blake be so obvious about it? Why would Blake murder a girl and then stuff her into the boy's box-spring? That's something kids might do, not a man in his right mind. I don't believe these kids, they're lying."

"I don't get it, why would they frame Blake Rappaport for the murder if he wasn't the one that came to the kid's house?"

"Because they did it and they're scared and they needed a scape-goat. I don't think anyone came to the door."

"I disagree, Clarissa. The boy was awfully scratched up from jumping out of a tree. When the police first saw those scratches they thought for sure they'd solved this crime. But Ike was frightened and he kind of scurried down, got cut up. Then he was beaten up by this kid named Bodean Frasier. We can't tie his scratches to Millie. There wasn't much DNA under the girl's nails. It seems she punched and slapped whoever killed her. She didn't scratch him. Not sure they got any DNA at all. Even if they did it wouldn't prove anything substantial, the boys could have been hanging out with her before she got murdered. Maybe they were all fooling around and they're just trying to protect her reputation."

"Why? She's dead."

"Ike has mentioned sleeping with Millie as well. I

think they were both fooling with her that day."

"What about the other boy?"

"John Peter? Not a mark on him."

"Any finger prints on the scarf?"

"Yes, but the scarf was a mess, lots of fingerprints on it. If she was in John Peter's bedroom that day, both boys could have been in there with her and both of them could have touched the scarf."

"I think the police are overlooking something very important. Ike said he was in the tree, not in the room. Now you tell me his fingerprints are on the scarf?" Clarissa could feel her frustration level rising and she knew she was speaking loudly.

"The fingerprints are inconclusive."

"I've got no love for Blake but I'm not sure he's our killer. At least I don't think he killed Millie Grady. And Ike was in the tree, he wasn't hanging out with them at all, now he's changing his story? If he was just spying on them why would his fingerprints be on the scarf?"

"He said he was sleeping with Millie too, that she let all the boys sleep with her."

"Oh, come on. I can't believe this. Even if it were true, you expect me to believe she was wearing the same scarf when she fooled around with Ike?"

"Could have been."

"Look, they proved the murder weapon was a scarf and they've got both boy's fingerprints on it? Am I missing something here?"

"Yes, that's been confirmed, but it doesn't prove those boys murdered her. A defense attorney could have a field day with that."

"Look, Dom, could this have been an accident?"

"If it were an accident why would the boys come up with some ridiculous lie about a man coming to the door and killing her?"

"They were afraid. Maybe they felt they were going to hang for this. You know how kids are."

"No one has said anything about accidental death."

"By the way, how did the police know Blake molested Chloe? Was it Graham that told them?"

Clarissa head the doorbell ring just as Dom answered her.

"No, it wasn't Graham. I don't know who told them. Someone came down to the station and demanded to see the lead detective on Millie's case. I can find out who it was."

"Yes, I'd be curious to know."

"Well, Blake is denying ever molesting anyone, much less killing anyone. Of course that doesn't surprise me, his career is on the line. The papers got wind of this and now it's all over the news. There's a snitch down at the station that must have gotten a bundle for leaking Senator Rappaport's perverted fascination with children."

"Why would the police question Blake for Chloe's death? Is it official that they are re-opening the case now?"

"Well, Philip Wiley just recently told the police that Randall Holmes never committed Chloe's murder, so this bit of news about Blake is important. I meant to tell you that."

The news startled her. She must have made a much greater impression on Philip Wiley than she thought.

"Will wonders never cease?"

"What's that?"

Whoever was ringing the doorbell was now knocking on the glass.

"Just a minute," she called out. "Philip Wiley finally told the truth?"

Dom laughed. "Look, with the investigation of

Graham Day, and Wiley's admission, Chloe's murder is now being considered a cold, unsolved case. Strange bit of luck, this person coming forward and telling them about Blake being a child molester. He's a suspect now. Graham may be off the hook, despite the fact he took the baby. Problem is, we might not find anything tying Blake to the scene of either crime."

"Someone is at my door, Dom. We'll talk later."

"I'd like to come by. There's something I'd like to discuss with you."

"Sure, Dom. I'll be here."

Clarissa saw her face through the pane of the front window. There was Savannah, peering in and knocking the way she used to when Clarissa had not answered the door fast enough.

"Savannah?"

Clarissa stared at her as Savannah took off her hat and ran her fingers through her hair. She also took off her sunglasses. Clarissa had the thought that she was incognito and didn't want to be seen slumming around Summerford.

"You said that as if you really didn't think it was me."

"I wasn't questioning your identity. It was more like surprise, shock even."

"Yes, I would imagine I wasn't expected. Are you alone?"

"Yes, I'm alone. I was on the phone when you rang."

Savannah stared at the paper on the end table and walked into the living room without an invite.

"I see you've read the morning paper?"

"Yes, I know that Blake is being questioned for two murders."

"Nice house."

"Thank you, Savannah."

"I don't think my brother killed that teenage girl. Just thought I'd mention that. I don't think he killed either of them, actually."

"Neither do I, but you read the paper, apparently the girl confessed to John Peter that Blake Rappaport had molested her."

Savannah sighed and sat on Clarissa's sofa, again without an invite. Clarissa wondered what the hell she was doing there until it hit her, it must have been Savannah that told the police about Chloe and her uncle Blake.

"It was you then?" she asked. "You went to the police?"

"Strange coincidence," Savannah said. "I must have told the police about my brother the same time they discovered that my brother had molested that young girl that was murdered in Hollow Creek. To my surprise, they told me they were reinvestigating Chloe's death."

"Whatever possessed you to tell the police anything?"

"I did it to protect Graham, to protect my granddaughter's father, to protect someone very dear to me. I wanted them to take the attention off Graham and I wanted to give them someone else to suspect. I love that boy like a son and he didn't kill anyone."

"I know that."

"Yet you meddled in my affairs until you got him investigated?" The two women glared at each other like boxers in a ring about to take their first punch. "I didn't want Graham arrested, so I did what I should have done years ago. It wasn't easy to do, Blake is still my brother. I knew this little bit of information would ruin him. But when it comes down to it, he's despicable and I can't let myself care about Blake."

"You've always known about Pleasant, haven't you?"

"Yes, I've always known. I don't know what I would have done without her in my life. She's kept me going, she really has."

"I see."

Clarissa felt let down, she'd missed out on having a relationship with Pleasant all these years, but Savannah had not. Clarissa was angry that she hadn't been told that Pleasant was Savannah's grandchild, alive and well and living in Hollow Creek. But of course, she realized, how could she know, the two women hadn't been friends for years.

"I have to protect my relationship with Pleasant. I don't want to see her hurt. Unfortunately, I think it's inevitable."

Clarissa felt like a meddling fool, perhaps she'd had no business looking into anything. Chloe was not her daughter, she was Savannah's daughter, but then again, she thought, she owed it to someone she'd cared for. She'd loved Chloe as well. "You know what Chloe meant to me. I was only trying to....."

Savannah's features seemed to soften. Clarissa hadn't expected a positive response and was surprised by it.

"I know you loved her and I know what you were trying to do. I always appreciated how much you loved Chloe, like your own. I just wished you'd stayed out of it."

Clarissa didn't know what came over her but she began to cry. "I'm sorry, but can't you understand why I had to look into Chloe's murder? I know that Graham didn't kill our girl but I also know that Blake didn't. I thought he did, I really did, but I have a feeling now that he didn't, despite the connection between Chloe and Millie. I don't think he did it."

"How do you know that Blake didn't kill her, is it just

a feeling?"

"Yes. I know it as a certainty."

Savannah patted the seat beside her. "Sit by me."

Clarissa was surprised, but after she took a tissue out of her pocket to dry her eyes and blow her nose, she sat beside Savannah. After a moment or two, she felt Savannah's hand over hers.

"You always called Chloe our girl," Savannah said.

Clarissa felt the squeeze, felt Savannah's warm skin against her own. "That's what she was."

"There were a couple of other people that could have killed our girl, you know."

Clarissa turned to stare at her. "What other people?"

"A week before she was murdered Martha Day paid Chloe a visit. She was very angry and she threatened Chloe, said she'd shoot her if she didn't stay away from Graham."

"Chloe wasn't shot, Savannah, she was stabbed."

"I heard that she and Graham were about to reconcile right before Chloe was killed, that would have broken Chloe's heart."

"Really? Anyway, Martha didn't do it. I keep seeing a two headed man."

Savannah let go of her hand. "Well, Blake only has one head, doesn't't' he?" She laughed. "A two headed man?"

Clarissa got up and went to the window. She didn't like being made fun of but she decided to ignore it. "Blake's career will be ruined over this. One more politician bites the dust, can't say I'm sorry."

"My brother is a goddamn pervert. I'm not sorry for anything that happens to him. But this could all blow over, you know how it goes."

"Look, I don't think Blake killed anyone, not Chloe or Millie Grady. I hate Blake, but I don't think he did it."

"Well, there is another suspect but I'm not sure I want to tell you about that."

Clarissa turned to her. "I wish you would."

"Come back and sit beside me."

Clarissa did as Savannah asked and sat beside her. Savannah stared straight ahead and did not look at Clarissa as she spoke.

"Chloe had this night of truth about two months before she died. She decided to share a dirty little secret she'd been carrying around for years. She sat Dennis and I down in the living room and confessed that her Uncle Blake had molested her when she was a little girl. She told us she was going to go public with it, that he was a hypocrite and shouldn't be running for office, that he might harm other little girls and she had to prevent it. I was horrified. I wanted to kill Blake with my bare hands but I didn't want my daughter put in the lime light like that. I begged her to forget it and go on, that the universe would punish him enough. She told us that Graham was also begging her not to go public, he was afraid that Blake would retaliate in some way, maybe prevent her from getting a job anywhere in the state, Blake has a long reach. I promised to talk to my brother, to threaten to expose him. I said I would insist that he get help so he wouldn't hurt any more children. We all begged her to keep quiet and not bring a scandal to the family."

"A scandal to the family? He was a child molester."

Savannah turned to look at her. "I spoke to Blake. I told him that Chloe had told us everything. He denied it at first, but he knew I didn't believe him, I believed my daughter. I made him go into therapy and he did. He did go into therapy."

"Well, it didn't work, while he was sitting in a shrink's office he was molesting Millie Grady."

"I'm sorry about that," Savannah said softly. "If I had only known….."

Clarissa sighed and stood up. She returned to the window and looked out. "So who's the other suspect?"

"Dennis," Savannah said almost inaudibly.

"What?"

"He decided to blackmail Blake. The bastard saw opportunity."

"He didn't need money, he was married to you." Clarissa was puzzled, horrified.

"I was divorcing him, we had a prenuptial agreement. He wasn't going to get much, not nearly as much as he could get out of my brother. But aside from that, nothing was ever enough for Dennis."

"But how could he back himself up?"

"It wouldn't matter, Blake didn't want anything like that getting out. Besides, he was guilty. It there was talk it might have brought another victim forward. He wanted to just shut him up."

Clarissa sank into a chair. "Oh, my God."

"Dennis is a very convoluted man, he's diabolical. I swear, he doesn't have an ethical bone in his body."

"You married him."

"Well, so did you."

"I always thought he was so ordinary."

"He taught drama, he was good at pretending he was someone other than he was. Dennis always wanted what other people had, you know. I guess we were alike in that way."

"He blackmailed Blake?" Clarissa was still trying to digest it.

"Yes. I have no idea how much money Blake paid him to keep his mouth shut. Dennis and I divorced right after Chloe was killed. In all honesty, I didn't care about either one of them after that. I wanted both Blake and

Dennis out of my life entirely and I didn't speak to either one of them ever again."

"Why did you ever marry Dennis, Savannah?"

"I did you a favor."

"Care to explain that?"

"I don't mean to be glib. Look, Dennis had a little hobby aside from blackmailing. Did you know about that, Clarissa. Did you know what his hobby was?"

"No."

"Phone sex."

"What?"

"The man was obsessed with phone sex."

"I can't believe this, that's disgusting."

"It's true. I found his phone bill, found all the 800 numbers."

Clarissa turned away. She couldn't digest what she was hearing, it was absurd.

"You're telling me why you divorced him, not why you married him."

"He seduced me."

Clarissa glared at her. " I thought it was you who seduced him."

"I'm sure that's what he told you."

"Why didn't I know this?" she finally blurted out. "About his obsession with phone sex?"

"You married him pre mid life crisis?"

"A leopard doesn't change his spots."

"Maybe he didn't have a thing for it in those days."

Clarissa sighed. "What did I ever see in him?"

"He was handsome. I know what he saw in me, my money. I insisted on a pre-nup; he wasn't happy about it, believe me. He seduced me for my money. He envied the way I lived, you know he did."

"What the hell did he see in me then? I certainly wasn't rich."

"You were very naïve, very independent. And you did get him that job at the high school, didn't you? He's an opportunist, Clarissa. But aside from that, men were always attracted to you. You were like a young Eleanor Roosevelt, passionate and smart. Anyway, I'm not sure he was into phone sex back then. I told you, he had a midlife crisis. He lost his hair and gained weight, the man is a mess."

"The man was a teacher, for God sakes. He had no morals?"

Savannah raised an eyebrow. "Love is not only blind it's imbecilic. Don't be hard on yourself."

"So Dennis is a pervert too."

"Well, I don't know if I'd call it perverted, creepy for sure."

"Perverted for sure. And he's a blackmailer. I mean, how low can you sink?"

"He's going to have to retire from that. Blake is all over the news now. Dennis has nothing to blackmail Blake about, not anymore."

"You think Dennis is a killer?"

"I suspect him. He could have wanted to prevent Chloe from talking. If she did then he couldn't get anything out of Blake."

"Have you said anything to the police?"

"Not about that, no."

"Perhaps we should."

"Yes, we probably should."

"My head is spinning from all this."

Savannah looked up. "I'll never live long enough to forgive myself for what happened to Chloe."

"There was no way you could have known, unless she told you, and children are usually threatened into silence in some way."

"I meant her murder, but that too, of course."

"How could I have been so fooled about Dennis?" Clarissa whispered.

A silence lingered in the room for a long time. Clarissa felt so sad, felt the absence of Savannah though she sat across the room from her, her thoughts as heavy as an anchor. What had been, she felt, was never going to be again, the innocence and joy of their early friendship. The ugliness had colored it too much, there was too much darkness in the people around them. They were connected by all the wrong things.

Clarissa said, "I always thought we were stronger than we turned out to be. I thought our friendship was stronger than anything. You never spoke to me after Chloe's death, never answered my calls though I did reach out to you."

"I was ashamed, Clarissa. At first I was ashamed that I had an affair with Dennis and doubly ashamed when I married him. I knew we couldn't be friends after that. I'd hurt you too much. I don't know why I did that to you. I was young and flattered that Dennis found me attractive and I always admired you. If you had something or someone, I wanted what you had. Remember? That's just the way we were."

"Then after the divorce we could have connected, don't you think?"

"No, we couldn't have. I knew what Blake had done to Chloe and I was ashamed to face you, ashamed that I had not protected my daughter from that. I knew you'd blame me."

"I wouldn't have blamed you."

"But I blamed myself."

"All during Chloe's trial, you never once looked at me."

"I blamed myself for her murder, how could I look at you? I wanted to go to the police and tell them that

Blake had molested her, that Dennis was blackmailing Blake but I couldn't. I buried myself behind closed doors and turned my back on everything. Don't you know what a recluse I've been all these years? It's only been Pleasant that keeps me from jumping in the goddamn river with rocks in my pockets."

Clarissa smiled. "Still the drama queen, aren't you?"

"I put a lid on all of it. Case closed. As far as I was concerned someone was being punished for Chloe's death and that was enough for me."

"But you didn't think Randall did it either, did you?"

"Back then I did. I couldn't deal with any of it. I just wanted the closure."

"But you never got it."

"No."

"And now you think Dennis killed Chloe to keep himself in designer clothes?"

"Chloe was threatening to expose Blake. He couldn't have that, he couldn't extort any more money out of Blake if Chloe talked. He wanted to silence her. He had motive."

"I don't think Dennis is our man."

"Why not?"

"I've been tapped with other information."

Savannah smiled. "I have missed you so much. You and your taps. I hope you don't think I haven't."

"And I have missed you."

"The ashes of our mistakes are between us. There's still smoke from the fire, isn't there?"

"You know we can never be friends again, don't you?" Clarissa stared at Savannah a long time.

"Well," Savannah sighed as she got to her feet, "the good news is we usually make all our mistakes when we're young, the bad news is that they bury us when we're old."

"Oh, Savannah," Clarissa whispered as her friend walked out the door. "Oh, Savannah."

Chapter Nineteen
Pleasant Day

Daddy was the last person in the world I wanted to see. I guess Sawyer didn't want to see him either because he said he was going over to Augusta to get drunk. After I told him not to forget his fake ID he hugged me fiercely. I don't think either one of us wanted to talk about the photograph I had shown him or the remnants of memory sticking in his head about a sister other than me.

I hopped on my bike and peddled over to Summerford. If anyone was going to take my mind off of Daddy's sins it would be Clarissa. She was removed from my circus of ghosts. She would distract me from my heartache and maybe together we could find things to talk about other than the distance between Mama and me. Maybe I could just spend a few hours beating her at jeopardy.

Unfortunately, Clarissa looked like hell, like she'd had her own bad news. Her eyes looked swollen from too many tears and she seemed weighted down with the burden of distress. She tried to smile when she opened the door but I saw the effort it took to welcome me. I almost jumped back on my bike and rode off.

"Why, Pleasant, come in, come in."

I might have been just the medicine she needed for I noticed that her energy picked up a bit and she smiled a full set of teeth for me.

"I was just riding by," I said.

She cocked her head to one side, and raised an eyebrow, as if she read my lie clear as day.

"Glad you were."

Clarissa led me into her living room and I sat in the big overstuffed chair that welcomed me with pillows soft as a love song, and plush as a cloud would be if you could float away on it. She sat across from me on the couch. Looked to me like she was trying to clear her head and focus on me but I could see her thoughts running all over the place like little maniacal Mexican jumping beans.

"Is something wrong?" I asked.

"I could ask you the same. You been crying."

"You too."

"Well, anything you want to talk about?"

"No, you?"

"No, Pleasant."

I sat there sighing 'till I finally heard her say I must be proud of John Peter. Well, that perked me up. I hadn't heard a thing from John Peter about anything.

"What do you mean?"

"Well, he went to the police and told them about Ike, how Ike saw the murder and they identified the man that came to the door."

I didn't think I heard her right. "There wasn't any man that came to the door."

Now she looked like she wanted to get the wax out of her ears.

"Did I hear you right? You told me that John Peter told you a man had come to the door and Ike saw him murder Millie."

"What do the papers say?" I jumped up and grabbed the paper she had on the table.

"That both boys identified a man by the name of Blake Rappaport as the killer."

"Senator Rappaport?" I felt myself getting riled up like water in a pot over a high boil.

"Yes, that's who they identified."

"That's not the truth," I said. I was shocked and horrified at this bit of information. It meant that John Peter was still protecting Ike.

Clarissa watched me as I walked around the room.

"Do you know what the truth is because I don't think there was any man at the door either?"

"No, I don't know what the truth is," I said, lying and not knowing why.

"Ike said that Millie slept with a lot of boys."

"Horseshit is what that is." I couldn't believe my ears. "Ike is lying."

"Ike told the police that he had slept with Millie."

I felt the blood rush to my head and I thought I'd pass out but instead, I laughed. "Ike is gay, he has no interest in sleeping with any girl."

Clarissa stared at me for a while and I could tell she didn't want to go there, didn't want to get into Ike's sexual preferences. She asked me if I wanted a chicken sandwich kind of out of the blue. I think she was letting me off the hook. I was too furious for any kind of confession, I had to think this through. John Peter had not told the truth and I couldn't imagine why not. Why the hell hadn't he told the police that Ike committed the murder? And now Ike is lying and telling the police he slept with Millie? Why the hell would he say that? I couldn't believe this terrible web of deceit.

Clarissa knew I was thinking too hard to get my lips

to move because I just sat there with the chicken sandwich in front of me. I decided I needed to come clean because John Peter certainly wasn't. I had to get the truth off my chest before the weight of it buried me.

"Got anything you want to talk about, Pleasant?" she asked, reading my mind. It was spooky how she knew I was ready to talk.

I nodded my head. Someone other than me had to know what had really gone down. I figured burdening Clarissa with it was the best thing to do.

"I got the truth out of John Peter and I made him promise to tell the police that Ike was the one murdered Millie. But I guess he's so afraid of Ike that he made up a ridiculous lie. Ike killed Millie, Clarissa. John Peter told me he did."

I broke down and cried. I couldn't stop crying. Everyone was lying to me, was playing me for a fool. I wondered if Clarissa was my only friend but maybe not, maybe her perplexities would drown me too.

Clarissa had her arms around me and like a dam falling to pieces from a rush of water, everything came spilling out of me, I told her everything I was burdened with, well, almost everything.

"My life sucks right now, Clarissa." I couldn't stop crying.

I told her Mama had left and Daddy had always two-timed her and still was. I told her that Mama and Daddy had a baby I was named after, and she died, and that was the baby Mama grieved for.

"All through my life she grieved for someone else."

I felt Clarissa hug me tighter. "I'm sorry. Oh, Pleasant, I'm so sorry."

"Mama left me 'cause she didn't love me enough. Maybe she didn't love me at all."

"Sometimes we have to turn away from the people

who hurt us."

"What do you mean?"

"Well, your daddy hurt your mama and she's turning away from him, not you."

Her words rung really true for me and I decided that that was exactly what I was going to do, turn from him who had hurt me.

I finally ate the chicken sandwich and went into the living room. I could have fallen asleep in that big overstuffed chair I felt so tired, so emotionally drained. Clarissa had gone to answer a phone call and I sat there alone trying to chase away the feeling of emptiness that had overtaken me. I wished Clarissa had been the one to restore my faith in people but she had her secrets too.

I walked across the room and reached for the photograph I saw sitting there on the end table. Funny, but I had never noticed that photograph before, though it must have always been there. The girl looked familiar. Of course she did, she was the girl with Daddy in the photograph that mama had put an X through. She was Chloe. She was smiling. I never saw a woman smile so wide in my life. She was the most beautiful girl I'd ever seen and she looked like me. Maybe Angus was right, I was beautiful. Is that a picture of me? I wondered. Have I been dissected into many parts? I slipped the photograph into my pocket and walked out the door. Everyone around me was a conspirator in the drama of my life and it was the masks of tragedy they hid behind. I had not one friend to tell me the truth about anything, not anything.

~

The photograph of the beautiful woman was in my hand. Daddy was out there on the porch looking down the road, looking for me, wondering if I had returned with too much ammunition against him.

I sat on the railing and stared at his dejected self. I saw his eyes, sadder than a heifer's stare 'bout to be sacrificed by the sword.

"Mama went to visit Aunt Lou."

"Mama went to get away from you."

He didn't say anything for a good minute. I guess he was going to let me get away with the truth.

"I found the bag, your mamma's bag," he finally said. "I assume you went through it?"

"Yes, did you?"

"I did."

"I hope you won't profess to see me then. For I am not here. Surely you know that now."

"Pleasant, I never knew the bag was there."

"Don't look under the bed much, do you?"

He tried to smile. "No, guess not. But now I wish I had."

"What little girl have you loved all these years? Not me, for sure. I died a long time ago. So who have you loved, Daddy?"

I saw his confusion. He did not yet know all that I knew. He only wondered.

"I love you more than anything in this world."

"It's only half a love. For I am in half. Where's the pool that took me under?" I stood up and looked around. "Have you ever told me the truth?"

He stood to his feet, as well. He too, looked around, dazed. He was so dazed that when he turned back to me I could see it in his expression. I threw the photograph at his feet. I heard the glass shatter. When he bent to pick it up I kicked at his hand.

"Bastard, I never thought you'd deceive me but you deceive all women, even her. You couldn't save her from whatever took her, maybe a broken heart. The one who died, you said. You should have said, the one I loved, the one I betrayed your mother for."

Daddy stepped back and held his hand. I knew I'd hurt him. "I know how angry you are so I'm going to let you get away with calling me a bastard."

"I'm not going to apologize either."

"Let me tell you the whole story, Pleasant."

He reached out for my arm and held it tightly for fear I'd run and not hear the truth, the truth of swords aimed at my heart.

"Chloe was your biological mother, she died when you were a month old. I took you, your Mama and I, we raised you."

"What?" I said and clutched my heart, for truly it had been shattered. "I really don't belong to Mama?"

"I would have told you one day."

"Then I'm an orphan."

"Nana is your biological grandmother, Chloe's mama. You are from us, from Chloe and I. You are not an orphan."

"Do you forget my sister, who took Mama down to the depths of that pool and never let her up?"

He stared at me and what I saw in his expression weakened me, tore me apart and I needed to run from my Daddy's pain, my pain. I needed clear air and the pure scent of day.

"I'm going to Mama, the only Mama I know," I shouted. "She doesn't lie to me. She never had to love me, to deceive me with lies. She told me the truth all my life. Well, I need her now, and damn you for hurting her and damn you for hurting me."

"How did I hurt you?"

"Omission."

He only held me more tightly. "Pleasant, stop it. I

know how you feel. I had to protect you."

I managed to release myself from his grasp. "From what, the dead?"

I saw my Daddy speechless. I saw the way he must look when Karlene McFaddy asks if he loves her. I saw the way he must have looked when Mama insisted on being the only one.

"You're a cheat. I'm the result of your weakness. You can never turn from me because I remind you of who you are. You keep thinking of that dead woman like she's some sort of saint, she was just a woman whose heart you would have wound up breaking."

"You remind me of her."

"Her? Who? The only Mama I ever had is the one you've driven into indifference."

"Pleasant," he shouted as I started running. "Pleasant!"

"Go to hell," I screamed over and over again until my throat was raw. When I looked up at him I saw that he had dropped to his knees.

"I never meant to hurt anyone," he yelled out at me.

"Whatever we do in this life is exactly what we mean to do, Daddy."

I turned on my heels and ran for my bicycle. I biked the three miles to Bodean's door and he found me there heaving up the words I'd thrown at Daddy and the words he'd thrown back at me.

～

"Take me to Sumter," I said through my tears.

He was staring at me like I was some Martian that fell to earth in his path.

"I can't do that."

"Please, Bodean, take me to Sumter."

"What's wrong with you?"

"I need to get to Sumter."

"Why can't Sawyer take you?"

"I don't know where he is, he ran off."

"Why you crying?"

"Life."

"I'm not taking you to Sumter, Pleasant. It's too far away."

Well, hell, I knew how to get what I wanted. My role model was Karlene McFaddy, she knew how to get a man to betray his wife and go home and slide into bed like he don't stink with her perfume.

"C'mon Bodean, it will be an adventure." I opened my eyes up big and fluffed my hair. "We'll have fun. I'll kiss you as much as you want, as a reward."

"Kisses ain't enough."

"Well, then..." I let my expression linger on his. My smile was the little wicked one I had practiced in the mirror one day for the sole purpose of attracting boys. Bodean reached into his pocket for his car keys. I guess the smile worked.

"I'm going to hold you to what you're saying in that smile, Pleasant."

"Hold me to it."

I always liked Aunt Lou's house. It had a picket fence and a garden trellis and it was on a little road all by itself. Mama said it wasn't by itself at all, just looked that way 'cause Aunt Lou had a corner lot.

I'd told Bodean to sit in the car and wait for me, that I wouldn't be long. He was pissed off that I didn't invite him in but I said it was family business and I was going to make it up to him. He asked me how I was going to make it up to him just as I closed the car door on my answer so he didn't get to hear me say, with a stick of gum and a buck for gas.

I didn't even know why I had come. I guess I wanted to save Mama, to bring her home and deposit her in the living room of our house, where she was queen over her kingdom, and Daddy was still king.

I hadn't seen Aunt Lou since the last holiday, she always showed up with the most disgusting food, some kind of yellowish potatoes with lots of marshmallows in it. Sawyer wasn't always polite after eating Aunt Lou's holiday pudding and her Yam pie, after he made an ugly face he said it stuck to the walls of his stomach and wouldn't go down so he'd just pass on it, if she didn't mind. The rest of us were stuck having to eat it. I always used my napkin to get rid of those lumpy yams before they hit my belly.

"Why Pleasant," Aunt Lou said, "what on earth?"

Mama must have heard my name 'cause she showed up pretty quickly and stood there looking at me like I was butt naked.

"Hello," I said and walked in. Aunt Lou stood aside and started in on me like she always did. I was getting so tall, I was looking so stunning, must be at least a bra size bigger than the last time she'd seen me, better watch all those boys going to follow me home, etcetera, etcetera.

I heard Mama sigh and we stood there taking ourselves an uncomfortable moment or two. She finally led me into Aunt Lou's den and closed the door. Aunt Lou was still going on about me, we could hear her through the wall, how she'd gotten wind of my straight A's and how I was going to become some big shot doctor or lawyer after I graduated college. I didn't shout back at her like I usually did, no sense telling her I was going off to some big city to be a no account writer living on promises and dreams. I'd yelled that at her one too many times and the fool woman always thought I was kidding.

"How are you, Pleasant?" Mama said.

"You mean under the circumstances?"

She remained quiet. I saw her biting her lip and looking out the window.

"I'm sorry." I went to her and stood close. "I'm sorry for your loss."

She was confused, I could tell how confused she was, but then she realized I'd seen something I shouldn't have. I knew something I had never known before. I'm sure my expression gave it away.

"What loss?"

"I found your purple bag."

Her whole body seemed to sag a moment before she stood up straight again. "I forgot it, left in haste. I'm sorry."

"I never loved Chloe so I can't grieve for her. I grieve for you though. I grieve for the daughter you lost."

To my surprise she started crying.

"I came to tell you that. I came to thank you for never pretending I am like Sawyer, worthy of your attention. I'm sure no one could take her place."

You'd think I hit her over the head. She was so startled she stepped back and nearly tripped.

"Daddy cheats because he feels the same way, that you're missing. I don't think you were like that once but that was a long time ago. You're really just barely present with Sawyer. If you weren't my mama I'd shake you to death."

I think she started getting angry 'cause a blush came to her skin. "I don't think you understand."

"No, I do understand, Mama. Daddy is a cheat. Your baby daughter died. Well, I got disappointment in my soul too. You can hide here at Aunt Lou's or you can take yourself off the missing person's list and come home."

"I'm not going to come home just because you think I should."

I guess I couldn't believe she said that, it made me feel hopeless. "How many lights in my life are you going to dim?"

"You go on home. Your Daddy can't take care of himself, he needs you."

"Mama, she was my sister. She's in me, however small, she's there. All you've got to do is find her in my words and in my deeds, just find her. We all die, you know, some sooner, some later."

"I'm just hurt, Pleasant. I'm just hurting, been hurting too long."

"We are all hurting."

"I'm angry at your daddy right now, very angry."

"Why now? What did you learn that you never knew before?"

"It's not what you know, it's what you do with what you know. Action takes forever sometimes."

I went to her and put my arms around her and something about the gesture softened her. She turned around and held me. I was standing in the happiest moment of my life. I was holding my mama and feeling the warmth of her. I was comforting her. We were so close. I didn't know that all my dreams were about to come true when Mama looked up and searched my face and there beyond the blue of her eyes I saw what I'd always longed to see. I saw her love for me.

"Come home," I whispered.

"Did he tell you the truth? The truth about Chloe?"

I thought I knew what she was talking about. "Yes," I said.

She sat back and stroked my face. "You look like her."

"I look like me."

"She was murdered, Pleasant. It was a horrible thing. I hated her so much but no one ever deserves to be murdered. That's what has me so angry, I can't hate her anymore."

I felt like someone had put a sword through my heart. Mama must have seen my expression.

"He didn't tell you that?"

"No."

"I don't think your daddy ever got over it. He was going to leave me for her, at least that's what the rumor was, but I don't think he would have. Actually, I know he wouldn't have. I honestly think he would have realized that she was just a childhood crush, something that wasn't altogether real, but after she died, Chloe became so much larger than life. She was always between us after that. Funny, if she'd lived she wouldn't have been. Your father has loyalty. He wouldn't have left me alone with Sawyer. He loved that little boy too much. He never would have done that to me or to his son. He would not have let that woman ruin our marriage. He brought you to me because he loved me and he loved you, not because he loved Chloe."

"Who killed her?"

"Chloe? They say it was a serial killer."

I got chills all over my body.

"I'm sorry I upset you." Mama started crying again. "Every time I look at you I see Chloe, you are so much like her. She was smart as a whip, everyone wanted to be around her. Your father was infatuated. That's all it was, infatuation."

"You were friends?"

"Lord, no."

"You're my mama. The only mama I know."

She put her arms around me and we stood there holding each other for a long time. I knew she was making up her mind to do something, I just didn't know what it was.

"How did you get here?" she finally asked me.

"Bodean drove me."

"Well, I want you to tell Bodean to take you home before it gets late."

I took her hand. "Please," I said. "Don't make me go home without you."

"Give me some time, Pleasant. I promise, I just need time."

I walked back into her arms. "I know who your father is," she whispered in my ear. "He comes with no surprises."

I kissed her cheek. I had never done that before. She had the scent of lavender about her and her skin had a creamy feel, like butter or body cream or the petals of a rose.

~

When I got back outside Bodean was slumped over the wheel. I think he fell asleep. He jumped a foot when I got in and slammed the door.

"Take me home," I said.

"I don't take orders from you."

I realized he'd gotten angry sitting there counting the minutes I'd been gone. I surmised it must have been an hour or more.

"Sorry it took so long. My aunt Lou hasn't seen me in awhile, I had to make small talk."

He pulled out of the drive while I stared at him a bit. I wondered what he was thinking. I wondered if he cared for me at all. If he cared he would have sensed my despair.

"You owe me a kiss," he said.

I had recently learned that I was in pieces, that my Daddy's heart was elsewhere and my Mama's tears were a river wide and my biological mother was murdered and all Bodean can think about is getting it on with me.

"I owe you? Well, Daddy owes the government, doesn't mean they're going to get their money anytime soon."

"What the hell does that mean?" He scowled at me like something wild, something that lived in the woods and feasted on flesh.

"We all got a debt to pay is all it means."

I had too many tasks in my young life to perform to think about what I owed or didn't owe Bodean. I had to make an honest man of my daddy and convince my mama that this was an opportunity to start over. I even had to convince that goddamn John Peter to tell the truth.

"I'm here to collect."

"Yeah, I don't doubt you'll attempt to do that."

After we'd been driving for about ten minutes Bodean pulled off onto this little side road that dead ended at a patch of woods. I realized pretty quickly he intended to hold me to my word.

"Well, would you look at this. Lover's lane."

I sighed long and I sighed deep. "Take me home. My daddy is probably worried."

"Well, I have to take a leak," he said and got out of the car. I saw him up by a tree with his back to me. I saw it then, the hump on his back. I leaned forward and stared. It wasn't there just because I wanted it to be. It was there because it was his Karma not to be perfect, to have some disfigurement that was keeping him from the beauty that could have been his. I hadn't seen it before because I didn't want to. Angus hadn't seen it, or Daddy, 'cause no one sees anyone all that clearly 'till you absolutely have to.

Bodean got back in the car and reached over for me like I was a bag of groceries he had to carry inside. I pushed him off.

"It will be getting dark soon, please take me home, Bodean. I fixed my hair and looked away from him. I felt his hand around my neck as he forced my head toward his.

"Just a kiss. You owe it to me."

"I don't feel well, 'bout to throw up."

He stared at me for a moment, wondering if I was telling the truth, and I hoped my wits had proven right. Who wants to kiss a girl under those conditions? However, that didn't stop Bodean. He got over me in the passenger seat and started touching me all over. I kept pushing him off but he was straddling me. He opened the car door 'cause he kept hitting his head on the roof of the car, and we both fell out on the ground. He was on top of me with his hands on my breasts. I guess that's just what he wanted, some room on the ground to have his way with me.

"You don't want my Daddy to hear about this. You do not have an invitation to touch me."

"Aw, come on, give me your hand, I got something for you to feel."

"Keep your goddamn hard-on to yourself." I screamed and kicked him off me.

But he came right back and tried to get my shirt up over my head. He was moving all over me like he was trying to scratch himself and couldn't find where it itched. He started to move faster, pumping away at me like some crazy male dog. Then he started groaning. I knew what he was doing and it disgusted me same way a rodent would have if it had snuck up behind me and started kissing my ear.

"Get off me, Bodean," I shouted.

He kept moving, he was moving right into me and I felt his hard on right there between my legs and I felt his hands on the zipper of my jeans.

I was fuming. "Take me home this instance," I yelled. And with one good kick I had him screaming and holding himself between the legs. I had no doubt he was wondering if his little riot rod would ever work proper again.

Bodean got back in the car after hopping in one spot for five minutes. "You didn't have to do that, you hurt me."

"Serves you right."

"I didn't rape you." He was still breathing heavy and holding his genitals like they were worth something. "We didn't do nothing that warranted the injury you might have caused me."

"I didn't do nothing but give you what you deserve," I said through my teeth as I got in the passenger seat.

He turned the car around and drove down the road. We didn't speak to one another. I felt slimed by the son of a bitch. I could see that hump of his as he slouched over the wheel.

When we finally got to my front door it was nearing dark, a dusky light shown into his eyes, which no longer looked pretty to me but kind of menacing, like the eyes of that little girl in the movies that had the devil inside her.

"I don't want you to think I don't like you, Pleasant, 'cause I do. But I realize you're too young for me. I need to find a girl my own age. Maybe I'll come back in a year or two. You're worth waiting for. But, Pleasant, everyone fools around. It doesn't mean anything if you like one another. I see you are too young to understand that. You should have just gone with it. You know, it was fun, wasn't it? We weren't going all the way or anything. We were just going to have some fun."

I stared at him and didn't say a word.

"I hope I don't break your heart. It's just that there wouldn't be any older girl that would have been angry at me for just fooling around. They would have enjoyed it. You angry?"

I opened the door and got out without answering him. When I was outside the car I looked back in the window.

"I didn't invite you to slobber all over me. You are a pig, Bodean, a total pig."

The son of a bitch laughed and drove off. I went inside the house feeling like shit. Maybe he was right, I should have enjoyed it. Maybe I would have enjoyed it if I didn't have the stress I did. Truth was though, I hadn't been in the mood for it.

Daddy was in the living room when I got back. I walked inside and stared at him. He looked at me like he didn't know what to expect.

"You don't know women and you don't know men. You don't know anything."

"What's that, honey?"

"You're a bad judge of character," I said.

"Maybe, but I never thought so."

"That Chloe woman must have been as cheap as Karlene McFaddy. Is that what I'm destined for, Daddy, men like you, men like Bodean Frasier?"

"What are you talking about, what did that little son of a bitch do to you?" He got up and came toward me.

I turned around and ran up to my room and I heard him yelling behind me, "What did that little son of a bitch do to you?"

I turned the lock to my bedroom door just as Daddy got there. He pounded on the door but I wouldn't answer him. For the first time in my life, I dismissed him. Yet I could not escape him. I felt him suffering. I heard his footsteps pacing. I didn't want to feel his ache but I did. I felt his ache and mine. Murdered? Am I a magnet to this? Chloe was murdered? I put the pillow over my head; I wished myself to sleep but sleep never came. I put my clothes back on and walked outside. I found Chloe's photograph exactly where I'd thrown it at Daddy's feet. I picked it up and sat down in the wicker rocker. When I took it out of the broken frame I nicked my finger and stared at the blood as it ran down my palm. I took the photograph to my heart and cried. I had no friend to comfort me, no mama in the flesh to hold me. There we were, Daddy and I, and a picture of a dead girl I never knew—so connected, so damn connected. My grief drifted up into Daddy's heart with the loneliness in my soul, and his grieving heart drifted into mine like a river with too much force, and a ghost flew past my eyes and showed me her shadow. She glittered like silver stars.

Chapter Twenty
Clarissa Blackwell

Clarissa did not want Pleasant to overhear her phone conversation, it could have been Dom calling her, so she ran up the stairs to answer the call. In her haste, she knocked into the bed frame and hit her knee on the wood.

"Shit," she said, as she reached for the phone.

"The Nancy Drew of my youth would never say that."

She couldn't believe it, it was Philip Wiley.

"Mr. Wiley?"

"Call me Philip."

"You told the police that Randall didn't murder my goddaughter, right? I can't thank you enough, they're going to reopen the case."

"That was my intent, I had felt your passion."

"What did you tell the police?"

"That Randall had confessed to me, quite recently, that Chloe Rappaport Holly was the only woman he didn't murder. It certainly got them interested."

"You knew that he didn't kill her years ago, you lied to the police back then?"

"No, I didn't. But who doesn't lie to the police? Perhaps I did, can't remember."

Clarissa sighed and stretched herself out on the bed. Her knee felt sore and she wondered if she'd have to limp back down the stairs, or slide down on her ass.

"I appreciate what you did, that you did the right thing."

"Now, how are we going to find the man that really did kill Chloe?"

Clarissa was taken aback. Her brain was on overload and her knee was on fire. She felt she should be downstairs comforting Pleasant instead of talking on the phone to anyone, much less Philip Wiley. She silently berated herself for running up the stairs, wounding her knee, leaving Pleasant alone, all because she thought it might have been Dom calling her.

"Did you hear what I said, Clarissa, how are we going to find this degenerate?"

"Well, I don't know, Philip, but neither one of us are detectives. You're a retired attorney and I'm an ex English teacher."

"I was a defense attorney, and a damn good one, I might add."

"Yes, everyone says that."

"You should be happy to have me on your side, so let's work together on this. I always thought I'd make a fine detective."

"But you're retired and...."

"I'm bored is what I am. My Dottie makes the best jam in the world but she's going to have to get out there on the road herself. Selling jelly is making me softer in the head than I already am."

"We'll talk about it."

"It's never too late to solve a crime, you know."

"We'll talk about it, but right now I have a guest I must attend to."

"Tomorrow at ten you'll come for breakfast and we'll

start from scratch, go over every detail together."

"Well, I ah…"

"I will not take no for an answer, you want to solve this or not?"

Fine, she thought, now she'd have two retired men working on a crime that seemed to have run out of suspects, that is, unless she could find a two headed man.

"I'll be there," she said.

～

Getting off the bed hurt more than getting on but Clarissa managed to hobble to her feet. Pleasant had been so upset, she never should have left the room. She had been so uncomfortable to learn that Pleasant knew about the other baby, but she hadn't said anything about her father and Chloe's affair, at least she hadn't mentioned that Chloe was her biological mother. Clarissa wondered if she knew about that as well.

"Pleasant," she called. "I'm so sorry, I'll be right down."

She hobbled out into the hall wondering how she'd make it down the stairs.

"I hit my knee as I ran for the phone so I have to hop down." She laughed at the vision of herself hopping like a bunny. "I don't think this would have hurt as much ten years ago."

When she finally reached the bottom landing she realized Pleasant was not in the living room.

"Pleasant, are you back in the kitchen?"

When Pleasant didn't answer Clarissa managed to hobble into the kitchen, only to find it empty, only to find that the whole house was empty.

She never should have run for the phone. She sighed as she sat down in the chair with the comforting arms and the soft, plushy cushions. "Poor Pleasant was so confused and unhappy."

Clarissa leaned back and thought of everything Savannah had told her, everything Pleasant had learned about her past. She wondered how she could have been such a fool about Dennis, how some dysfunctional need kept him hanging on to her, perhaps because he was getting old and had no one else. Perhaps it was because she was actually the only person on earth who did not know him well.

As she lifted her head she felt the difference in her environment, the difference in the room. She who had everything in its proper place sensed the missing object like a finger that might have disappeared from her hand.

"Oh, no," she whispered as she stared at the absence left by the photograph that was no longer there. It was obvious that Pleasant had taken it.

Shit.

~

Clarissa fell asleep in the chair and was awoken by her front doorbell. As she tried to shake herself from the groggy fog she was in she realized it must be nearing eight in the evening.

"Dom?" she said as she stepped aside to let him in, but he stopped just inside the door.

"Remember, I said I would be by later?"

"Oh, yes. Yes, now I remember"

"Can I come in or is this a bad time?"

"No, no, it's fine. Please."

Dom walked into the living room and sat on the couch. For a moment she felt as if her memory had left her and she had no idea that there had ever been a murder, or that a teenager named Pleasant Day was Chloe's daughter.

"Can I get you something to drink. It's cocktail hour, how about some wine?"

"Yes, red if you have it."

"I do, I do."

As Clarissa got up to decant the wine she wondered why he wanted to see her. They had just spoken earlier.

"Has anything come to light?" she asked, sitting next to him on the couch.

"I'm afraid I have some bad news."

"What is it?"

"You look like hell, Clarissa. Are you all right?"

She was startled and sat back. Instinctively her hands went to her hair and she brushed it off her face. That was hardly the thing she wanted to hear from a man she found attractive.

"I've had an upsetting day."

"I'm afraid I'm going to upset you more."

Clarissa took a sip from her wine and felt her body tense. Was it Pleasant, was she all right?

"Please tell me Pleasant is okay?"

"As far as I know she is. It's about John Peter, he's in the hospital, shot himself."

"What? Oh, my God."

"He must have been aiming for his heart but nicked his shoulder instead."

"Then he's going to be all right?"

Dom nodded. "Looks to me like a sign of guilt."

"How did he get the gun?"

"His mother kept a gun in a drawer by her bed."

"It should have been locked."

"I know. Mrs. Clottey told the police he'd never shown any interest in the gun, always said he hated them. She's a bit of a wreck now, blames herself."

"Is he talking?"

"No, not a word."

"I need to see him, Dom. I think I know what happened but I need him to own up to it."

She knew he was wondering if she'd had a vision of what had happened. She volunteered the information even though he hadn't asked for it.

"I don't really see anything clearly in my head, Dom, not clearly at all, but there's been so many inconsistencies that I think I can intimidate him into telling me what really happened that day."

He looked at her for a long time. "Okay, I'll bring you over to the hospital tomorrow. You can talk to him then, I'll make it happen. But if he confesses to anything you've got to inform us immediately."

"Of course. Oh, it will have to be in the afternoon. I have a morning appointment."

"That's fine."

"I'll be alone with John Peter?"

"Yes, I'll get an okay on that."

"Thank you, Dom."

"This makes the boy look very bad."

"I know"

They sat in silence for a while. Clarissa went in to the kitchen and brought out some crackers with cheese. She had noticed that Dom was downing the wine like it was punch.

He poured himself yet another glass and stared at her. She sensed his discomfort about something. The bottle was nearly empty and she'd barely had a glass. The sun was setting in the distance and the colors of dusk made their way into the room, as if sneaking toward them, an offer of unparalleled beauty in their arms. Clarissa turned on the lights.

"I love dusk," she said.

"Care to tell me just why you've had an upsetting day?"

"Well, I'm happy to discover that Chloe's murder is being reopened."

"That shouldn't upset you. I asked you what upset you."

"I discovered today that my ex husband is a rather dis-gusting man with a rather disgusting hobby, and he seduced my best friend. I always thought it was the other way around."

Dom smiled. "Hard to ever get at the truth of something like that."

"Perhaps. He was also blackmailing Blake."

The expression on Dom's face was almost humorous. "Your ex-husband was blackmailing Blake?"

"Yes. He knew about Chloe, and that Blake had molested her."

"Unfortunately, Blake is getting a public apology from the police and the papers, and WIS TV, the first to leak the story."

"What are you saying?"

"Just that, there is nothing to tie Blake to the scene of either murder; there is no proof that he ever molested anyone and on the evening of Chloe's murder he was in Washington. He was able to come up with proof of some meeting, a rather vital meeting at the time. I'm sure there are records of his being there, people who will swear to his presence."

"Dennis and Savannah could swear to what Chloe told them, that Blake had molested her. John Peter has already told them that Blake molested Millie, that Millie told him that."

"Savannah?"

"Chloe's mother, my former best friend and my ex-husband's ex-wife."

"You're a complicated woman."

"I just have a complicated life. Look, Blake needs to be prosecuted for what he did."

"I agree but it's hearsay, unfortunately."

"Yes, unfortunately."

"It would be better if we had a child that could testify against him."

"Perhaps we should work on finding such a child? I'm sure there is one."

"Do you suspect Dennis of anything more heinous than blackmail?"

"Like murder?"

Dom nodded.

"Well, Chloe threatened to go public about Blake, which would mean that Dennis could not get away with blackmailing him, thus ending his new found wealth."

"I could make a case out of that, grounds for murder."

Clarissa stared at him, he seemed to find courage in the wine. He unbuttoned his blazer and crossed his legs. He leaned back as if he'd been in the room a hundred times, as if he owned the furniture.

"If not for my visions my ex-husband would be high on my list, but he didn't do it."

"So what do your visions tell you, who killed Chloe?"

"A two headed man."

Dom seemed disappointed. He poured the last of the wine into his glass. "There are no two headed men."

"Things aren't always what they seem."

"No, Clarissa, that's true."

"You mentioned something you wanted to talk to me about? I remember now, you wanted to come by and talk to me about something."

"It can wait."

"Okay." Clarissa bit into a cracker. "Philip wants to

help me solve Chloe's murder."

Dom laughed, as if the thought of Philip making sense out of anything was ludicrous at this point. "Hell of a person to have on your side." That surprised her.

"Do you think he has anything to offer or do you think I'm being a fool for involving him?"

"As far as I can tell, you have not one suspect, but it will keep you both occupied for a long time to come, that's for sure."

"You don't think her murder will ever be solved, do you? You think we'll just chase out tails? So it really doesn't matter if Philip is senile or not, or even if he's helping me or not."

"Clarissa, I think you can do anything you set your mind to do. I admire you. You're one of the best people I know and you are tenacious, and so is Philip."

She caught his expression, sensed his discomfort. She felt her stomach take a dip, she felt her mind race ahead, her psychic instincts kicked in. He was going to tell her something else that was unpleasant, something about him. She had a very, very uneasy feeling.

Dom sat forward and put his empty wine glass on the coffee table. He cleared his throat before he began to speak. This is it. He was about to say something she wasn't not going to like.

"Ah, the other week, when you came by and there was a woman there. I know this is uncomfortable but I am a single man and Millicent is a single woman and…"

Clarissa stood up. "You're defending yourself to me, no need to do that."

"Well, I know that there's an attraction between us, Clarissa. At least on my part there's an attraction, but I've been single three years and I'm not very good at being single, but when women are available you've got to snap the good ones up when they come your way and

Millicent is a nice woman, a good woman."

"What in the hell are you trying to say?"

"I'm engaged to her, Clarissa. I'm sorry. If I weren't I'd want to see more of you."

She watched as he wobbled on his feet. For some strange reason, she felt sorry for his discomfort, sorry he had put himself in the position he had. His face was as red as a fire truck. She wondered why he brought it up at all.

"Are you okay to drive? You can sleep on my couch."

"No, I can stay with my ex-wife."

"Be careful, Dom."

"Yes, yes, thank you."

"Oh, good luck," Clarissa said as he stumbled by her. "I'm sure she's a very nice woman, like you said."

"Thank you, thank you. Yes, she is."

Clarissa felt relieved, the pressure of having wanted a relationship had waned in an instant. Perhaps she never wanted a relationship at all, she just liked to fantasize. She imagined her feelings would change and she would feel let down in the morning, but for that moment it was like getting over a fear of the water. She felt buoyant and light as air. She felt she could swim for miles, unencumbered and free.

Whew, he's engaged. Saved by the bell, dodged a bullet.

Chapter Twenty-One
Clarissa Blackwell

Clarissa lay in bed thinking about her dream. She felt it was important to recapture the images, for she was quite sure of their significance. In the dream, the two headed man who had killed Chloe would not turn to face her though she asked him to reveal his features; she demanded that he reveal his features but her demands went ignored. There was something odd about him, aside from the fact he had two heads, he was slight of build, so slight in fact that he didn't seem to have the strength to raise the old wooden window. It was stuck and he struggled with it, though it finally managed to give and he wiggled himself through it. Clarissa wondered how Philip would react to her visions, to her theory about a two headed man who was slight of frame.

As she dressed for her breakfast date with Philip she racked her brain for some visual clue. Her past visions were always so clear but these recent ones were blocked. The killer must be very good at not revealing himself, very clever at disguise. Perhaps that was it, she deduced, perhaps the killer had come to murder Chloe in disguise.

Philip was up and dressed when she arrived and Dottie had set out a fine breakfast for the two of them.

"I can't work on an empty stomach," he said, as if the disclosure was somehow significant.

She agreed, crunching off a piece of bacon. "Yum, I haven't eaten bacon in years but I couldn't resist it, it smells so good."

"My Dottie has turned the head of many a health food fanatic." He winked at his wife.

The sun came through the yellow curtains and threw sun spots on the wall big as quarters. Clarissa felt enveloped by the heat and the pleasant aromas from Dottie's kitchen. It was so fairy tale cheery. It was as if the little house was a fictional place that when entered, banished all evil. Sometimes she could feel when houses were less than inviting, dank and oppressive, usually revealing the inhabitants as akin to irate ghosts. She didn't enter too many of those kinds of houses very often, fortunately.

She smiled at Philip, once they were seated in the living room. He settled in and put a notebook on his lap.

"You'll be happy to know that I have finagled my way into police records, old notes on the crime."

"How did you manage that?"

"It pays to have friends." Philip held up his hands and ran his thumb across the tips of his fingers.

Clarissa was sufficiently shocked. "Are you insinuating you paid someone to steal these notes?"

"You may interpret my actions that way, entirely up to you but I would hardly call it stealing."

Clarissa wondered what she was getting into but her instincts told her to stick with him. She couldn't do this alone and Dom was acting like a typical detective, he was assuming that every tip given meant guilty until proven innocent. He'd been ready to throw the book at John Peter and jumped on Graham's guilt. She was feeling very, very disappointed in Dominic Sacco.

But on the other hand, she didn't entirely trust Philip either, his behavior was so erratic.

"Philip, I have to ask you, why do you throw pebbles at Pleasant?"

He looked at her as if she might have been a bit off her rocker, but then he laughed. "She's a plucky little thing, isn't she?"

"Yes, but why do you throw pebbles at her?"

"I like her."

Clarissa was surprised and sat back. "So you throw pebbles at her?"

"It's a throwback from my youth, whenever I saw a pretty girl back then I'd make a fool of myself. Sometimes, when I look at Pleasant, I'm a teenager again. I was such a fool for the fairer sex. Pleasant is a little beauty, makes me think I've still got a skip in my step, but alas, I'm stuck in an old man's body."

"I interpret that to mean that you throw rocks at women when you find them attractive?"

"Pebbles, dear. I threw flower petals at Dottie, who married me. I threw sticks at a little girl in grade school, oh, how she scowled at me, but after she realized that the sticks were tokens of affection, she became my first girlfriend. Oh, I even threw pennies at a girl I went to college with, she gathered them all up and threw them back. She was rather plucky too."

"I'd say she was smart to get rid of you."

"Get rid of me? Oh, no, ten pennies got me a kiss, twenty pennies got me a feel and I'm sure you can imagine what a hundred pennies got me."

"I don't know whether to believe you or not."

"And remember, I got it all back, in spades, at least two hundred bucks by the time we broke up. I still have her phone number if you'd like to ask her."

Clarissa sat back. She decided it was best to let him have his illusions, he might still be able to solve Chloe's murder, eccentric or not, somewhere under his puerile remarks he was still brilliant. "Before we begin, I have to tell you about my visions."

Philip looked shocked for a moment but then he took a pen out of his breast pocket and snapped down the point.

"You do know that it was my vision of Randall Holmes that got him arrested, a forensic artist took my description of his face and he created the most amazing likeness."

"You're one of those strange psychic people?"

Clarissa never really referred to herself as psychic even though she imagined she was, nor would she have referred to herself as 'strange.' "Look, I must tell you up front that I've been having dreams about Chloe's murder."

"And so?"

"She was killed by a two-headed man."

Now it was Philip's turn to sit back. He stared at her as she uncomfortably stared back at him. Neither spoke for a good minute or two.

"A metaphor?"

"Of course."

"Okay, who are our suspects?"

"I don't know. They all seem to have alibis."

"Well, we have to start with who had motive. Her husband had motive."

"He was out of the country."

"Perhaps he wasn't."

"I'm sure the police covered that."

"Don't be so sure, the police are often inept."

"Can you look through those stolen notes of yours and see how well they covered it?"

Philip put his fingers to his lips, "discretion, my dear," he said. As he rifled through his notes Clarissa wondered how many people he'd paid off over the course of his career.

After about ten minutes watching Philip scan the pages of what appeared to be handwritten notebook pages he found what he was looking for, only to reveal what she'd always known, that Martin Holly had left the country a week before his wife's murder and he did not return for another ten years.

"His alibi is solid," Philip said. "There's a passbook stamp and an airline ticket that puts Philip too far away to hurt his wife."

"I think I remember that there was DNA found on the murder weapon, am I correct?"

"You are, belonged to Martin Holly but he was out of the country and the knife may have come from their kitchen."

"Interesting."

"Randall always wore gloves. Besides, the evidence could have been tampered with."

"Okay, okay, perhaps, but there must be another suspect other than Chloe's husband?"

"Graham's wife."

"But Chloe was stabbed."

"Women don't stab?"

"Well, I suppose they do but my vision reveals a two-headed man."

"Which is only a metaphor, not real."

"A metaphor of what?" Clarissa said, rising to her feet and walking a bit around the room.

"Two heads on one body, two headed, meaning

dishonest, like two-faced....two-headed meaning different in appearance but the same, twins perhaps, two headed, male-female?"

"There's Blake Rappaport."

"Who was in Washington at the time of her murder and does not have two heads."

"I think we need to verify his whereabouts. Dom tells me that Blake can prove he was at a meeting in Washington, but I want to see the proof of that, speak to witnesses."

"Yes, that's right. Let's start by verifying the testimony of all of our suspects. Were they really where they said they were?"

"Was Martha Day ever questioned?"

Philip shuffled through his notes as Clarissa sat back down.

"Home with her family according to her husband."

Clarissa's back stiffened and she bolted upright. Her husband hadn't been home that night, how could he have vouched for his wife's whereabouts? He had been the one to find Chloe's body.

"I'd say we have our first real suspect, Philip. Martha Day's whereabouts couldn't have been verified by her husband."

"Are you sure of that?"

"Sure am, right from the horse's mouth sure."

"Care to explain."

"This stays between us. We're only trying to solve Chloe's murder, nothing else. Promise me, Philip."

"You have my word."

"Graham could still go to jail for withholding evidence and I don't want that."

"What are you talking about?"

"It was Graham Day that found Chloe's body, the police don't know that. The killer was still there when

Graham arrived but he was so shocked by what he was witnessing that he rushed to attend to Chloe, and the baby."

"And the murderer?"

"Got out the back window."

"But the baby was never found."

"The baby is Pleasant Day, was Pleasant Day. Graham took her, he was the father."

"Ah, ha," he said. "Good work, Nancy Drew."

Clarissa thought a moment, something felt askew. "Philip, can you go through your notes and see if Graham was ever questioned for Chloe's murder back then? Before Randall's confession they must have questioned everybody who knew her. I mean, Martha was questioned, Graham must have been as well."

It took Philip a while to find what he was looking for, but finally, in his excitement, he held up the notes. "Well, well, well. They were both lying. Philip vouched for his wife and she vouched for him but they could have both been out."

"Well, one of them had to be home with Sawyer, their son."

Interesting, Clarissa thought, they had lied for each other, probably because they didn't want anyone to tie them to the missing baby.

"Philip, I think that Graham suspects his wife of stabbing Chloe to death. And what is more ludicrous is that I think that Martha suspects Graham of the same crime. It was all over the papers that there was a missing baby and all of a sudden it showed up in his arms. She must have known that Graham took that baby."

"You mean that after Graham took the child he and his wife raised it as their own?"

Clarissa nodded. "Martha must have put the pieces together, it was all over the papers that the baby was missing yet Graham told me that his wife believed he purchased the child."

"Why would Graham kill Chloe if in fact he loved her?"

"Do you think Martha wanted to admit to herself that her husband was in love with Chloe? No, she'd rather believe that Chloe was threatening him to get out of his marriage, threatened to tell his wife about their affair and he killed her."

"And he covered up for Martha because he thought she did it?"

"The police may or may not have known about the affair between Chloe and Graham, but if they questioned Graham and Martha about the murder, they certainly heard the rumor."

Philip looked back through his notes. "Graham was brought in to the police station for questioning, Martha was questioned in her home."

"So, you're saying that they might never have known at the time that the police questioned the other one?"

"No, they might not have, especially if neither mentioned it and why would they? Randall confessed to the crime and the case was closed. So which one of them killed Chloe?"

"Neither," she said.

"Then we are sitting here with no suspects."

"Precisely."

Chapter Twenty-Two
Pleasant Day

Morning sounds came in through my window like the world made sense. Consistency should alleviate anxiety but it sure as hell didn't that day. The sun streamed in with its perfection breathing in my ear, as it has done so many mornings before, but the sun's congruity did not soothe me either. The breeze danced with my curtains and swayed, uncomplicated and simple, as it should be. I tell you, nothing on this earth should be arduous or complex, not when simplicity is needed.

Birds sang out as they did every morning. I could set my watch by their song, so consistently loud, but melodious and cheerful all the same. Nana calls birds God's most precious creatures. I wonder what Nana means by God. I know instinctively that I have only limited experience of who I call by that name, a name with a measly three letters to define him or her. Nana says that too, that God is indefinable, certainly an androgynous entity. No, I do not believe that God the Father and Mother Nature got together to create the Earth. If God is omniscient then he or she wears the face of all of us. Anyway, I think birds know God better than I do, that's why they don't have a human language of description, no good telling us there's a God and God looks like this or that. Well, unlike a bird, perhaps, I will never know God in total, not until I am holding Millie's hand, not until I am a soul with no more human bullshit weighing me down, and maybe, not even then.

We give a simple name to a profoundly limitless entity is what Nana says. Nana loves to talk about those things. We impose logic and science and theory on how we all got here, she says. We close the book on our answers, that's what Daddy says too, that we think we know what we will never know. We think we understand what we can't imagine but we need to understand it so much that we give weight to all the puzzles on this earth, none of which we really have figured out. That's where Daddy and Nana and I are a lot alike, always trying to describe the indescribable but not too proud to know when it's time to give up. Truth is, you can't figure out life or God, you just can't figure it out. Life is too much of a mystery and God is too unfamiliar to ever be known. I guess, if you ever had God figured out the universe would be split in thousands of pieces and it would disappear and we who have dreamed ourselves alive would all fade away in all those splintered parts. What I mean to say is, it isn't meant for us to know anything.

"What you thinking about, little girl?" Daddy asked as he entered the kitchen where I sat with a cup of coffee and a donut from Mama's last trip to the mall, where there's a Dunkin Donuts, a Wendy's, and my favorite, a Cheese-cake Factory right there on level One.

"I hope you have noticed recently that I am not a little girl, I'm too tall to be little and I'm too old to be a girl."

"You'll always be my little girl."

"I'll remember that when I'm losing my teeth, when my hair becomes see through to my scalp, and my bones are too brittle to hold me up. Perhaps it will give me some solace knowing that I am still your little girl."

"I bet it will."

He eyed the last donut in the box but I reached for it and took a big bite, the cream fell on my lip. How heavenly it was to lick it off.

"Oh, did you want that last one?"

Daddy turned to the coffee pot and poured a cup. Mama is the only one that ever gets Daddy's coffee just the way he likes it. Well, Sawyer does too but Daddy usually complains that Sawyer's coffee is too rich and makes him pass wind all day. I hope he nearly gags on the way I made it, maybe then he'd realize that Mama has served many a purpose in this house, loving him for one and making good coffee for the other.

Daddy slumped down in the kitchen chair and stared at me. I knew he wanted to talk, wanted to make amends, wanted to pretend that things are just the way they were before Mama walked out the door. But he surprised me and didn't talk about Mama at all.

"Did Bodean get fresh with you last night?"

"What do you mean by fresh?"

I was feeling guilty for taking the last donut and I wanted to give him half of what was left. I felt selfish and nasty, but I didn't offer.

"How was your Mama?" he asked, so I guess he was going to talk about her after all.

"Fine."

He nodded his head up and down a few times then he reached over and took the last half of the donut off my plate. He didn't need my offer, he was King and this was his kingdom.

"You snooze, you lose."

I glared at him.

"So was Bodean fresh with you? You were pretty upset when you got home."

"I'd just seen Mama and she was pretty upset."

"You just said she was fine."

"I lied, just like you, I lied."

"I didn't lie, Pleasant, I omitted the truth."

"I live in a world of lies, I might as well learn early that lies come with the territory. You befriend people, you grow up and marry, you work and you lie to everyone, your boss, your spouse and your best friend. You tell big lies, little lies, the world is a bunch of lies. You teach your children to lie because you believe that the only protection they will ever have from any kind of harm will be in the lies they tell."

"Lies are necessary sometimes."

"Where is the truth then? Where does truth exist, behind the lie, within the lie? Is truth that which we seek to know or that which we avoid knowing?"

He smiled. I watched him sip his coffee, knowing that it tasted like mud to him but he wasn't' going to tell me that, he wasn't going to lie. So maybe he was right, lies are necessary."

"I would like to know if Bodean was not the gentleman he promised me he would be with you. I would like to know that."

"You think Bodean is different than any other boy? You think you are different from any other man?"

I could see he was getting exasperated with me. Maybe he thought I'd been completely violated, or worse yet, that I'd relinquished my own free will to Bodean.

"He does have a hump on his back," I said. "You lied about that."

"I never saw a hump on Bodean's back. I said he

stoops, that's all."

"Protecting me from the truth, are you?"

"When the truth hurts I will always protect you from it."

"Like I really care that he's ugly."

Daddy laughed like I'd told a joke. I felt myself getting angry. "Why the hell did you ever try and fix me up with him anyway?

"Because my beautiful nearly sixteen year old daughter needs a boy who appreciates her, not like John Peter and Angus, who like her in jeans and hiking boots. You need attention, honey."

"Well, Daddy, that's just what I got. Bodean tried to get into my pants but I imagine every boy I'll ever date will try the same thing. And maybe I would have let him if I wasn't so depressed to learn that I am an orphan with a murdered mother and a no account cheating father who lies to me."

"I told him to keep his hands off you."

His face turned a deep red. I didn't know if he was angry or embarrassed but he got up from the table and walked outside. A few minutes later I heard his car. As I went out onto the porch to watch him drive off I saw Angus peddling up the drive.

"Real bad news, Pleasant," Angus said, as he leaned his bike on the ground and stood there looking up at me, breathing hard.

I really didn't think I was in the mood to hear any more bad news. "Keep it to yourself."

I could hear Sawyer in the kitchen and watched him through the window. He was pouring coffee. Angus joined me up on the porch, looking at me like the last thing he wanted to do would be to reveal whatever bad news he had come to depress me with, but he was going to do it anyway.

"Did someone's mother find another frigging body inside someone's frigging box-spring, Angus?"

Angus remained quiet for the moment and dropped his head. Sawyer came outside and stared at the two of us. After he took a sip of his coffee I watched him spit it out over the side railing. "You make this shit, Pleasant?"

I threw him a dagger look, which he threw back at me.

"My God." Sawyer gagged a few times for dramatic effect. "You 'bout to kill me."

"You're not going to like this, Pleasant," Angus said.

"I'm in no mood for any of your stupid bad news."

"You depressed about something?"

"It's a long story." I sat on the porch steps. Angus came down and sat beside me. I felt him take my hand.

"I don't want you to get upset but did you hear?"

"Hear what?"

"John Peter is in the hospital, tried to kill himself?"

I felt myself crumbling into a million pieces. Angus squeezed my hand.

"He tried to what?" I asked softly. I don't cry easy but I was raw and my tears could not be squelched behind bravado. I let loose a wail that put the fear of God in Angus's expression and he stared at me open mouthed and shocked. Even Sawyer came down from the porch to stare at me.

"Pleasant.....I'm sorry..." I heard Angus say, but he never finished his sentence.

My brother and Angus stood around uncomfortably as they watched me cry, screaming out sobs loud enough to wake the dead. Poor Angus was walking around in little circles, clueless on how to comfort me.

"Pleasant, I didn't mean to upset you like this. If I'd only known to keep my mouth shut, but I just thought you'd want to know."

Even through my tears I could see the pained expression on his face.

"God, why he'd do something so stupid?" Angus yelled.

Sawyer came down and put his arms around me. He held me and rocked me as I cried. I think it was a good fifteen minutes before I could talk.

"He's alive, Pleasant," Sawyer said, looking over at Angus. "Isn't he Angus? That's something, that's good news."

"Yeah, yeah," Angus said, shaking his head like it was an iPod with a dead battery that he was trying to extract music from. "They won't let us in his room at the hospital though. I tried, I went over there."

"Why not?" I asked, getting to my feet. "If he's okay, why not?"

"The police told me he doesn't want to see anyone."

"The police? What the hell do they have to do with anything?"

"He tried to kill himself, Pleasant. Thank God he can't shoot straight."

I put my face in my hands, I could not believe that my life could get any worse but it had.

"Go on home, Angus. I need to figure out a way to get in to see John Peter."

"I can't leave you in this state. It's my fault you're feeling so bad. I should have kept my bad news to myself, like you said."

"I got a lot of people to blame for my tears, least of all you. Go on home, now."

Poor Angus looked horribly upset. I felt sorry for him walking off, feeling useless. I knew that's how he was feeling. He looked back at me with this awful pathetic look. Then he jumped on his bike. Angus was a jackass but he was a harmless one. Angus had been hurt deeply by what John Peter had done, that he might have lost a friend in such a horrible way. I could see that. But even aside from the stupid thing John Peter had done, Angus was hurting for me, feeling my pain, taking it with him as he rode off. He might not have understood all of what I was feeling but he had embraced it. He didn't get it after Millie died, but now he knew what loss could do to a person. Empathy just might save the world one day.

"Kid's in love with you," Sawyer said.

"You don't know shit. You need to disappear."

"Sure, sure, I'll disappear, but not before I teach you how to make coffee."

"I've got to get inside that damn hospital to see John Peter. I don't have time for coffee."

"You better make time before you grow up and some lover boy like Angus expects a good cup of java from you." Sawyer shook his head. "You will fail miserably."

He grabbed my hand and forced me into the kitchen, ignoring my protests.

I was out on the porch with Sawyer drinking the coffee he'd just taught me to make. He was right, the difference between a good cup of coffee and a bad one was like the difference between a filet mignon steak and raw seaweed. Sawyer had a special stash from Jamaica that he hid away in the refrigerator behind Mama's Eight O'clock Coffee, Jamaican Blue Gold he called his, said it cost him a bundle. He ground the beans and put the ground coffee into a pot that you didn't even put over the fire. He got me to stand in the middle of the kitchen to savor the aroma. Sawyer called his coffee maker a French Press and he kept it so clean that I could see my reflection in it. I thought his coffee took a lot of time to make because after you ground the beans you had to boil the water, then pour it in the press and then wait three minutes before you could smash the damn thing down and get your coffee. I will have to admit though, I could have sat in the sun all day drinking cup after cup of Sawyer's Jamaican Blue Gold. Even Mama's coffee couldn't match his. Mama didn't mix hers and she didn't grind the beans either.

I was thinking that even if John Peter wouldn't see Angus, he'd see me. I was hoping that was the case anyway. I had to get over to the hospital to find out why John Peter would actually shoot himself. I knew he was bipolar but I never really believed he was suicidal. I was about to ride my bicycle into town when I saw Daddy driving up the drive. I watched as he brought the car to a quick stop. I had an uneasy feeling, and if I hadn't sensed something bad was about to happen, I would have kept on going. Daddy started honking his horn at me. Next thing I knew he was out of the car dragging Bodean up to where I was standing with my bicycle. I was flabbergasted. He had Bodean by the neck and Bodean looked so angry I thought fire was going to come flying out of his mouth. I was mortified, too shocked to even run off.

"Go on up and apologize," Daddy said and pushed Bodean up to me. The expression on Bodean's face was frightening, like he was harboring the Incredible Hulk.

"I'm sorry," Bodean muttered.

"What's that Bodean, sorry for what?" Daddy said.

"Sorry for disrespecting your daughter, Sir."

"Damn it, Bodean, say it to her, not to me."

Bodean's eyes were in little slits. I'm sure my mouth

was hanging open so low that I might have looked like a spastic 'bout to spit up all over herself. Bodean couldn't stop glaring and looking like a bull 'bout to gore me. He finally got some sort of apology out that sounded like he was sorry for trying to take advantage of my innocence. I was too shocked to even understand what he was saying. But I watched with some kind of horror as my daddy pointed his finger in Bodean's face and told him he was lucky not to get strung up to the Oak tree gracing our yard.

I vowed never to speak to Daddy again, I felt so humiliated. I'm sure my face looked like a tomato on my neck as I watched Daddy shove Bodean back in the car and screech off. I didn't know how I was going to show myself in school, which was about a week away from starting. I knew Bodean would tell everyone my Daddy was about to lick him 'cause I was a crybaby and wouldn't let him kiss me, or feel me up, or give himself a thrill humping me. I ran back in my room and slammed the door. I could hear Sawyer on the other side telling me not to worry about it, that Daddy would keep the wolves away. Hell, Daddy's words and deeds were going to keep everyone away, who the hell wants to hang out with a girl who can't take care of herself?

It wasn't that Daddy had humiliated me, was about to make me look like goddamn Mother Theresa in front of all my friends once Bodean opened his mouth. It wasn't even that he never told me my mama wasn't my real mama or that I was sprung from his sordid affair, or that I had a sister drowned in the pool, or that I had a mother murdered by a serial killer. It was because I needed distance, maybe even a fresh start. It was because the halo atop my daddy's head had turned to rust, and his indifference to Mama's feelings got under my skin. I got my cell phone out of my knapsack and called Nana, told her I was moving in and I wouldn't take no for an answer. I told her I didn't want to live with Daddy anymore and I knew she and I shared blood. I told her that I was a responsibility she couldn't shirk.

"How long will it take you to pack?" she asked, after she told me she'd have to tell Daddy where I was.

After probably taking a punch at Bodean, or threatening him within an inch of his life, Daddy must have stopped over at Lilac Gardens so Karlene McFaddy could ease his troubled spirit, 'cause he never came back that day. Ain't that just the luck, he wasn't even present to see my exit in Nana's car. I didn't leave anything behind either, not even that crumpled up photograph of Chloe, or my mama's purple bag.

Chapter Twenty-Three
Clarissa Blackwell

Clarissa stared at the boy crumbled in a heap before her, his eyes so swollen he looked physically beaten up. She didn't know if she believed in reincarnation but one thing for sure, she didn't want to go through adolescence again, that painful period in one's life in which a bully can taunt another weaker spirit into murder, into suicide, into complexes too embedded to ever dissolve.

What would the courts say, she wondered, that he was afraid of Ike Lewis who was built like a bull, who was capable of painting black children white and drowning gays for sport.

"The truth is going to set you free," she told him.

All the while John Peter was confessing to her he kept begging her not to tell Pleasant, that Pleasant had loved Millie and he had strangled her, strangled her because Ike kept telling him to pull, pull, pull the scarf around her neck tighter, tighter, tighter, to see her face turn red, to see her eyes bulge. "She's going to hate me, Pleasant is going to hate me," John Peter kept crying.

"Start at the beginning, John Peter, tell me what happened," Clarissa asked softly while she held his hand.

John Peter said that Ike was mad 'cause after he

jumped in the window, Millie hit him with her one arm and starting yelling at him. Ike punched her good, broke her nose right away and she screamed and cried, started hitting him again and again with her one arm. He became furious and punched her over and over again. Millie was naked, she was standing there with blood running down her face. Ike took her scarf and wound it around her, he told her that her body was too ugly to expose and she needed to get dressed. Millie was scared by then. She ran down the stairs with Ike in pursuit of her, slapping her ass and laughing and pulling on the scarf as if it were reins. She was so scared she never put her back clothes on.

"What were you doing while this was going on, John Peter?" Clarissa asked.

John Peter shook his head, he said that he wanted to help Millie, Oh, God, he really wanted to help her. He didn't think Ike was hurting her that badly, he didn't think she was going to die that day. Ike kept saying that he wouldn't tell anyone in school that he was fucking a freak. And he was afraid of Ike, he was so mean. He watched as Millie ran around his living room trying to get out the front door and Ike kept pulling on the scarf. You got to play the game now, John Peter. What game? What game?

Millie got out the door but Ike was still holding on to the scarf. Millie tried to get out of it and it had slipped to her neck. "Let's take this cow home," Ike yelled and he dragged Millie out back and pushed her down on the ground. He gave John Peter the other end of the scarf. "Pull it, you faggot," Ike screamed and John Peter pulled it and Ike pulled on his end and Millie wiggled on the ground and the boys laughed because she looked like a naked fish with her one arm hidden behind her and her body flailing back and forth.

John Peter said he didn't want to laugh but he couldn't help it. "I caught me a big one," Ike screamed. "Pull her in, John Peter." They pulled and pulled and pulled. It was just a joke. Millie would forgive him. Everyone knew Ike was a bully, they'd laugh about it.

But then her eyes got big and still, her mouth hung open. She looked shocked. John Peter said he screamed 'cause she looked dead. "Oh, no," Ike said and bent down to inspect her. Then he looked up at John Peter. "You get to do me, cause you're such a bad ass, John Peter. You killed her." John Peter didn't think he'd heard him right.

"You leave this to me, John Peter," Ike said. John Peter kept crying and Ike told him what they were going to do with the body. "Stuff it in a big, black bag. Stuff it in your box-spring. You can fuck a corpse tonight, big man, ha, ha."

Then Ike told him he was going to come back with his Daddy's truck and they'd take Millie to the woods," and he threw John Peter across the body and John Peter screamed again. Ike came back with a bag while John Peter kept trying to wake Millie up but she didn't wake up. Ike made John Peter help him stuff the body into the bag. Ike lifted her up to the bedroom, ripped the box-spring apart and shoved her in there. "You going to keep your mouth shut, faggot?" Ike asked and John Peter nodded and nodded and nodded till Ike left.

Clarissa put her arms around John Peter, told him he had to tell the truth to the police, that Ike couldn't hurt him, that Ike needed to pay for Millie's murder. She told him he'd have to repeat everything he'd told her in a court of law.

"But when he couldn't get his Daddy's truck and after Mama found the body, I told him what Millie had told me, about that man molesting her, I told Ike that so we could use the information to blame someone else," he sobbed. "It's all my fault, my fault. I should have told the truth from the beginning."

He held on to her and she stroked his hair. Clarissa wondered what his life would be like after this, a sensitive boy carrying that horrific day around in his mind, carrying it into adulthood, carrying it to his grave.

"I'm sorry, John Peter," she said. "You really liked the girl, didn't you?"

"Yes, yes, yes I did." He wept, and she held him until his tears subsided.

~

Dom was waiting outside the room with two other detectives. She relayed John Peter's confession. One of the detectives informed her that Ike was in custody but he was blaming John Peter for the murder. Clarissa assumed the truth would prevail here, John Peter was hardly the dominant one of the pair.

She noticed that Dom was uncomfortable and could barely look in her direction. She felt there was something more to his discomfort but she couldn't put her finger on it. Maybe he wasn't as much in love with the woman he was engaged to as he thought he was. Maybe she made him feel guilty for finding her attractive, and he did find her attractive, she felt that pretty strongly, psychic knowing, maybe. She wanted to just go on and enjoy her life the way she'd been doing before Pleasant ran her over on a bicycle and good ole divorced Dom Sacco came back into her life.

Millicent, good name, she thought. She wondered what Millicent looked like. Clarissa hadn't gotten a good look at her, just saw a pretty woman that was fifteen or more years younger than she was. And did they fall in love right away or was it a gradual deepening of affections, a comfort level because they loved the same things, like old black and white movies, long walks on the beach, shrimp and grits with champagne? Clarissa wondered what she really had in common with Dom, did he like mystery novels, antiques and rainstorms? Who knew, probably wasn't meant to be. But maybe, if she'd met him first, who knew?

Clarissa had just put down the phone when she saw the car drive up the drive, a very beautiful car. From where she was standing it looked to be a BMW with a convertible top, nice cream colored body with brown leather seats. The two nearly identical blonde heads in the front surprised her, Pleasant and Savannah seemed to be paying her a visit. She had just called Graham and told him it was important that they meet up and he told her he'd be waiting for her at Buck's in fifteen minutes.

Clarissa could see them through the glass panes on her front door, both in jeans and baseball caps turned backwards. Savannah was taller for now, but Clarissa surmised that Pleasant would catch up pretty soon. They were thin, both in t-shirts. Clarissa knew that many charming strangers in their futures would graciously mistake them for sisters.

"This is a surprise," Clarissa said, opening the door. Neither of them hesitated but filed in, stopping abruptly in the foyer, clearly not there for tea and cake.

Clarissa noticed that Pleasant had something in her hand. After a moment she recognized it as Chloe's photograph.

"Here," Pleasant said. "I believe this is yours." She held the photograph out. "What were you doing with it?"

she asked.

"Chloe was my Goddaughter. Your grandmother and I were very good friends once and I was made Chloe's Godmother."

"Then I guess we're related too." Pleasant smiled at Clarissa, her pretty hazel eyes went into a slant. "In a sense."

"Do you want to keep the photograph, Pleasant?"

"You keep it for me, I might come back for it one day."

Clarissa agreed to keep it and promised to get the frame repaired. She shot Savannah a glance and thought about the date she had with Graham that she was about to be late for.

"Why didn't you tell me who Chloe was?" Pleasant sounded more forlorn about it than accusatory.

"It wasn't my place to tell you." Clarissa put her arms around the girl. Pleasant did not pull back, a welcomed sign, much to Clarissa's surprise and relief.

Savannah announced that she was taking Pleasant home with her, at least for a while, at least until she got back on good terms with her father. Then they said they were going to make a stop at the hospital so Pleasant could see John Peter.

Clarissa felt her stomach drop to the floor. "I have to tell you something about John Peter, I've just come from the hospital. I've just seen him."

Clarissa knew that she had to tell Pleasant what had happened to Millie, she didn't want her hearing it from anyone else, or reading about it in the paper. She knew it might sound as if John Peter had been as much of a monster as Ike, and that really wasn't the case, not entirely.

She sat Pleasant down and recounted what had happened to Millie that day. She softened John Peter's involvement as much as she could. She made it sound like he had been completely bullied into hurting Millie. Pleasant was probably going to wonder why John Peter hadn't done more to help her. Clarissa wondered the same.

Pleasant looked too shocked to cry, or maybe she was just all cried out. Clarissa felt sorry for her. She'd tried to be as gentle as possible in describing Millie's death. Pleasant didn't say anything in response, nor did she question Clarissa for any details. "Now, at least I know what happened," was all she said.

"I just brought the truth to light."

Clarissa watched as Pleasant turned and walked away. She got into the front seat of the car and looked off. Clarissa imagined that Pleasant's thoughts were sad enough and heavy enough to leave an impression that only time would fade, yet never erase.

"She'll be okay," Savannah said. "I'll take good care of her."

"I don't doubt that you will."

"You know," Savannah said as she stared at Clarissa. "We will always be in each other's life."

"Do you mean, you and I or you and Pleasant?"

"All of us. We will always be in each other's life."

"And so too, the betrayals. They'll be there too."

Savannah seemed stunned but Clarissa noticed her quick recovery. "And so too, the laughter," she said as she began to close the door behind her. "And so too, the love," she added as the lock caught.

~

Clarissa pulled her car into the driving lot at Buck's. She was over forty minutes late and she prayed he'd still be there. He had to know that his wife had lied for him.

Maybe he'd been harboring a resentment against her all these years because he thought that Martha had flown into a jealous rage and murdered his mistress. She didn't think he really believed that but then again, he must of fantasized that it could have happened. Clarissa herself wasn't so sure of anything anymore, maybe Martha had done it. What the hell did it all mean, a two headed murderer? Perhaps, she concluded hastily, Chloe had had more than one enemy.

Clarissa noticed right off that Graham almost looked as bad as John Peter, like he'd had the shit kicked out of him. She slid into the booth and tried to read his expression. She had something important to say to him but it sure looked to her as though Graham had his own bit of bad news.

"Pleasant has gone to live with her grandmother."

Clarissa didn't say anything, just nodded her head, didn't tell him that she'd just seen both Pleasant and Savannah.

"She's probably already packed and gone as we speak, got a call from Savannah a couple of hours ago. My daughter no longer wants to live in my house so she's going to live with her grandmother."

"She'll come round, Graham. Give her time."

He held her eyes for a moment or two wondering, she was sure, what she'd come to tell him.

"So which is it, am I going to like what you have to say?"

Graham ordered Clarissa a beer and sat forward in the booth. His hands were over his mouth. She knew he was upset about Pleasant.

"Graham, did you know that Martha lied for you fifteen years ago when she was questioned about Chloe's murder? She said you were home all night but you and I both know you weren't. She obviously knew it too. She was home and you weren't."

Graham's hands came away from his mouth quickly and he shook his head. "What are you talking about?"

"Blake wasn't the only one you suspected of murdering Chloe, you suspected your wife of doing it, didn't you?"

Graham rubbed his forehead like he was rubbing off a stain.

"My wife threatened to shoot Chloe if she didn't stay away from me. Chloe told me that. That's what made me realize I couldn't walk out of my marriage. I had some crazy idea that I was going to keep Chloe as my mistress and Martha as my wife. I really didn't know that my wife knew about my affair with Chloe until then. It was like I was hit with a brick."

"Graham, Martha thought you might have killed Chloe. She lied for you, gave you an alibi when the police questioned her because you hadn't been home that night, but when you did show up, you showed up with a baby. She didn't really believe that bunk you told her about purchasing a baby from a down and out woman. It was all over the news that Chloe's baby was missing."

"What are you saying?"

"She thought you did it, you thought she did it."

"That's crazy. I didn't think that, and why should she? Why would I have killed Chloe?"

"Well for one, Martha believed you were just having a fling. She thought you loved her, and Chloe threatened your marriage. I'm going to go out on a limb here and assume you've always been a player, never faithful to any woman. Martha knew what she was getting into when she married you, but at some point, she became fed up. Maybe Chloe threatened her more than the others. And let's not forget, you took the infant.

In Martha's mind you did everything for her, even brought her a little girl to take the place of the one she'd lost, even murdered her rival, maybe. She knew you cheated on her but she always believed you loved her."

"Jesus," he said and put his head down. Clarissa thought he was going to cry but he didn't, he just raised his head and looked up at the ceiling. "How does life get so fucked up?"

"I don't know, Graham, but I tend to think we always have something to do with the way it turns out. I think resolution is always a possibility though.

"I never really thought my wife would do such a thing, that she was capable of murdering anyone, but every now and then I wondered about it."

"Every now and then you resented Martha, maybe she did kill Chloe. You knew she threatened to shoot her."

"I was very confused back then. I don't really think I would have gone through with that divorce. Yet, I loved Chloe."

"Well, I know you and Martha have separated, Pleasant told me. I do know that Martha loves you very much, I'm psychic that way."

"I was never a good husband, I don't deserve her."

"You probably need to tell her that."

"After our daughter died things changed. Martha never got over it. There was this distance that just appeared between us. Chloe made me feel less empty."

"Martha stood by you, no matter what. She didn't kill Chloe so don't even go there. She thinks you wanted to give her the child she lost so she accepted whatever you told her. You harbored resentment toward your wife all these years for nothing except suspicion. I don't know who killed Chloe but it wasn't you or Martha."

"I did resent her but I'm not even sure why."

"Chloe died, Martha lived?"

"No," he nearly shouted.

"Chloe is gone, time to stop feeling guilty, Graham."

"I'll always feel responsible for Chloe's murder."

"You bear no responsibility."

"Why do I feel responsible then?"

"I'm not sure. We don't know who killed her. But you're not to blame, not even if your affair were the cause of her death in some way."

Graham downed his beer and ordered another. She sensed his distress, his confusion.

"Truth is beauty, beauty truth, that is all ye need to know on earth." Graham stared at her.

"What is Ode on a Grecian Urn by Keats," she said spontaneously, and laughed at herself softly.

"I never really understood those words before now." He raised his head to the ceiling again. "Have I caused this,? I'm losing everyone I love."

"There is a cost to deceit," she whispered, "a price to pay," and reached over to hold his hand.

PART II

Green-Eyed Monster

Chapter Twenty-Four
Millicent Holly Linder

She ran the brush through her hair, her highlights caught the sun. She'd paid a good price for the color, rich brown with honey golden highlights. Her natural hair was the color of a bleached stone, listless and lifeless. For years she'd had it dyed by a master colorist, Albert the Great, she called him. He was absurdly expensive but she'd been coming up with his London prices for years. Imagine, being robbed blind by a goddamn beautician in small town South Carolina, she scoffed. But the rich brown he gave her made her look less like her brother, more vibrant.

Poor Martin's thinning, nearly white hair and sallow complexion made him so average looking, barely noticeable. She'd looked less like Martin for a long time now; she had an envious figure, he was so thin he seemed fragile. She'd had her nose perfected at twenty, he'd succumbed to the length of his, calling it regal. The lines around his eyes made him look harried. Her eyes were clear and her lids did not droop like his did. His teeth were dull and looked grey when he smiled. Hers shone white from the bleaching she got every six months from the Whitening Clinic in Edgefield.

She no longer looked at Martin and saw herself. When she was younger she thought for sure she must be a boy, they weren't identical, but still, they were twins. Therefore every line of his body, the length of his fingers and the muscles that formed on his arms should appear on hers as well. She was always a bit perplexed that her arms were soft, not firm like his. She did not have a penis either, nor did he have breasts as they developed on her quite nicely. She was able to separate then, see herself as unique, different.

The further away she could get from Martin's identity the better she felt. But even though she wore her hair long as a teenager people still mistook them for one another. It made her angry, furious even. Why the hell couldn't they tell who she was, that she was feminine and he was not so at all. He was plain and quiet and his shoulders stooped. He wore loafers and plaid pants and shirts with stiff white collars and she did not, but still, other people were startled by the resemblance. She reinvented herself out of necessity, she had to. She was determined to remove herself from the womb they'd shared. She became loud to his quiet, noticeable to his shyness, flirtatious to his conservative approach to women. She painted her nails and her toes bright red and wore low cut blouses and short skirts, and so she became different than Martin, so very different, a Marylyn Monroe to his Clark Kent, one might say.

Still, she could not escape their intrinsic bonds, the thought processes and opinions that could have been uttered from her tongue as well as his, the emotions that dictated his sometimes erratic behavior also dictated hers. There were days, she would pick up the phone and call him. "I feel your distress, Martin, are you all right?" And he, in his male aversion to feminine sentiments would feign ignorance and yet, she knew, she knew he was distressed.

And it worked both ways, he would call, "Millicent, are you well?" She would always tell him the truth. She wasn't afraid to be unwell, or unhappy or distressed. She wished he was more like her in that respect but he was, after all, a man and she was a woman and she told the truth about what she was feeling and he didn't. He hid his emotions and she expressed them. But they were still tied, he had been at one end of the womb and she had been at the other. They could never hide anything from one another, they had been revealed to each other in the misty chasm that had held their embryos. It did not have hiding places, that chasm. She would never escape her brother Martin, no, not entirely.

And when he announced one day that he was moving to America, that he had a job offer in a small city in the south, she knew that she would join him. He'd always wanted to live in America, he found it fascinating. She really had no desire to separate that far from Martin anyway, she didn't know what she would do without him. They each had a desire for sophistication and adventure and assumed that their impressive degrees in finance would insure them success. Perhaps he would even get her a job in the USA, recommend her to his superiors at that impressive bank he was going to be working at. And so he did get her a job, only a few weeks after her arrival. He was happy that she would be so close and of course she knew that he would be. She rented a small house not far from his that was somewhat similar to the area near the River Cuckmere where they had grown up. The town was pretty, not exactly as lovely and interesting as the village of Alfriston but still charming. It would certainly do for Millicent, she would be near her brother and she found Americans, if not altogether stimulating, at least, helpful and gracious.

Martin rarely socialized, he was shy with women but he liked them. He always had a woman that he was fixated on, whether she returned his affections or not. She, unlike Martin, went out often and had no trouble at all attracting men, but she was fussy, she didn't really like the American male demeanor. She wondered if she would ever marry with so few men to choose from. She wanted to marry. She didn't really want children but she did want someone there that validated her, made her feel that she was loved, made her feel that she was worthy. Of course, she never would have chosen a married man as her lover but Graham was unlike the men she'd been meeting, he was a southern, soft spoken gentleman, not at all rowdy or opinionated, not at all misogynistic.

She and Graham had met in a bar and he found her eyes despite the crowd. Well, she knew she was beautiful. How could he not have noticed her? She had made herself beautiful. She would not have had it any other way. Now, when people asked how closely she resembled her twin she could reply, "Oh, not much at all anymore." And that is what she'd said to Graham when he'd asked her later that evening. "You're a twin? Oh, that is so interesting, do you look like him?"

Their affair began that night in the back seat of his old car on a dark deserted road. The moon had been full and it shone down in his eyes. He looked at her with such sincerity, his desire for her not yet apparent below his belt. He tipped her chin up and kissed her lips lightly, not as other men had done, shoving in their tongues and making their intentions obvious. Aggression in men was something she detested. When a man wanted to fuck there was nothing else to discuss, and they seemed so entitled about it. Graham was not like that, he was too sensitive for obvious advances. Yes, before he took her into the back seat to slip her skirt above her waist and her panties down below her ankles he told her that he was married. Millicent felt her disappointment, was this to be just a brief connection, a one night stand, she wondered. But she did not think of it at that moment, she liked him too much. She guided his hand between her legs and she fitted herself under him. He was a master, she thought, as he slipped inside her and took her not only to the surface of the moon but within its glow, the sweet encompassing glow of sexual euphoria.

~

She was hooked from that night on. But is lust love, she pondered? For her, it could be nothing else for it brought absorption, obsession and near delirium. There would be many trysts on dark roads in the months to come, many nights in her bed before he snuck out her back door to the car he had hidden two blocks over. She was curious about his life, of course, was he really happily married? It was only a matter of time before she would try and see for herself. So, one day, she took off from work and drove to his house. She knew where his house was because she had stolen a peek at his driver's license while he was showering, he never would have told her where he lived on his own, though she had asked him many times. She hated how he kept that part of his life separate, as if by sharing it with her he would somehow soil it.

She parked across the street from his little white Colonial. She wanted to see his wife with her own eyes. She only had to wait five minutes or so before Martha emerged in the most ungainly clothes. A little boy of one or two toddled along beside her. Martha Day was no beauty queen, Millicent thought instantly, as she stared distastefully at Martha's old cargo pants and some faded blue jean shirt she had on, tied haphazardly at her waist. When Millicent recognized that she was the superior woman, she felt a sense of confidence. But was Graham the sort of man to love her just because she was beautiful, to leave his wife for her just because she was beautiful? No, she decided, he was not. He loved what about his wife, she wondered. She would have to ask him the next time his long, lean body was over hers and the sweet scent of his after shave made her nearly drunk with passion for him.

Graham wouldn't tell her what he saw in his wife anyway. He refused to talk about his marriage. The only thing he did tell her was that they had just lost their little girl, she'd drowned in the family pool, and his wife was so distraught, that he was so distraught.

He'd only told her that after she'd pleaded with him to get a divorce, after she'd injured his shoulder with the ashtray she'd thrown at him when he said that he would not get a divorce. Millicent had lost control of the emotions she was trying so hard to hold back, the anger at his apparent disinterest in leaving his plain Jane wife. "I will never see you again," she'd shouted. "Go home and fuck your ugly wife. I will never have you again." That's when she flung the ashtray at him and she heard him say "Ouch," and she heard the door slam behind him.

She should tell Martha Day that her husband was unfaithful. Yes, she certainly should. And that is exactly what she decided to do, especially after he said he wouldn't get a divorce, that his marriage was solid. "He's madly in love with me," she would say to Martha. But Graham wasn't madly in love with her, he was in love with his wife and it was infuriating to Millicent that he would be so blind. She was the woman to make him happy; it was obvious that she was the one. So when she finally cornered Martha in the parking lot of the Associated Market she said that Graham was fucking her, not in love with her, as she had planned to say, but fucking her and that was the truth at least.

She hated what she saw in Martha's eyes. It was contempt. There was not anger or sadness or the devastation Millicent had hoped for. There was not even shock. Martha Day held her in contempt, it was in her stare, it was in the way she moved her body after a slight pause; it was in the way she looked back briefly and started her car and drove off without a word.

Millicent became more and more depressed with her situation, with the nights and weekends she sat alone and thought about Graham with his family. Millicent woke up every day feeling as if her heart were going to burst out of her chest from the stress it was under. Her brother should, at least, be as unhappy as she was. They were twins after all. She wanted to share her misery with him. But, no, Martin was happily in love.

Millicent had no idea what Chloe Rappaport saw in her brother, the girl was quite beautiful in an all American girl sort of way, with her athletic gait and her billowy blonde hair, but Millicent imagined it was her brother's dry wit and his intelligence that had snared her. Her brother could be very charming and he was not altogether unattractive. But she was so distraught, so furious with Graham, that he had lured her into loving him, made her think that yes, of course he would leave his wife for her, that she couldn't be happy for her brother. How could she be happy for Martin when he was talking marriage and there she was, contemplating her life as the other woman?

After the ashtray incidence, she got Graham back

into bed by apologizing profusely, swearing never to do such a thing again. She also promised not to bring up divorce after he told her it was not an option. "You must accept us the way we are," he said and she reluctantly agreed that she would. But it wasn't like it had been before she'd tossed that ashtray at him. He still fucked her but he seemed to like her less. He seemed more distracted, focused only on the sexuality between them.

She wondered if Martha had ever mentioned that she'd been accosted in the parking lot of the Associated Market by his lover. But no, she doubted it. Graham still came to open her legs, to kiss her neck and to whisper his passion for her only to leave with dusk. Her love for him turned angry and bitter because he would not acknowledge how much he needed her. He showed up at her doorstep because he liked to have sex with her. Well, okay, she would not turn him away, but like a prowling cat she would find a way to stick it to him, him and his precious Martha.

※

Millicent really tried to be happy for Martin but she herself was so miserable. She did tell him it wouldn't last, this marriage between a Southern American Belle and her British brother. She told him out of concern and foresight. But of course Martin wouldn't listen. The wedding was planned and he was ecstatic, so she pretended to come around, pretended unbridled delirium for him. She kissed him and she put her arms around him, "I wish you much happiness," she whispered, but the words came out so flat that Martin looked at her with pity. "It's not working out for you?" he asked and she shook her head. "No, he will not leave his wife," she told him. Martin had no idea who her lover was because Graham had insisted that she tell no one, and she honored that, but she did say that her boyfriend was bound in marriage to an unhappy woman who had just lost her child, and his divorce would take time.

Martin begged her to cut it off, "It will do you no good. You have got so much to offer, find someone new, someone single, he may never leave his wife, for God's sake." But she was too focused on Graham, too preoccupied by her fantasies to lure him from his marriage, her fantasy of hearing that poor Martha had died in a crash of some kind, or by the hand of a madman, a Ted Bundy. It could happen, she told herself. He would be free one day. She simply needed to wait for that day.

It came as quite a shock to see Graham there at Martin's wedding to Chloe. Graham was there with Martha, smiling, shaking hands, kissing the bride like he wasn't torturing Millicent with his distance. He avoided looking at her, she avoided looking at him, but still, she could see him in all his married glory, affectionate with his wife, remaining at her side, holding her hand. She finally pulled Martin aside, "what is he doing here?" she whispered, indicating Graham with her gaze. Martin followed her gaze, slowly realizing who she was talking about, the recognition that Graham Day was the man his sister was seeing. "He's the one? Graham?" and Millicent nodded. "What is he doing here?" she repeated. Martin led her further away, out of anyone else's hearing and he told her that Graham and his new bride were friends, "childhood friends," he said.

~

Millicent wanted to stop seeing Graham but she knew she wouldn't. He was like too much candy, making her crave the sugar. But Graham kept coming to her bed, kept enjoying their sexual tryst, swearing to her that if he weren't married he'd take her away, he said that in bed, in the act of lovemaking. "Where?" she'd ask breathlessly and he would say, "to an island in Hawaii where you'd tan and wear next to nothing all day." Then he'd laugh after he said it. It was so amusing to him to fantasize and so painful to her. What was she to him, she wondered? She tried not to hate him for the hold he had over her but mostly she did, in his softest moments, when he was tender with her she wanted to kick him in his groin, those moments when she felt he owed her something and he felt that he owed her nothing. When she became nasty, sarcastic, even violent during sex he seemed not to notice and why should he? She was merely fulfilling his fantasies, creating arousal games, soothing his lust, taking him where Martha couldn't, or wouldn't.

It lasted nearly a year between them and then he broke it off, as if she'd been nothing to him, nothing more than a whore. He broke it off just like that, around the time her brother had his nervous breakdown. For awhile she thought it was for the best, she would get over Mr. Graham Day but that didn't last long. She began to follow him, to see for herself who he was fucking now, for she knew there had to be someone else. If he no longer wanted to have sex with her then there must be someone else. He said no, it was because his wife was grieving so deeply over their daughter's death; that his wife needed him and his little boy needed him. He said he wanted to turn over a new leaf; he wanted to be faithful to his wife. Millicent wanted to laugh, she didn't believe him. He'd found another woman and that was the truth, she'd decided.

Martin had been admitted to a psychiatric center for

a month. It seems he tried to kill himself by jumping out a window, only a fifth floor window but none the less, a window. Something broke his fall and he didn't even get a bruise or a scratch but it was quickly determined that he was mentally unwell and needed supervision. When she visited him in great distress, he looked at her so forlornly. Eventually he told her that life was stranger than fiction. He said that Chloe wanted a divorce because she and Graham Day were going to marry. "Can you believe that? he asked. "Your lover is now my wife's lover?" He laughed like a madman.

Now she understood. She needed to sit and quickly found a chair. She held her heart. Her blood ran cold. Was that why Graham had broken it off, the real reason? The room began to spin and she thought she would faint. "That bastard," she whispered and Martin stared at her, his face looking unfamiliar and frightening. "That bitch," he said.

So the Southern American Belle had captured her Mr. Graham Day? Well, she wasn't going to kill herself over it. Martin was much more fragile than she. She wasn't going to forget about it though. She'd find a way to retaliate.

Millicent paced the floor night after night. Chloe had taken Graham from her. It was clear that he never would have stopped seeing her if not for Chloe. Chloe had broken Martin's heart, as well as hers. Her brother might have succeeded in doing himself in, and then Chloe Rappaport would have been the cause of her brother's death. God, how Millicent hated her.

Well then, if Graham would leave his wife for Chloe Rappaport then surely he would have left his wife for her at some point. Yes, of course, if Chloe had not been in his life he certainly would have left his wife for Millicent. But she'd made demands on Graham, whereas no doubt Chloe hadn't. Perhaps that was the only difference between them. What a fool she'd been. Chloe probably never insisted he divorce his wife. She had badgered him so much that he got disgusted with her. She hadn't even been sensitive to his daughter's death, how painful it must have been. But maybe that's why he wanted to be with her, to take distance from his grieving wife, and maybe that was the only reason.

But why had Graham fallen in love with Chloe, and not with her? What did Chloe have that Millicent didn't? Chloe had ruined her life, ruined her brother's life. Martin was not the same man since Chloe had screwed with him. Millicent didn't know who he was half the time. He kept opening and closing his hands, he stuttered, something he'd never done before. He did odd things, like forget to turn off his gas stove, forgetting in what direction down a one way street he was going. Millicent had to take hold of him. His lack of clarity would overtake her, would become her lack of clarity; would find its way inside her very being. She couldn't tell his emotions from hers, they were the same. She couldn't sleep because Martin's emotions were bubbling in her veins along with her own.

Chloe Rappaport had caused them deep despair, both of them. Chloe would not make Graham happy in the long run; no one would make Graham happy but her. Why couldn't he see that? Chloe was nothing more than an insensitive slut. She was dispensable.

Millicent decided that there would be no future at all for Graham and Chloe. She planned it carefully. She would orchestrate it, Martin's rage would drive the act. All she had to do was give Martin a plan, an opportunity.

She would return to England with his passport, thus giving him an alibi. She would dress like a man, cut her hair. She would look exactly like Martin Holly. Then he would be off the hook. He would sneak into Chloe's house and stab her to death. But how could he have done it the police would deduce? He was back in London. He would then dress as a woman and use her passport to leave the country. It was a perfect plan. But Martin wouldn't have it. He begged her, he could not do it though he wanted it done, he would not do something so heinous, even in his discombobulated sense of disorientation he would not murder anyone, not even his adulterous wife.

Well, that was the difference between them, he was a coward and she was not. Millicent sent her brother back to London with his own passport, it would be best for him to have a cut and clear alibi. One week after Martin's return to England she went to Chloe's house wearing her brother's clothes. She looked so much like Martin with her short hair that not even Chloe noticed that she was not Martin. She would do this for her heartbroken brother; she would do this for herself. By looking like Martin it would be as if Martin and she were both extracting revenge.

Chloe opened the door to exasperation. "Martin," she said. "We've been through all this; you need to stop badgering me about the separation." Chloe left the door open and walked ahead, still talking, still telling Martin to leave her alone. Millicent closed the door. She walked behind Chloe with a knife that she rose up in her right hand. Chloe did not turn around. My God; she was still going on and on, talking about how unfortunate it all was as Millicent plunged the knife into Chloe's back.

It was easy after that. She plunged the knife into Chloe's back over and over again, and again and again.

When Chloe fell to the floor, Millicent stabbed her over and over until she realized that the body was still. She had done what she intended to do, she had killed Graham's lover. She had killed her brother's bitch of a wife.

She noticed the infant in the crib, now crying. The baby was Graham's, Martin had told her that. She remembered his tear streaked face as he said it. She walked to the crib. She would suffocate the child. She raised the pillow over the baby's head, but then she heard the car approach and the footsteps on the drive.

She dropped the knife near Chloe's body and ran through the open window in the back bathroom. It stuck but she got out and fell to her knees. Her leg was bleeding and hurt like hell; she must have cut it on the glass that had shattered.

She heard his scream, Graham's scream, and she smiled. She would bear the pain. She would heal. He would not.

Chapter Twenty-Five
Dominic Sacco

The restaurant was loud, he'd turned away and then he felt her hand on his. "What are you thinking?" she asked him.

He had been thinking of Clarissa but he certainly wasn't going to tell her that. "You were a million miles away," she said.

"Oh, I was just thinking about a cold case I'm investigating. An old acquaintance and I have gotten together to try and work on it, a murder that happened years ago. We've gotten quite friendly trying to—"

"Please, Dom, this is to be a romantic evening. I can't think of a bigger deterrent to a romantic evening than discussing a murder."

He smiled. "You're right, darling,. No talk of murder."

The trendy restaurant made conversation difficult and he wondered why she'd picked it if she wanted a romantic evening. His idea of romance was soft music, candlelight and gentle mutterings from the environment, not the shit that was being piped through the speakers posing as music, nor the obnoxious little corporate go-getters who spoke too loudly, obviously drawing attention to themselves and their thousand dollar suits.

He hadn't seen Clarissa since she'd gotten that confession out of John Peter, and right before that, that evening he didn't like thinking about, when he'd made a fool of himself telling her that he was engaged. He'd seemed so guilt ridden over it, but he'd decided it was the right thing to do, especially since he'd noticed the developing attraction between them. He wondered if she was aware of how uncomfortable it had been for him to tell her that he was going to be married.

He was furious at himself when he was alone later that evening, furious that he told Clarissa anything at all about his personal life. He'd made a huge assumption, how the hell did he know that what he was feeling went both ways? She may think of him as a big jerk for all he knew. It was absurd to have told her anything, she didn't need to know that he was seeing someone. He should have just gone over for that lasagna dinner and tested the water, was she interested in him or was it just his imagination? Maybe she would have flirted with him, though he couldn't imagine Clarissa flirting. She was too sensible a woman and flirting, in his opinion, was frivolous, certainly could be interpreted as frivolous.

He looked over at Millicent. She was sipping her wine and looking out over the crowd, perhaps easedropping on the mutterings of conversation around her. Now she was the master flirt, he thought. He assumed every man in the restaurant had noticed her; that should make him proud, after all, he was going to marry her. But he was indifferent to it. At least he'd very recently become indifferent.

"I think I would like to go to Belize for our honeymoon. I've been gathering information." She turned back to him. "We can get a villa on the beach. Oh,

I'd love that." Her eyes twinkled in the light of the room. She looked starry eyed to him and he wondered why he didn't want to rip off that low cut dress she was wearing and make love to her. He usually had those thoughts, but he realized the only thing he was thinking about was getting into his own bed and having a good night's sleep. Oh, who was he kidding, the only thing he was thinking about was getting an invitation to Clarissa's for that lasagna dinner she'd promised him.

He smiled again. He didn't want Millicent to know that he didn't really give a damn where they went, if they were even going to go at all. He'd been in a real quandary over it. He'd seen a side to Millicent that shook him to the core; it was a rather frightening side. She'd accused him of flirting with a stranger, a woman who happened to sit next to them in a bar. She said he gave the woman too much attention, spent too much time talking to her and couldn't he tell it was improper to insinuate that he'd like to fuck her. He was shocked because he had no such intention at all.

"I was only being polite," he'd said.

She'd slapped him hard, and then, before leaving, she'd tossed her drink in his face. He sat there mortified as she stormed out. His face stung, his anger seemed to rise like a great fever. *I can't marry a crazy woman like that,* he thought.

She apologized that night. The minute he got home the phone was ringing and he picked it up reluctantly. She begged his forgiveness and he gave her that. It was easy to forgive mentally unbalanced people when they did something completely ludicrous. They were, after all, not wrapped too tight. That's what he thought about Millicent after that, that she wasn't wrapped too tight, yet he continued to see her. He thought he owed her a chance to redeem herself, but despite her apparent heartfelt apology, he had become leery of her. He wondered if she had emotional problems that would strain their marriage. But he wasn't comfortable with his snap judgments. Perhaps she was simply upset about something entirely unrelated to her overreaction in the bar, and whatever it was had made her act out of character.

He noticed she was staring at him and realized she expected him to say something. He spoke without thinking. "I don't like jealous women."

She looked at him like he'd said something obscene.

"You're still angry at me?"

"Well, I keep thinking about it. It disturbed me."

"Jealousy is a human emotion," she said with a smile. "If you weren't jealous if another man flirted with me I'd be terribly disappointed."

"I would feel completely confident that you would handle it."

He could tell she wanted to get off the subject because she changed it abruptly and went back to talking about Belize. She was clearly dismissing him. He didn't like that either. He certainly hadn't gotten over what he'd been calling 'the incident.'

"We can go to Caracol," she said.

"Ruins?"

"Yes, Mayan ruins." She took a sip of her wine and met his eyes over the rim of her glass. Her eyes were the deepest shade of green, like some sort of reef one might find at the bottom of the sea.

He'd been flattered that Millicent found him attractive. They'd met in a supermarket when she'd asked if he could reach the pasta, then they found themselves in the same line at check out, and lo and behold, he'd parked right next to her in the lot. He never thought she'd find him in the least bit interesting, she wasn't much older than his sons, or his daughter, but after she asked if he was married or seeing anyone, she asked for his phone number right out. It was a bold move and he couldn't help but smile. He hadn't felt that flattered since the chief of police once told him he was the best cop on the force.

They'd been dating for about four months when she broached the subject of marriage, about a week before the 'incidence.' He hadn't been prepared for any discussion of marriage, it was too soon. He never thought he would marry again but then again, they were having so much fun together, and it was so pleasant to have a steady sexual partner and a partner in general, for the movies, for dinners and all those social events he hated going to alone. But when Clarissa came back into his life, he felt a shift away from Millicent, even before she embarrassed him by accusing him of wanting to fuck a total stranger.

His attraction to Clarissa wasn't at all surprising. He remembered how he'd felt fifteen years earlier when he'd met her for the first time during the Holmes investigation. She'd been an enchanting deterrent to his failing marriage, not that he ever gave her the slightest inclination that he found her attractive back then, but there was that one time when their hands touched quite by accident and she flushed so deeply. His instinct had been to draw her close into his arms and kiss her endearing lips. He loved her lips. They seemed to have little wings at the end of her mouth that went up when she smiled. Her face completely changed when she found something amusing, she became impish and vulnerable.

He really wanted to break it off with Millicent when he realized he was attracted to Clarissa, and even more than that, he genuinely liked Clarissa. And then, when

Millicent showed such volatile behavior in that bar he was sure he wanted to break it off. But his best friend, Charlie, had insisted he give Millicent another chance, "Everyone has a bad day, Dom," he'd said. Well, he wanted to do the right thing. He assumed he was getting cold feet, only imagining he wanted to drop Millicent in order to date Clarissa because he was scared to death of getting married again, of getting trapped into living day in and day out with a woman he didn't really enjoy.

~

"Darling, have you heard a word I've said?"

He realized he hadn't but he nodded anyway and mumbled something about how much fun it would be to snorkel with her, that he loved to scan the underwater world. He surprised himself by taking her hand and telling her she looked beautiful. He could tell how much compliments pleased her but she didn't blush, as Clarissa would have. Damn, he wondered, what is all this thinking about Clarissa?

"Why do I still get the feeling you really weren't listening to me?"

"Damn headache," he said. "This music doesn't help. Might have to call it an early night."

Chapter Twenty-Six
Clarissa Blackwell

She and Philip were getting nowhere, just going round and round in circles. They didn't have any suspects in Chloe's murder, but they were confident that she knew her killer. It was clear that there was a missing part of the puzzle and Clarissa knew she had the clues, if only she had the interpretation to go with the clues.

How to define a two headed monster, one perhaps, of slight build, she wondered. She also felt pretty certain that there was a connection between Millie's murder and Chloe's but she had no idea what it was. She spent so much time trying to figure it all out that her head actually hurt from the effort.

Of course she tried to tie Dennis to the crime, how she'd love to see him behind bars, if for nothing else than just being a bastard. But Dennis didn't tie into her vision. Dennis was a large man who would not have fit through the bathroom window in back. When she and Philip went to examine the scene of the crime they discovered that the murderer had gotten out of a small bathroom window. The police had found DNA all over the place but none that couldn't be tied to Chloe, and to Martin, who had once lived in the house. Clarissa assumed that the only reason the murder weapon was left behind was because the murderer had been surprised and had dropped it. The police had also found a blood stained hand print on the baby's crib and the baby's pillow. Dom told her that the handprint was small, again attributed to a man who was slight of build. Dom also told her that the fingerprints lifted from the house could not be matched to anyone.

Clarissa felt that that should have exonerated Randall but it hadn't.

Chloe's murderer could have been Martin Holly, who was barely five feet seven, but Martin had been safely tucked away in London, England. He had a stamped passport, a receipt for his ticket, and many people who could place him thousands of miles away. The police were not yet bringing a case against Graham Day and Clarissa applauded them in that decision, but that could change at any moment. For now, they assumed that a good defense attorney would point out that the bloody handprint on the crib was too small to have been Graham's and any DNA of Graham's, or hair particles, could have been explained away by their affair. And most importantly, Savannah would have testified that her daughter was planning on marrying Graham, so why should he have killed her? Clarissa was relieved that Martha was spared that public embarrassment.

Unfortunately, Graham was not altogether in the clear; he was still a suspect and could be brought to trial for a crime she knew he didn't commit. Clarissa was furious that fifteen years ago the police had overlooked the bloody handprint and the size of the escape window, where more blood was found. The police had simply ignored the fact that Randall Holmes was over five foot ten and his hand would not have matched up to the print either. It seemed preposterous to her that

Randall's confession put a lid on the case and Chloe's murder went unsolved. But at least, the police were now looking into it. She wondered if they'd stumbled across any suspects that she hadn't.

"Could Chloe have been seeing another man aside from Graham?" Philip had asked her and Clarissa told him she would have no way of knowing that but she doubted it.

"This was not a random crime, either, Philip. Whoever committed the murder knew exactly what he was doing. I think it was planned, premeditated."

Philip had disagreed with her there, saying it could have been a spontaneous act of passion. He kept going back to Dennis. His scenario was that Dennis had pleaded with Chloe not to go public with the molestation charges against Blake and she had refused and Dennis killed her.

Clarissa insisted that Dennis would never have fit through the back window. Philip came to the conclusion that Dennis had tried to fit out the window and couldn't, so he waited until Graham left and went out the front door. Clarissa wondered if any shoe impressions outside the window were preserved as evidence, she'd have to check on that. Maybe she was missing the significance of the two headed man she saw in her vision, but try as she might, whatever significance there might have been evaded her. If shoe impressions had been taken it would only eliminate the suspects they had, suspects she already knew were not guilty.

～

Clarissa decided it was time to confront her ex-husband. She'd been putting it off, probably because she was so used to relying on him for one thing or another.

But she didn't want him in her life anymore and that was certain. She didn't want the gifts, or the phone calls or the unplanned visits. She didn't want anything to do with Dennis. He'd been hanging around her ever since Savannah had kicked him to the curb and she realized that it had been a mistake on her part to have allowed it. Dennis didn't seem to realize that she would never forgive him. Yet she had accepted the car and the picket fencing he paid for, and the new roof he put on her house, among so many other things over the years. Maybe she was just complacent because there was no one else in her life she could call at the drop of a hat to help her with one thing or another. But this she knew, whatever strange relationship she had with Dennis had to end. She took the keys to the Escalade and drove the fifteen minutes to Dennis's sprawling ranch.

~

"How could you...how could you...." He couldn't even finish his sentence after she'd asked him if he'd killed Chloe. He was so completely taken aback she thought he'd faint.

"Well, did you kill her?"

He looked at her with abject horror, his face contorting into an expression of despondency, a saddened mass of confusion.

"How can you think that, you don't really, do you?"

"Well, you're a blackmailer, an adulterer... why not?"

He hung his head. Seeing Dennis speechless was an anomaly for her.

"I never want to see you again, Dennis, you truly turn my stomach."

He reached out to balance himself and slid into a chair. She thought he looked weak enough to pass out.

She knew that Dennis had nothing left in life but his blackmail money and a slew of relationships that only lasted a couple of months at best. She knew now that he never loved Savannah, he had simply wanted the lifestyle, the beautiful, sophisticated woman on his arm, and most importantly, Savannah's money.

"That's what you are, isn't it, a blackmailer and an adulterer, not to mention, a phone sex freak?"

It didn't surprise her when he pulled himself together and came to her, taking her arms.

"Say you don't mean that."

She looked into his eyes, the once handsome face, and she remembered for one brief moment the happiness of her youth when Dennis had asked for her hand in marriage.

"I do mean it. My God, Dennis, those are all the things you are."

"You're the only woman I've ever loved. I've made mistakes, I'll admit that but I always loved you."

"That's not what we're talking about. Your very presence disgusts me, so it doesn't matter a damn whether or not you ever loved me."

Ah, the true Dennis took hold of himself, she observed, as his face took on a red blush and his graying eyebrows went in to a pensive dip.

"She's a liar, whatever she told you is a lie," he said with a scowl as she watched him cling to whatever life boat he could find. "I never blackmailed anyone."

"Oh, I almost forgot, here." She tossed him the keys to the Cadillac.

"I don't want it back. What would you do without it?"

"Get a Durango."

"Clarissa, Clarissa. Please, please hear me out. Savannah is jealous of our relationship, she always was. She'd say anything to make me look bad. She told you a bunch of lies."

"You don't need Savannah to make you look bad."

Clarissa would not argue with him further, there was no defense. She walked through his door and out into the day. She took the back roads home on foot, with the companionship of the wrens, doves and cuckoos. The sky was a slate of blue and the perfection moved her, the sky's consummate color, the sun's balmy heat, the entwined dance of moss covered plantation trees. I will never need anything else but this, she thought as she walked with a brisk pace down the winding lanes that took her home.

Clarissa felt the relief of absence as she settled into the embrace of her living room. That's what Dennis was now, a true absence. The sublime choice she'd made to cut whatever ties she'd allowed over the years gave her a sense of her own strength. Dennis had no right to her, not anymore. He had understood her need to hold on, to pretend that she wasn't a woman alone in the world, she had him, who would show up with a wink and a seductive comment, keeping the illusion of himself alive in her heart. Clarissa breathed a sigh of relief. He was gone, like summer to fall, he was gone.

She thought it was cause for celebration, a glass of wine to toast the exit of the last player on the stage of deceit. She poured the wine and took it out on the porch to watch the last rays of the sun fade away. There is glory in life, just watching a sunset.

The phone was a sudden distraction and she was slow to rise, to walk through the door, to reach for the damn thing. It had pierced the silence with its wail of entitlement, its promise of connection.

"I almost hung up," he said.

"Dom?"

"I'm going to hold you to your word, Clarissa."

She was surprised, what had she promised him?

"The lasagna dinner?"

"Oh, of course, tomorrow night?"

"Seven?"

"Perfect."

She stood for a moment with the phone in her hand. She had a psychic flash. He's in love with me. But then she laughed at herself, she couldn't trust her psychic flashes anymore; they made no sense, like this one. After all, the man was engaged. She smiled. Ah, well, I could use a friend.

Chapter Twenty-Seven
Millicent Holly Linder

Millicent was angry and was trying not to show it. She knew another bad move on her part and she'd be dumped. Dom had been horrified that night she'd shown her temper, which she had every right to show. She knew he'd wanted to fuck that fifteen-year-old tart that had sat next to them in the bar. Well, maybe not fifteen, she acquiesced, but at least only twenty-three or so.

What was it about men who can't deal with a woman's anger, makes them feel too threatened, makes woman appear too much like men, to whom anger is a natural emotion, like lust and aggression.

She knew that Dom had feigned that headache. She almost laughed and said, isn't that a woman's excuse when they don't want to get laid? She didn't say it, just nodded her head and smiled and told him to call her if he needed anything. That had taken an ungodly effort on her part. She really wanted to push him off a cliff.

She knew she'd fucked up badly by throwing that drink in his face, slapping him in front of a room full of people. She also felt he'd get over it. It would just take a little acting on her part to present herself like the even tempered lady she really wasn't. And then, after they were married, would it really matter?

Truth was, she really hadn't wanted to marry Dominic Sacco; he was no Graham Day. But God, she was over that, Graham was still married to Martha. Who'd want to go there again? But she was curious to know how much Dom knew about Chloe's murder. That's why she looked him up. Marriage just seemed like a good idea after she started seeing him. He wasn't a bad bloke at all and he seemed to have a good deal of money. She'd love to stop working and on his pension and savings and whatever else he had, she could probably afford to.

After she'd returned to England, she didn't forget about what she'd done. She'd been assuring herself, almost daily, that Randall Holmes was still paying for the crime she committed. Even when she was married to Stanly Linder, she kept herself abreast of any news from America, any new turn of events in Chloe Rappaport's murder. Millicent wanted to make sure there was never a glitch in the verdict. After all, they were blaming the wrong man, who could have a change of heart and admit that he didn't do it, get the wrong people asking too many questions. That's all she'd need, to have that case reopened. But chances were, it never would be.

She'd followed Martin back to England right after the trial of Randall Holmes. She'd been at the trial every day watching Randall plead guilty to twelve counts of murder, including Chloe Rappaport's murder. She couldn't get over it when Randall confessed and called Martin in giddy hysteria. The wrong man is going to pay for it, she'd screeched out. Martin, in his impassive demeanor remained quiet, and she wondered if he had any regrets. God, Martin, the bitch is dead and we're both off the hook. Show some emotion.

She remembered Dominic Sacco from the trial, of course. She'd watched him take the stand. She was never noticed, not sitting in the back under a hat she did not remove. She also remembered the weird one, the so called psychic, who took the stand and testified that she'd given the forensic artist the impression of Randall's face.

It all fell into place. After Randall's conviction, Millicent felt a momentary safety. She'd been stupid that night, leaving the murder weapon on the floor. Were there fingerprints on the handle of the knife? She couldn't be sure, but even if there were, her prints weren't in anyone's database. She'd gotten away with murder. Just enjoy it, she told herself.

She had only been back in London a year when she met and married Stanly Linder. It was a bad marriage from the start. Every year he became more and more of a chronic alcoholic, the one thing Millicent thought of as an intolerable weakness. They argued incessantly until Stanly divorced her three years later, for what he termed her 'psychotic temper.' Two years after her divorce, Martin was asked to return to the bank he'd worked for in Edgefield and he agreed. Millicent thought it best to accompany her brother and return to the states as well. Her bad marriage had soiled her taste for British men.

When she was being honest with herself she had to admit to having a very macabre side, but she couldn't help it. She wanted to sleep with a detective, specifically the one who had investigated Chloe's murder. It was titillating. She remembered Dom Sacco quite well, his good looks, his serious demeanor. Once she learned of his divorce, she planned on running into him and coming on strong. What man could refuse a younger, beautiful woman, especially a divorced lonely one? She followed him into that supermarket. God, he was easy.

What fun it was. Mr. Detective was sleeping with a killer. Ha! The killer was sleeping with a detective, the very detective who had unknowingly saved her from a death penalty by being too stupid to realize that Randall Holmes had not murdered Chloe Rappaport.

She was never sorry she had looked Dom up. He would be the perfect lover. When she'd planned that serendipitous meeting in the food market he had no idea who she was. He fell hard for her, could barely keep his hands to himself. Things were going very smoothly, in fact, until that psychic bitch began to meddle. She remembered reading the statement that Clarissa had made to the Post right after Randall's trial, how she didn't accept Randall as her goddaughter's murderer. Then, years later, she saw Clarissa the day she'd come out to Dom's house, recognized her immediately. It wasn't difficult to put the pieces together. Clarissa was still clacking over Chloe's death.

"What did she want?" Millicent had asked.

"Oh, it's just about an old case, she wants it reopened."

Millicent's blood ran cold but she pulled herself together quickly.

"Well, good luck with that." She'd laughed.

"Yeah."

Clarissa wanted the case reopened? It couldn't be any other case but Chloe's. Millicent wondered if she should have any cause for concern. Briefly, she remembered her brother's call, something about Clarissa Blackwell coming to his house and asking about Chloe, telling him she didn't believe the right person was paying for the crime. At first, Millicent thought nothing of it, it was simply an annoyance, nothing could be proven, but now it seemed there was reason to worry because Dom had gotten involved and it was being 'looked into.'

Millicent probably should have paid more attention to what was going on with Dom's retirement interests. Surely she could have gotten all the inside details if she'd questioned him. Dom had told her the other night at dinner that he'd been thinking about a cold case. Idiot that she was, she didn't ask about it. She'd been too eager to get him excited about the honeymoon. Was it the Rappaport case? She had an uneasy feeling in her gut that she should return to England.

When Dom called the next day to tell her he still wasn't feeling well, she knew he was lying. She sensed that she would soon be told to get lost. The bullshit headache of the other night was proof of that. Millicent would have to find out if her instincts were correct. She drove to his house and parked out of sight. Maybe she was just being paranoid. She would wait the night if she had to but she had to know if he was lying to her. At precisely six p.m. he got into his car. She could tell he was dressed for an occasion. He wore a sports coat and nice slacks. She followed behind. Just where was that crafty bastard going?

Millicent was sufficiently shocked to see him pull into Clarissa's drive and emerge from his car holding a bottle of wine. She could see Clarissa when she opened the door. Millicent could tell that Clarissa had on make-up and some sort of silky lounge outfit.

Jesus, she's old and batty. He couldn't possibly be interested in her.

Sure enough, as the hours went by, it was obvious that Dom was not leaving Clarissa's house. It was obvious when the downstairs lights went off and Dom did not emerge. When dawn broke, Dom's car was still in Clarissa's drive.

That utter creep she thought as she got out of her car.

Chapter Twenty-Eight
Dominic Sacco

He felt the heat on his arm as sunlight entered the room. Slowly his eyes adjusted to the wall paper, a vine like pattern with a touch of lavender flowers, like bluebells. The distressed looking dresser on the wall was green. He smiled as he noticed several bottles of lotions and perfumes. He would never have imagined that Clarissa was the type of woman to pamper herself. He had so much to learn about her; he was looking forward to it.

He smiled more broadly as he turned to find her shoulder, tanned and slightly boney. Her hair was thick, such a rich brown. He touched her hair and leaned in to kiss her neck. Her hair smelled like lemon. He liked that it was streaked with grey. It made him feel comfortable, like the laugh lines around her eyes and the fact that she remembered type writers and the Platters, like the confidence he felt that any vows he'd make with her would be forever.

He heard the birds outside her window and found a sweet analogy. He would become a part of her life, as predictable as the song of birds. He thought back over the evening, the lasagna had been spectacular and the wine had been rich, smooth as velvet, as they finished off the bottle in the comfort of her parlor.

At one point she took his hand and said, "what of your engagement?" Yes, just what of my engagement? Certainly he would never marry Millicent. He would break it off the minute he got home. That was clear. It was clear the moment he'd taken Clarissa in his arms and kissed her and told her that his engagement was over.

Well, not quite over yet, but he'd made up his mind to break off with Millicent so it was as good as done. He closed his eyes again and tried to recall how they made it up the stairs and into bed. He did remember how they never got to the dirty dishes, how long their first kiss lasted, but damn if he could remember how they actually wound up in her bed. Well, what's important, he told himself, was that he remembered every detail of their lovemaking, from watching her undress to the feel of her skin against his.

He seemed to sink into the yellow pillows. The comforter was so soft and seemed to hug him. He reached his arm around Clarissa and snuggled into the crook of her body. He smelled the lemon scent. He wondered what they would do now, as lovers, what plans they would make. He was excited by it. He fell asleep thinking about taking her on his boat, biking on the back roads of Hollow Creek and going out into the world together holding hands.

~

When Clarissa awoke she realized quickly that she'd have to remove Dom's arm from around her in order to get up. He was snoring softly and she was careful not to wake him. She stared at how disheveled his hair was, waving down on his forehead, the long length of his legs.

But he wasn't asleep, either that or her movement had woken him. He pulled her back onto the bed. He was smiling, there was mischief in it.

"And just where are you going?"

She turned to look at him, to appreciate the fact she had a man in her bed after how many years? She shuddered to think.

"The dirty dishes. I must get to them."

"And you will, all in due time."

As his lips found hers she felt the familiar yearning, how it had enveloped her the night before, how eagerly she'd given into it.

"You are all I want," he whispered, "in my future, my heart, my life."

One door had slammed shut and another had opened. Clarissa felt herself overtaken with happiness, so much so she started to laugh. He held her tighter and joined her laughter with his own.

It would be another few hours before Clarissa would even give the dirty dishes a thought. They made love, came up for air, and made love again.

"Do you like wheat berry bread?" she asked.

"I'll learn to love it."

"That's good, I'll toast us some."

She reached for her robe and slipped out of bed. The only thing on her mind was Dom, the sweet memory of everything he'd said to her, their passion for each other surprising both of them.

She didn't know what it was at first. She was seeing it beyond the curtain, there before her front door. Something was hanging, moving slightly. It seemed so strange.

"Dom," she called.

He had thrown on his pants. He joined her at the step.

"What's that?" she asked.

He shrugged his shoulders. "Don't know."

As he walked to the front door she held her breath, almost knowing what it was before he opened the door.

She heard herself scream. A cat had been hung on her porch.

～

The police were questioning the neighbors but no one had seen anything, must have happened around dawn.

"You hear anything?" a young police officer asked.

Dom shook his head. "No."

"You ma'am?"

"No."

Clarissa was shaken to the core. The cat had belonged to a neighbor and whoever had done this must have snatched it from a back yard. Dom held her hand tightly. She couldn't stop crying, the cruelty to the animal was so disturbing that she didn't know if she'd ever be able to sleep again, or not feel guilty for the rest of her life, as though it had been her fault.

"Do you have any idea who might have done this?" The officer asked.

"No," Clarissa said quickly but she thought she did know, she just couldn't give a name to the person responsible. But that person must know that she and Philip were investigating Chloe's murder. Maybe this was a warning to back off?

After the police left she mentioned that to Dom and he adamantly disagreed. "There couldn't be a connection."

"Who would do this to me then?"

"Dennis? Didn't you tell me you told him you never

wanted to see him again? Would he have reacted this way?"

Despite what she thought of Dennis he would never have killed an animal, she knew that. "He loved cats. He has two that live in the house. He has a dog also, a big mutt of some kind. He's an animal lover, he would never do this."

Dom didn't look like he believed her. "I told the police to question him."

Her head sprang up. "He has nothing to do with it."

"Then who?"

She put her face in her hands. "I don't know."

"I'm staying with you. Until we find out who's responsible, I need to stay here."

Clarissa reached for his hand. She wanted that. She felt she was in danger and she needed him near. It was surreal, but from that point on she felt stalked.

The police hadn't come up with any leads on who might have hung the cat on Clarissa's porch.

"You should go home," she said to Dom.

"I like it here." He smiled at her.

"I need to go to the market."

"Let's go then."

She wanted to think of nothing else but Dom. But she wanted the space alone to go over it all in her head. Her life was changing and the man before her was the reason. Oh, how she wanted to enjoy it. But she couldn't enjoy anything. Someone was giving her a warning, someone capable of murder.

"Chloe's murderer did this."

"No, you don't know that."

"I do know it. Someone thinks we're getting too close

but I don't see how. We have no new suspects and we haven't publicized anything. I mean, how would it get out about Philip and I and what we're investigating?"

Dom kept disagreeing, saying it was a kid's prank. Maybe she'd pissed off one of the neighborhood boys, did she remember doing that?"

Clarissa felt exasperated. "I need to buy a car. I've given the Escalade back to Dennis."

"We'll use my car."

"Not just for the market. I need a car to get around in."

That afternoon, Clarissa bought a new Durango and they went to the market and stocked up on food. Later that day she made him a vegetable stew. She discovered how witty he could be, how much he knew about history and how much he loved Classic literature. They seemed a perfect match. She trusted him. God, she hadn't trusted anyone in so long.

His cell phone rang a good deal, certainly more than hers. She clearly remembers the call that brought him outside, how he paced as he talked. When he came back inside he was pale.

"I've broken off with her," he said.

"I thought you'd already done that."

"Not altogether."

"How did she take it?" Clarissa stared at him pensively. He didn't look upset; he looked more worried than upset.

"She was fine, just fine."

Clarissa didn't believe him. She thought back quickly to the cat and dismissed her thought. "Couldn't be."

"What couldn't be?"

"Jealous ex-girl friend hangs a cat on my porch?"

Dom laughed. "I wouldn't worry about it. Besides, how would she know about us?"

～'

Dom stayed with her for four days. On the fifth day he had to take his son to the airport.

"Do you want to come?"

"No."

"Well, maybe I can get him a ride with someone else."

"I'll be fine, Dom. Please go."

"Call me at the drop of a hat, it will only take me forty minutes to get here but I can call an officer in the area that can get here in three."

Clarissa didn't really want to go anywhere but she needed some dirt and mulch for her plants and some touch up paint for the back yard patio furniture. She also needed a distraction. She was jittery and could barely sit still. What had happened with the cat had deeply disturbed her. She drove over to Home Depot trying not to think that someone had hung a cat on her porch. She wanted to think about Dom without anything else in her head, what a wonderful surprise he was, just when she thought that life had become static and predictable he had appeared. Yet she felt there was a dark shadow around her. She didn't want to be afraid but she was.

She'd called Philip, she wanted to tell him what had happened and he agreed that it was possible someone knew that they'd been digging into Chloe's murder.

"Who would know?" he asked her. "Who have you been talking to?"

Clarissa wracked her brain for the answer to that.

"Savannah, Dom, you and Dennis but not really. I never told Dennis anything."

"What about Savannah?"

"Oh, Philip, she'd wants me to solve Chloe's murder."

"I guess you're right."

"What about Dom?"

"Don't be ridiculous, Philip."

"Well, who does he talk to?"

She had gotten off the phone feeling a bit angry. Philip grabbed at straws. Dom did that too, though. She pulled into the parking lot at Home Depot thinking about Graham. She spoke to him at least once a week now, just to see how he was doing without his wife and daughter. He seemed sad, as if he were struggling with the weight of the world. She realized she didn't tell him much about what she and Philip had discussed, if anything at all. She felt it would just be a burden to him at this point. He had a lot of his own to think about.

She spent longer in the store than she planned and bought more than she'd wanted to buy but there had been a sale on garden tools and she'd run into two neighbors who offered their condolences about the cat, which wasn't her cat, but still, she grieved over it as though it were.

Clarissa started the car and felt the drag. Flat tire. When she got out of the car to check she discovered that all four tires had been slashed and someone had written 'bitch' in large bright letters across the passenger side.

It hit her in a flash then, a clear, bright thought. A woman did this.

The woman who killed Chloe did this.

Chapter Twenty-Nine
Pleasant Day

I didn't think I'd ever be happy again. The whole world was falling in on me and the weight of it was unbearable. John Peter had written me a letter that I couldn't bring myself to open. Ike was going to be tried as an adult for what he'd done to Millie but John Peter was getting off with a juvenile offense. I heard from Angus that his mother was moving out of the state and taking John Peter with her. I guess no one in Hollow Creek was going to forget what he'd done anytime soon so they needed a new start. I'd never see John Peter again and that made me so sad. He was weak, I knew that, but he was also kind and sweet. I knew that too. But I guess pleasing Ike had been a lot more important to him than trying to save Millie's life. Maybe he was so afraid of Ike he wasn't thinking straight. I wasn't in a place in my life where I could justify or forgive what he did anytime soon, but maybe, one day I would be.

Angus came up to see me at Nana's a lot. He and Clarissa were the only visitors I got aside from Daddy. Daddy was up there every weekend trying to make amends. I was too unhappy to forgive him. I had fallen into an odd state of mind where feeling bad seemed so normal, and much more comfortable than feeling good.

The first time I saw Angus after about a month, he almost bowled me over. It seems Sawyer had gotten a hold of him and did a makeover. I never knew Angus could look so good. Sawyer made him grow out his hair and took him shopping for clothes. Angus came up to see me that first afternoon in tight jeans, designer sneakers and a tee-shirt that showed off his slim, muscled arms.

Sawyer called me later that day to ask me if I approved. "You're a miracle worker," I told him.

"Girls are chasing me now, Pleasant," Angus said and I assumed they were.

"Better not let them catch you, Angus."

"Why not?"

"What would you do with a girl?"

That made him blush and look off but when he turned back to me I read his mind.

"I know what to do." He grinned at me like I was a box of chocolates.

"Not with me you won't."

He jumped up in a huff and walked off. Poor boy didn't know that I knew how badly he wanted me to turn all warm and toasty and tell him I was just a pushover for him. He made me laugh, at least. He brought some joy into my dank existence.

"Well, maybe someday I will," I shouted out.

That made him smile and walk back to me. It was like I had some kind of magic in my hand and the older I was getting, the more potent it was becoming. I felt like I could say, Angus, if you jump off that cliff, I'll let you kiss me… and then some."

"Someday is good," he said and flopped beside me.

Better Angus than Bodean I was thinking, but didn't say, of course. Word got back to me that Bodean was going around town with this little girl who barely came up to his waist. 'they were an odd couple' people said, but I guess if odd translated into horny, she could have him.

⁓

Angus kept me abreast of everything that was going on at school. I was really missing being home, though living with Nana was great. It was like every day I was discovering my dead mama more and more. Chloe was all over that house. I was living in her room and I was surrounded by her pictures. I went through a dozen old albums. I felt real strongly that whoever killed her was in those photographs somewhere, I just didn't know where. I knew Clarissa was trying to solve the crime. She'd come up some weekends and talk to Savannah about her visions and the two of them would sit around scratching their heads. I could have told them that whoever did it was in the photograph album but since I didn't have any more information than that I kept my mouth shut. I didn't claim to be psychic like Clarissa but somehow I knew it. Every time I touched that album electric shots ran through me.

I never thought I'd see the day that Daddy would make me smile, but life is not altogether nasty, sometimes it's really good. One bright afternoon, Daddy came to right my world. He was so happy that weekend that before he even got the words out of his mouth I knew what he was going to say and I kept biting my lip in anticipation.

He took my hand and told me to take a walk with him. Colors were so vibrant, so much purple in the fields, and the air was fresh as newly washed laundry on a line. Daddy was quiet for a long while but he had a skip to his step. We sat down on Nana's wide lawn and he apologized to me. I didn't know what to say so I just nodded my head. Then he told me Mama was coming back home and I could have said something smart like you don't deserve her but I kept my mouth shut.

"We're retaking our wedding vows."

I couldn't get over that, but I hadn't learned my lesson in love yet, I wasn't yet aware of the risks it took.

"Will you come home, honey bun?"

"What promises are you making to me, Daddy?"

"I promise to be the man you deserve to have as a father. I want you to have a husband in your life someday that will never lie to you. I need to set an example, give you a proper role model."

I studied his expression, there were tears in his eyes. I didn't want to believe him but I did. I knew my daddy wouldn't ever want to see me hurt by some fool of a man that didn't respect me. I thought about him dragging Bodean up the drive and smiled.

"You turning over a new leaf?"

"And then some."

He was my daddy and he would always try and do good. That was just the kind of man he was. I had no doubt that his days of knocking on Karlene McFaddy's door were over. Just something in his expression told me he was like a man off the booze, hard as it was, he was going to wean himself of other women.

"I've missed you so much. You and your Mama. Me and Sawyer have nothing to talk about without you two."

"I'll be packed in five minutes, Daddy,"

I was so giddy riding back to Hollow Creek that I could have grown wings and flown just to pick up some speed. Daddy was singing to the radio but other than that we were being pretty quiet. I didn't question him about anything. All I knew was that my suitcase was in the back seat and I was returning from a semester of snot nosed high school students and rejoining the rednecks I was used to. Nana had sent me to some private school where everyone wore a uniform and spoke French.

Mama was waiting for me outside. I could see her from the road. The more I looked at her the more I sensed that a heavy weight had been lifted from her. I walked up the driveway expecting Mama to look away but she didn't. She stood up and hugged me. Her face was so clear; I'd never seen her face look that way before.

"I've missed you," she said.

I saw the glance that passed between Mama and Daddy and wished I knew what had transpired in my absence, and Mama's absence, but I'd never know that. The only thing I knew was that they had found each other again. What I saw in that glance between them was some sort of transformation. I saw the understanding between them and I understood in that moment the oceans that love can part.

"Think you've grown an inch," she said.

I may never know Mama as well as I wanted to but I knew how gentle she was. I had been a jig saw puzzle for her just waiting to be touched and made whole. But now, I was free from hurting her. She was looking at me, not as a loss but as a gain.

"I missed you too, Mama."

I crumpled in that moment when I said I missed her. I crumpled and fell to pieces but I did not want for completeness. We were a unit and within that unit there was no place for causing each other pain.

All of a sudden I heard the porch door slam and the

dog bark and there was Sawyer standing there with a Chew apron on and a platter of something that looked like a pie and smelled like a little bit of heaven.

"In your honor little sister, I have made Boeuf en Croute. Shall we dine under the stars?"

"Why not?" Mama grinned. "It's a perfect night. Just for us."

I looked over to see Sawyer showing me his Hollywood smile and holding that platter and that fool dog running around barking just to bark and I knew that this moment was ingrained in time and would live within me forever.

I found Daddy alone on the porch the next day. I had the photograph album with me, the one Nana had let me have with all of Chloe's pictures in it. It was the one that gave me the electric shots when I looked through it.

"Chloe is in here. Want to see the album?"

I opened it up and sat next to Daddy. Slowly we turned the pages.

"Does it hurt you to see her alive, the way she was?"

Daddy shook his head but I wasn't quite sure I believed him.

"You are a lot like her, Pleasant."

"Do you believe in ghosts, Daddy?"

Well, you'd think I'd stumped him on a Jeopardy question; he just sat there starting up at the sky. Finally, he answered me.

"I believe in more. In something greater than we understand. So, maybe, there are ghosts."

Then we got to Chloe's wedding picture. It took up the whole page of the album. Daddy studied it long and hard.

"Who is she?" I asked.

"Who?"

"That woman there," I pointed, "the one that's staring at you."

"The groom's twin sister."

"Why is she looking at you like that?"

He studied the picture again, then he shook his head. "I don't know."

"Everyone else is looking at the camera, Daddy."

He looked off and I watched his expression. "Doesn't look like she liked me too much, does it?"

"I think ghosts come into your head sometimes and whisper to you."

"What is your ghost saying, sweetness?"

"She's not saying anything to me. She's talking to you, Daddy."

"And how do you know that?"

"I just know it. Something Clarissa told me about intuition, that it's nothing more than knowing the truth."

He put his head up to the sky and closed his eyes. The tear that fell down his cheek glistened in the sun and remained there, like the impression of a scar.

Chapter Thirty
Clarissa Blackwell

Clarissa watched as Dom pulled up to the body shop. There were creases on his forehead she could see from a mile away.

"Who the hell would do this?" he asked, as if she would know.

"The same person that hung a cat at my door, that's who."

She took his hand and showed him her four slashed tires and the spray paint on the passenger side of her car.

"I don't get it."

"I can pick up the car tomorrow. Thanks for coming to get me."

"I'd bring you back to my place but I don't want Millicent showing up there. She's got a bad temper."

"Millicent?"

"She's been calling me every few hours, called me every name in the book each time. Now I don't take her calls but I wouldn't put it past her to show up at my house and start heaving things through my window.'

Clarissa shuddered. "Millicent what?"

"Millicent Linder. Why?"

Clarissa felt like she'd been hit with a rock. It wasn't a significant connection but still, Millicent had the same name as Millie Grady, real name, Millicent Grady. She dismissed it as a meaningless coincidence.

Dom drove for awhile in silence. She could tell by the tightness in his jaw how upset he was. She thought it best not to mention that she was being stalked by Chloe's killer. He didn't believe that what had happened to her recently had anything at all to do with Chloe's killer.

"I'm staying with you. My suitcase is in the trunk."

She smiled at him and reached out to touch his arm. "Thank you. I don't feel right about staying alone. Someone out there has it in for me."

As he turned into her driveway they immediately noticed Philip's old Buick. He was outside the car and looked agitated. He was pacing around in circles.

"Where the hell have you been?" he asked her as she approached.

Clarissa was startled but then again, Philip's rudeness shouldn't surprise her anymore.

"It's a long story. What are you doing here?"

"I've solved it." He looked at Dom and grinned. "Glad you're here, Detective, you'll need to make an arrest."

Clarissa exchanged an amused look with Dom as Philip followed them into the house. She wondered if Philip had really solved the crime. She at least had it somewhat solved. She sensed very strongly that Chloe had been murdered by a woman. But she had no motive and no suspect.

Philip produced a box of his wife's homemade banana walnut bread and insisted on coffee to go with it.

"You're going to keep us in suspense, Philip? It will take me twenty minutes at least to make coffee."

"I insist."

Clarissa was amused and curious. Was her stalker

going to be stopped and was Chloe's murder finally going to be vindicated?

They sat in Clarissa's parlor with the light streaming in, making the room look happy and light.

"So?" She raised one eyebrow at Philip as she took a bite of the bread. "Delicious," she said.

Philip sat back on the couch. "The other day I discovered that Martin Holly had a twin sister and a little bell went off. I was right about the husband, the husband always does it."

Clarissa felt her hands become tight around the cup. Two-headed? As in twins?

"There was an article in the newspaper about Martin, something about a promotion and about his family. It also mentioned his twin girls and that he himself was a twin. That's when the light bulb went off. So I did some digging."

"What are you getting at?" Dom asked.

"Well, I simply figured it out." Philip wiped his fingers on a napkin and put more cream in his coffee. "Martin killed Chloe Rappaport and it was his twin sister that took his passport and dressed up as a man and left the country. She made it look as though Martin wasn't here. But it was Millicent Holly that left America, not Martin."

"There's that name again," Clarissa said. "Millicent."

Dom gave her an odd look as Philip continued. "A day or so later, Martin dressed up as a woman and used his sister's passport to leave America. No one would have suspected."

"No," Clarissa said. "It was Millicent who killed Chloe."

Philip nearly leaped from his seat. "Why do you complicate things, Clarissa? Martin had motive, what possible motive would his sister have to do this?"

Clarissa looked at Dom, who seemed uncomfortable. "Trust me on this, Philip. We need to find out why but I have a feeling...."

"A feeling? A feeling? A feeling isn't enough." Philip came up to her. "We'll need fingerprints off the murder weapon. We can prove this." He turned to Dom.

Clarissa wondered how she was ever going to put the pieces together but she knew it wasn't Martin who had killed his wife, it was his twin sister. Her doorbell rang just as she heard Philip asking Dom what evidence still remained from the night Chloe was murdered.

Clarissa opened the door to Graham and his daughter, Pleasant. She was delighted in one moment and surprised in the next, what were they doing here?

"Come in, come in," she said as she gave them both a hug.

"I see you have company but this could be important," Graham said.

"Sit, sit, we've got coffee and banana cake." She led them into the parlor and they all acknowledged each other politely.

"I hope I didn't interrupt anything." Graham looked at them each in turn.

Philip laughed. "I have just put a feather in my cap."

Graham leaned forward and stared directly at Clarissa. "I think I know who killed Chloe."

They were all surprised and sat up a bit stiffer. "Well, so do we." Philip grinned as he looked around the room.

"I've discussed this with my wife and my children and we're in agreement that I should tell you, that I should be willing to take the stand if I have to." He looked momentarily un-comfortable but then he gained his composure. "Millicent Holly, Martin's twin."

Clarissa sat up straight in her chair. "Millicent?"

Graham nodded. "I had an affair with her years ago."

He looked at his daughter who gave him an encouraging smile. "She was a violent woman, very prone to temper. I broke off with her and she might have wanted to get back at me for hurting both her and her brother. She must have blamed Chloe for our breakup, for what it did to Martin." Graham took his daughter's hand and squeezed it. "I wished I'd known…I wished I'd known."

Pleasant said, "You couldn't know. Some things just have no rhyme or reason."

The rest of them sat in silence. Clarissa felt an odd presence around her, like an embrace. She turned to Dom. "How can we prove this?"

"That doesn't prove anything," Philip shouted. "Women don't go around stabbing people."

"I think you should at least look into it." Graham stared at Dom. "Martin had a breakdown around that time. He could barely brush his own teeth, much less murder anyone. He was on a prescription for anxiety, Xanax or Valium, I think. It wouldn't have made him violent. Besides, he was very passive, Millicent wasn't. It was a revenge murder. I'm quite sure of it."

Philip shook his head. "Well, maybe. Millicent lives here, not far, goes under her married name, Linder."

Clarissa noticed that Dom's head shot up. "Linder?" he asked. "Millicent Linder?"

"Twins share the same DNA but not fingerprints. If we can get the fingerprints that they lifted from the murder weapon, the back window and the crib and compare them, we've got our killer." Clarissa turned to Dom and noticed he didn't look at all well.

"I'm sure she's not going to willingly give you fingerprints or admit to this," Philip said.

Dom stood up. Clarissa noticed that his face was beat red. "I can get you her prints."

Part III

Yellow Leaves

Chapter Thirty-One
Pleasant Day

I been sitting here by Millie's grave trying to figure out death, but it's a hard mystery to unravel. I don't know why God gives it to us to bear 'cause it leaves so deep a scar when we lose a loved one. We make up all these dumb clichés to try and explain what happens after death but not a one of them makes a lick of sense to me. Thinking there's a heaven somewhere don't mean shit. I have no guarantee of any heaven and having faith in something I can't see makes me feel like a fool.

I been asking Millie what it's like to be dead and getting no answers. What is she to me now but a hollowed out place in my heart? What do I do with that as I go through life but remember and feel sad? She wouldn't want me to feel sad but how can I avoid that?

I guess one could say that our actions bring about our lives, like stepping stones toward the plans we make — choices, right or wrong, that lead us toward what we want or what we never would have chosen. Got nothing to do with fate, I don't think, but everything to do with choice. We're the artist with the brush, the writer with the pen. It's all about what choices we make to put on the page, or on the canvas. Kind of makes us God-like.

Well, living makes me feel like life is tenuous and fragile and I've only got so much control over it. I've got no crystal ball that's going to tell me whether I'm making the right choices or the wrong ones. But for the time being, I'm going to go on taking breath while Millie is stuck being in the ground, being a ghost. But how the hell did she know that Ike was going to jump through that window that day and choke her to death? How the hell did she know that John Peter wouldn't be there when she needed him most? How the hell do any of us know anything?

I could make myself feel better by pretending Millie can hear me talking but I don't believe she can. I don't believe she can see the yellow-golden world of Fall in Hollow Creek or hear the red and yellow leaves that crunch under my footsteps, snapping like the terra chips that Sawyer likes. And if I tell her that the sky looks like it's got white streams of brush strokes that resemble tails that have fallen from clouds that look like pigs. Would she remember? We used to look at the sky and name the shapes the clouds made, Rubenesque ladies, pigeons and wagon trains. Remember Millie?

Makes me angry she can't laugh and tell me she always saw clouds of doves. Clarissa tells me we all got souls and its souls that communicate. Clarissa says that's all any of us are, just souls. Maybe then, I need to be quiet enough to hear that greater language. One thing I've learned, we are born to lose, that's just the way life is, but what cruelty then must we bear trying to be healed by the dead and their impotent attempts to console us? Daddy says be strong and face whatever comes up but be righteous and responsible for who you are.

Based on those words, you'd think Daddy found religion but he didn't, he just found himself when he thought he lost Mama. I was proud of him at that trial but I was even more proud of Mama, sitting there supporting Daddy even though she had to hear all the gory details of his affair with that awful Millicent woman. Mama will always be an enigma to me, someone I aspire to, someone strong enough to allow love to be buoyant and forgiving.

I hope Chloe has some peace knowing that that woman who killed her was put away for life. They tried to get her off on an insanity plea but it didn't work. Philip Wiley is no longer in retirement. He helped prosecute her. He works for the District Attorney's office now and he doesn't throw pebbles at me anymore. I don't think old people should be put out to pasture anyways. I never seen that old man look so good as when he's getting up every morning to go kick ass down at the district attorney's office.

I think we all felt relieved that Chloe's murderer was caught and put away. Clarissa said that Chloe kept sending her clues as to who killed her. I asked her why it had to be so damn convoluted, like why couldn't she come right out and tell us who killed her, why'd she have to throw hints to Clarissa in her dreams? Clarissa told me it had to do with language, the dead speak differently. If they want to speak our language then they have to get themselves reincarnated so they can. The only way to participate in life is to be alive. I know Clarissa makes sense to herself but sometimes she leaves me a little confused.

She's still dating that detective but I don't hear wedding bells anytime soon. I just think Clarissa is her own woman, likes things her own way and maybe a man will just mess with it. I think she likes being with Nana a hell of a lot more than she likes being with anyone, even me. Those two can't seem to get enough of each other.

They're always going around picking up antiques and paintings and visiting old towns and inviting me over for one of their cook-ins. Clarissa says that her friendship with Nana is like a family heirloom, you start out loving it, then you absolutely hate it and then you recognize its value and you treasure it. I guess she means that whatever happened between she and Nana years ago had room for restoration.

Nana needed us all around her when her brother got indicted for being a pervert. There was a big scandal and I think it embarrassed Nana to be related to him. It seems like three or four women testified that Blake Rappaport had molested them when they were little. I was happy to see his sorry ass carted off to jail.

~

"What the hell you doing?"

I turned to see Angus standing there with a piece of straw in his mouth.

"Talking to my friend," I said, reaching out to touch the tombstone over Millie's head.

"She can't talk no more, Pleasant."

"Summer's lease hath all too short a date."

"What?"

"Shakespeare."

"I swear, you never make sense."

"You wouldn't know sense if it jumped up and bit you in the ass, Angus. You can't recognize it 'cause it's a foreign language to you. Sense is the coin in your pocket, not what should be there inside your head."

"I swear Pleasant, I don't know why I keep after you the way you treat me, like some kind of fool."

"The wise man knows himself to be a fool."

"Shakespeare."

"Good guess."

Angus walked beside me as I started home. Something felt good and serene, maybe like the world is supposed to feel.

"I was going to ask you to the Senior Prom."

"You were going to and changed your mind or you were going to as in any moment now you're going to ask me?"

"I swear, you rile me up."

I noticed his head was down and he wouldn't look at me. His hands were in his pockets.

"Senior prom isn't till June."

He looked away. I dashed his hopes, I guess.

"You hear that there was a body washed up behind the track field?"

"You really expect me to believe that?"

"Pleasant you never believe anything I tell you and I'm telling you the truth."

"You're the bearer of bad news, Angus."

He kept pace with me but his head was still down. He spit the piece of straw out of his mouth. There was a whole flock of birds that flew over us, came out of nowhere. Angus and I stopped walking and stared up.

"Ain't they something?" he said.

It was perfect. The birds and the sky and the yellow leaves of Autumn. This was what it was, this life. It was tenuous and frail and yet fraught with beauty, and with beauty comes sadness. If you opt in to loving then you opt in to being human, to having your heart break a million times over. It's a circle of sorts. The more you go round the more laughter you find, the more laughter, the more joy, the more sadness. That is what life is. I felt something warm in my heart and I reached for Angus' hand.

"The dead speak, Angus."

"Ha! What do they say? Get me out of the damn dirt?"

I laughed despite myself. While I was sitting by Millie's grave asking her to tell me what death was, I wasn't listening to the answer. Somehow walking beside Angus on Piper Hill, leaving the cemetery behind and heading home I knew what the dead know and it comforted me.

"What you thinking about?" Angus said.

"Death."

"You are so strange, Pleasant. I never know what's going to come out of your mouth."

"Sure I'll go to the prom with you and we'll dance all night."

"That's great, that's great." He did some little kick with his heels, took him off the ground about a foot.

The birds flew off and the sun threw streaks of gold across the sky. I could hear Mama's laughter as I neared the house. Fredo barked and Daddy was sitting on the porch rocking.

"See you tomorrow," Angus said, with a smile as wide as a meadow.

I walked up my drive and autumn's leaves fell on my hair. Daddy looked up and smiled in my direction and Mama stopped to stare at the setting sun.

"This is it," I whispered. "This is it forever."

And the ghosts walked into my memory, into the happiness, into the pain of my future, and they wished me well.

I turned, as though I saw them in the unfolding season, in the beauty and in the death of autumn. Perhaps I had, perhaps I had.

Vera Jane Cook
PLEASANT DAY

Pleasant Day is Vera Jane Cook's eighth published novel. Her first southern fiction novel, Dancing Backward in Paradise, received a five star ForeWord Clarion review and won the Eric Hoffer Award for publishing excellence in 2006 and the Indie Excellence award for notable new fiction, also in 2006. Her second southern fiction novel, The Story of Sassy Sweetwater was a finalist for the 2012 book of the year awards. The novel also received a five star ForeWord Clarion review as well as being an honorable mention winner in the 2013 Eric Hoffer Award for ebook fiction. Also by Vera Jane Cook, Where the Wildflowers Grow, Marybeth, Hollister & Jane, Lies a River Deep, Annabel Horton, Lost Witch of Salem and Pharaoh's Star. The author lives in New York City.

To learn more about Vera Jane Cook, visit her web site: http://www.verajanecook.com

www.ingramcontent.com/pod-product-compliance
Lightning Source LLC
Chambersburg PA
CBHW060228100726
47907CB00003B/555